'Ruth Leigh goes from strength
adventures of self-obsessed blog
Smugge. Issy faces a frightening
marriage collapses, her old rival
articles about her and she strugg_ _ ... ... with pregnancy,
single parenthood and her own looming fortieth birthday.
When even social media has to take second place, Issy finds
herself re-examining everything she has always taken for
granted. Touching, funny and cringe-making by turns, she is a
true (anti)-heroine for our times.'
Caroline Taggart, Sunday Times *bestseller*

'Ruth Leigh has done it again! With heart and humour Leigh
takes readers on another hashtag-filled ride through *The Trials
of Isabella M Smugge,* balancing life's unexpected with honesty,
hope and style. This is the sequel Smugge readers have been
waiting for!'
Lauren H Brandenburg – award-winning author of The Death
of Mungo Blackwell

The Trials of Isabella M Smugge

Ruth Leigh

instant
apostle

First published in Great Britain in 2021

Instant Apostle
The Barn
1 Watford House Lane
Watford
Herts
WD17 1BJ

Reproduced by permission of the Crown's patentee, Cambridge University Press.

Scripture quotations marked 'NIV' are taken from the Holy Bible, New International Version® Anglicised, NIV® Copyright © 1979, 1984, 2011 by Biblica, Inc.® Used by permission. All rights reserved worldwide.

Author's agent: The Tony Collins Literary Agency.

British Library Cataloguing-in-Publication Data

A catalogue record for this book is available from the British Library.

This book and all other Instant Apostle books are available from Instant Apostle:

Website: www.instantapostle.com

Email: info@instantapostle.com

ISBN 978-1-912726-50-9

Printed in Great Britain.

Dedication

This book is dedicated to my husband, Nick, and our children Alex, Robbie and Katie. Without you, life wouldn't be nearly as wonderful as it is. Thank you for everything.

Acknowledgements

Isabella M Smugge began life as a two-dimensional joke character in a blog I wrote in March 2020 for the Association of Christian Writers (ACW). In May of that year, I mentioned her again in another blog and was pleasantly surprised by the many comments from fellow writers saying they'd love to know more about her. My world changed forever the afternoon that blog came out, when Tony Collins (now my agent) got in touch to say he thought Isabella would make a good novel and would I like to write two sample chapters and a story arc. Huge thanks to him; to Instant Apostle who took a chance on me; to the best copy editor in the world, Sheila Jacobs; to my first readers; to everyone at ACW who encouraged and supported me; to my family; and to all the Smuggers who have taken Issy to their hearts.

September

This morning, I overslept and woke up just before eight. Once I'd got up, done a few half-hearted stretches and picked up my clothes from the floor, I said to myself, 'Isabella, you can do this. The cellulite will go, you've still got all your own teeth, you and Suze are friends again and you've got this beautiful house in your own name.' #bestfriendsforever

Suze is my younger sister. I hardly ever see her since she lives in Hong Kong with her family, but this summer we managed to restore our relationship, which has made me happier than I can tell you.

Outerwear is the key look for autumn. On the playground walking my children in, my on-trend tightly belted jacket drew gasps of admiration from the girls in the Year One line. My archenemy, the gossip columnist Lavinia Harcourt, was still peppering her stupid rag with bitchy attacks on me, but in spite of this, samples and gifts were still pouring in. Since this season's look is luxurious loungewear and cocooning, I should be all right. What better look is there for a secretly pregnant lifestyle blogger? It won't be long before I consign anything tightly belted to the very back of my wardrobe, but for now, why shouldn't I show off my enviable figure?

Once Finn, Chloë and Elsie had walked into their classrooms, I hung around in the playground chatting for a while, then wandered back to my delightful Grade II listed residence, the Old Rectory. We've been back at school for two and a half weeks now, and I'm starting to get used to the morning routine of breakfast, uniform and walk to school. None of us said it, but we were all looking at the place where our dear friend and fellow parent Claire usually stands. She had

11

collapsed and was rushed to hospital for an emergency C-section, hovering between life and death.

On my way back home, I sometimes make a detour through the graveyard. I know that sounds a bit morbid, but it's beautiful. The church spire soars up into the blue autumn sky, the old gravestones lean against each other like drunken aunts at a wedding, and the brightly coloured flowers and cards with childish handwriting mark the places where new grief lies.

I walked around, reading the faded inscriptions, as I often do. So much loss and yearning hidden beneath the moss and lichen.

Elizabeth, wife of Wm Harborne Esq, died in the twenty-eighth year of her age.

Here Lieth the body of John, the Son of Robert and Ann Smith, who departed this life on 12th May 1786 aged five years and of their Daughter, Mary Ann, who died in her Infancy. Suffer the little children to come to me.

Gillian Ling, beloved wife, adored mother, precious grandmother and friend to many. Died 1st December 2019. Sorely missed.

There's a long strip of grass which runs parallel with our garden, separated by a stone wall. All the new graves are there. Against all the odds, it's a cheerful place, embellished with fresh flowers, little rose bushes and pretty stones. How do vicars feel, I wonder, christening babies one minute, then joining people in matrimony, then trying to find something to say to comfort grieving families? It must be one of the hardest jobs there is.

Birds are crying out to each other and there's a tang of woodsmoke in the air. I left my phone at home so I can't take any shots, but that's OK. Somehow, I don't feel it would be appropriate.

I've got some work to do this morning, then I'm heading over to the vicarage with some delicious meals cooked by Ali, my housekeeper.

We've all been helping Tom, Claire's husband, out as much as we can. He's really got his work cut out, with three children and a newborn to deal with. I like to feel that I can give something back.

They've called the baby Benjamin, Ben for short. He looks just like Claire. **#helpinghands #newlife**

No one knows I'm expecting. And no one needs to know yet, thank you very much! For now, I look exactly the same, my toned figure giving away no clues to my real state. Underneath my carefully curated outfits, my stomach isn't playing ball, starting to swell in a most alarming manner, but for now, I can keep it under control. This isn't the way I planned it, with my husband off living with my ex-au pair, but the children wouldn't notice if I grew an extra head, and when Ali's here, I'm usually down at the studio. Eagle-eyed mums on the playground are my main concern, but as winter is drawing near, I'll be rocking the layered look.

I haven't decided when to tell Johnnie, but if I know my man (and I do), he'll come running back the minute he hears that a new little Smugge is on the way.

My sister-in-law Horsey Davina has been texting very nearly non-stop. Dear me, she's excited. Every last twitch, throb and spasm of her pregnancy is faithfully recorded and sent over to a reluctant Issy Smugge. Her due date is mid-October, and the latest excitement is her Braxton Hicks which are coming hard and fast. I was bracing myself for an invitation to be birth partner, but fortunately her husband, Toby, will be manning the head end while the professionals attend to the egress of the baby at the other.

It's been a terrible week. The children fight and squabble from the second they wake up in the morning until the blissful moment I finally manage to corral them into their bedrooms, then I crash out on the sofa. It was never like this when *she* (my former au pair and right-hand woman, Sofija) was here. Everything ran like clockwork. Mornings are hell, a flurry of half-eaten breakfast, missing shoes, last-minute homework and pathetic arguments over nothing. It drives me crazy. I need space and tranquillity if I am to continue being one of the UK's most respected and revered lifestyle bloggers. The children don't seem to understand this however many times I shout it at them. #generationgap

Sometimes, I don't know how I keep all my plates in the air. I've got my agent, Mimi Stanhope of Mimi Stanhope Creatives, of course, plus my socials' guru, Harpreet. He manages anyone who's anybody, and a few who are presently nobody but might shortly become somebody. I've got complete flexibility to post whatever I like across all the platforms, but I can fall back on him for the solid, everyday content. To maintain the meteoric success I've achieved over the years, the right support is absolutely vital.

It soon became apparent that as well as stealing my husband, the affection of my children, my chive-green gilet (I can't prove it, but *she* was the last person to wear it), my will to live and my belief in human nature, *she* has dumped a whole load of dull and repetitive tasks upon me. Isabella M Smugge has worked very hard to get to where she is today, and she cannot continue to shine brightly in the blogging firmament if she is constantly weighed down with repetitive paperwork.

From the minute I hired that woman, her job was to work alongside me, smoothing my path and taking mundane tasks away from me. Let me give you an example. Our primary school is renowned throughout the district for its Good

Communication Skills. Roughly translated, this means that it sends home enough paperwork to make an origami practitioner weep with joy. *She* used to go through it all on my behalf, extracting the goodness and recycling the husk. A brightly coloured newsletter detailing all the class activities, recent achievements, upcoming opportunities to part parents from their money and suchlike lands in my inbox each week. However, I never had to worry about it as *she* dealt with it all. Not any more.

The children were hardly back at school when smiley Mrs Hill, the school secretary, was on the phone. 'Nothing to worry about, Mrs Smugge, but we would very much appreciate payment for Chloë's class trip to the power station. And will you be joining us at the Year Six Residential meeting for parents after school next Monday? And if you could encourage the children to draw their self-portraits for the school calendar before the end of the week, we'd be ever so grateful. Bye!'

When I look back on last September, just twelve short months ago, I can barely believe how much has happened. Back then, I could swim before school, had virtually unlimited time to work and enjoyed a delightful relationship with the children. Plus, of course, I had a loving and attentive husband. Everything seemed perfect in Issy Smugge's world. Mind you, I also had no real friends and was estranged from my sister owing to the painful situation around how Johnnie and I met. Even though she's forgiven me, occasionally I still wake up in the night and cringe at the memory of stealing my sister's boyfriend.

I would say swings and roundabouts, but I can't bear clichés.

Time's a funny thing. When you're waiting for something wonderful to happen, counting the days off until a birthday or sitting in a dull briefing meeting, it drags. When you're living your best life and all is right with the world (not that I can remember what *that* feels like), it shoots by at breakneck speed. Right now, it's going as slow as it possibly can. In the same way, once Suze left our house for Hong Kong, after spending a blissful time with us in the summer, time dragged until the blissful day when the children returned to full-time education, leaving me at home with some much-needed peace and quiet.

On the first day of term, I dropped the children off at school and consulted my friend Lauren for guidance as to what was coming up in the academic year. I don't know how she does it. She seems to have a rolling calendar of events in her head, for three children (hers) and with auxiliary attachments for three further children (mine).

'OK, babes, so after school today it's Meet the Teacher. We signed up for it last term, so Sof – *she* (here she coughed) would have booked you slots for all three of them. We'll go round to the office and ask Mrs Hill. You can write them down, then I'll see you here at pick-up and we'll go in together. You've got that new man teacher in Year Six, you know, the tired-looking one with the five o'clock shadow, the Newly Qualified Teacher in Year Three and Mrs Jenkins in Year One (you've had her already, haven't you?). Monday afternoon after school you've got the Year Six Residential meeting. Have your three done the calendar pics? Don't forget we need to do the form for the Year One and Two school trip. We'd better go and sign up right now if we stand any chance of going along as helpers.'

My head was spinning. We waved to the children and trotted round to the front of the school to Mrs Hill's domain. As we approached the double doors, it became apparent that a demonstration of some kind was in progress. The reception area was full of parents, mostly mothers, some waving pieces of paper and all talking at once. Lauren pushed open the door and we were nearly blown backwards by the noise. I was utterly at a loss as to what could have brought so many women in their twenties and thirties to one cramped meet-and-greet area. Lauren mouthed something at me, stuck her elbows out and powered through the crowd. I was left uncomfortably wedged between a lopsided Perspex rack containing back copies of the school newsletter and a large, framed collage of recent entries to a local art competition. Most of them seemed to be mixed media, with a very strong leaning towards glitter.

Mrs Hill's voice could be heard above the racket.

'Ladies. Please! One at a time.' She might as well have been speaking Xhosa for all the good it did. The door opened and another squad of mothers swarmed in, including Hayley, the miserable woman with the eyebrows whom I had replaced as PTA secretary. For one terrible moment, I was back in my City Girl days, squeezed on to a hot, smelly tube train and far, far too close to my fellow man. And woman. My face uncomfortably pressed up against the wall, I began to feel claustrophobic. What if I had a panic attack here, at school, in front of all these women who would love nothing better than to gossip about that posh, stuck-up woman from London losing her grip? **#panic #whatshappening**

At that moment, Mrs Tennant's door flew open and the headteacher herself appeared. Raising one elegantly manicured hand, she looked ready for anything.

'*What* is going on? I can hardly hear myself think!'

Mrs Hill raised herself from her seat to reply. 'It's the Year One and Two school trip, Mrs Tennant. Parent helper forms.'

I saw the head's eyebrows twitch slightly. 'Ah. I see. Well, can I suggest that anyone who is *not* here about the Year One and Two school trip concludes their business with Mrs Hill, and everyone else forms an orderly queue. Thank you, Mrs Hill.'

'Thank *you*, Mrs Tennant.' Mrs Hill sank back down on to her chair. I took a deep breath and focused on a poorly drawn depiction of what appeared to be fireworks coming out of a chimney (rather dangerous, I'd have thought).

A sheepish-looking man made his way to Mrs Hill's hatch and pushed a brightly coloured lunchbox towards her, before turning tail and scuttling out of the reception area to freedom. Several mums handed her crumpled pieces of paper and departed. That left Lauren, myself, Hayley and about fifteen other mothers.

'Right.' Mrs Hill folded her hands and appeared to be ready for the fray. 'Are you all here with your permission slips for the Year One and Two trip, and to offer yourselves as parent helpers?'

There was a general mutter of assent and heads nodded like sunflowers in the breeze.

'One at a time then, please. After last year's... unpleasantness, we will be putting all the names in a hat and asking a child from another year to draw them. You will be notified by text. Thank you very much.'

And that was that. Lauren passed her slip over to Mrs Hill and requested another one for me. (I had no idea where the original was. *She* dealt with all such matters.) I duly filled it in, handed it over and walked outside into the fresh air. Most of the mothers were standing outside, talking animatedly. Hayley's piercing tones were cutting through the buzz of conversation like a circular saw through plywood.

'I'm not at all happy about her attitude. My Lysander won't be able to cope if I'm not there. He's so sensitive. I've *told* Mrs Hill again and again. He can't be treated like a normal child. He's far too intelligent.'

She looked around for support. Several of the women rolled their eyes and there was a general wave of tutting.

The group started to break up and I found myself walking out of the gates with Lauren, Kate, Maddie and a couple of other mums. I'm getting better at identifying people. An entire year spent in the Reception line has improved my grasp of names no end. Lovely Lou, a friendly girl who never speaks ill of anyone, was talking.

'I know she gets a bit overprotective, but he is a sweet little boy. And her hormones can't be helping, poor girl. She's due after Christmas, isn't she?'

Maddie snorted. 'She's a right royal pain in the rear end, and you know it! Thank goodness I'm not pregnant. Imagine having her in *two* of your kids' years. On and on like a broken record about the child prodigy. I happen to know he still wets himself when he gets excited.'

Lovely Lou smiled benevolently and pointed out that she still wet herself on a regular basis. The conversation moved on in a frankly scatological fashion, with lurid anecdotes of ill-fated bouncing on trampolines, unexpected sneezing and so on. *My pelvic floor is as tight as a drum thanks to my regular Kegel exercises.*

'Oh, speaking of trampolines, I'm party sharing with Kim in December.' Lauren whipped her phone out. 'We're going to Boing! for a trampoline party. Usual deal, drop-off, stick around if you like, hour and a half free play, food, cake, party bags, home. I know it's a way off, but I'm trying to be efficient. Just texting you all so that you can save the date.'

Kate grimaced. 'Are you inviting Hayley and the child genius? Better bring some wet wipes.' We all dissolved into laughter, even Lovely Lou grinned reluctantly. Everyone scattered in different directions, and I was left walking towards the village centre with Lauren.

I questioned her about the anarchic scenes in the reception area.

'It's the same every year. They book up a class trip to the fire station in Ipswich and everyone goes crazy. It used to be first come first served, but Mrs Hill got fed up of mums lying in wait for her in the car park at 7.30 in the morning. There was a punch-up last year. That's why they've introduced this new system.'

I was confused. 'Why does everyone want to go the fire station?'

Lauren gazed at me, open-mouthed. 'Because of the firemen, babes. The firemen. You know, fit, young, gorgeous-looking. It's an absolute treat.'

Issy Smugge has always prided herself on her absolute fidelity to one man and her wifely virtue. Suddenly, I was seized with a passionate desire to visit a fire station, to hear the sirens ringing out and watch handsome young men leaping into fire engines and racing off down the mean streets of Ipswich. Perhaps it was the pregnancy hormones.

Hard on the heels of my sudden urge to visit Ipswich, a familiar craving hit. When I was expecting Finn, all those years ago, I couldn't eat enough tinned sardines (organic, sustainably sourced, of course). Suddenly, I yearned to sink my teeth into the delightfully slippery little fish, feel the oil running down my chin, the bones crunch. I swallowed and felt myself salivating.

'I'm just going to pop into the shop. I need to pick up a few bits for tea.' I hoped that Lauren would head off back to her own house, but to my consternation, she followed me in, basket in hand, still talking eagerly about firemen. I was aware that seizing all the tinned sardines in stock would look extremely suspicious. I attempted to throw her off the scent by adding some low-fat Greek yoghurt, a handful of kiwi fruit and some blueberries to my basket.

'Babes, how can you even eat those?' Lauren was making gagging noises as she eyeballed my tinned sardines. 'Just the thought makes me want to be sick.' She ambled over to the reduced section and started going through packets of slightly damaged biscuits and cartons of juice coming up to their sell-by date. I paid and got everything packed away into my bag double quick before she could ask any awkward questions. I had a nasty feeling that I'd overshared about my pregnancy cravings months before, at a coffee with Claire and some of the other mums.

Claire. I would have given anything to be able to sit down with her and tell her my news. But there was no point in fretting. I waited for Lauren to pay then walked out of the shop, said goodbye and headed home. **#missingmyfriend #sadness**

At home, I sat down for a minute with a cup of tea, and the next thing I knew, it was lunchtime. I had only two hours to get all my work done before I had to be back at school for Meet the Teacher. I mean, you've got to applaud the school for their excellent communication, but really! How is a hard-working, award-winning lifestyle blogger like me supposed to get everything done? **#runningoutoftime**

Rubbing my eyes, I checked my emails. A whole slew from Mimi giving me chapter and verse on the reaction to my new, kindlier lifestyle feature, Open Brackets (generally good), the outcome of her drinks with Lavinia Harcourt's editor last night (bad) and what she thought about the increased sales of my newest book, *Issy Smugge Says: We've Got a Teenager on our Hands* (excellent). Harpreet had sent me the weekly report on my socials (very heartening) and there was an email from Johnnie's solicitor about the flat.

Grinding most of my teeth, I opened it. It seems that my husband and former au pair are finding the flat too small and wish to sell it. Since I own 50 per cent, I must give my permission. I never want to see it again as long as I live, and of course, I'll receive a healthy chunk of cash from the sale. That said, I don't see why I should smooth Johnnie's path any more than necessary. I replied, saying that I was far too busy to consider it now and would reply in due course. Let them sweat. Ha!

Briskly, I went through the rest of my emails, checked all my notifications across the platforms, replied where necessary and scheduled some posts. By the time I'd done all that, it was 2.45. I don't know where the time goes. I took a moussaka out of the freezer for tea (there's nothing Ali can't do with an aubergine), unloaded the dishwasher, went to the loo (the baby isn't even the size of a prune – how can it be pressing that much against my bladder?) and left for school.

I suppose Meet the Teacher is a good thing. We didn't do it last year, as we were in such a flurry with the move that all my interactions with the school were online. The girls ran off to play on the field and Finn and his best friend, Jake, wandered over to the back bushes to climb trees and hit each other with sticks. Lauren had Year Two first, so I bade her farewell by a battered-looking trolley full of reading books which had seen better days and positioned myself outside Chloë's classroom. I peered through the window. There was no sign of the newly qualified teacher, Mr Rycroft. Our appointment was for 3.20. I checked my watch – 3.22. Rude. Punctuality is the politeness of princes, as Nanny always used to say.

My eye detected a slight movement in the corner of the classroom. A teenage boy (smartly dressed, I grant you) was fiddling about with a pile of books. Honestly! What a time to let a work experience student into the school. I rapped smartly on the door and marched in. The boy jumped and turned around.

'Isabella Smugge. Chloë Smugge's mother. I'm here for my 3.20 with Mr Rycroft.' After losing half my day's work owing to pregnancy-related napping, I was in no mood to waste yet more time. 'Where is Mr Rycroft? Come along, my next appointment's in twenty minutes!'

The youth gulped and ran his hand over his chin. (Blotchy, I noted. He'd clearly just started shaving.)

'I am him.'

'What do you mean?'

'Him. Mr Rycroft. That's me.'

'You can't be. You look about fourteen.'

'But I *am* him. Honestly.' The young man was starting to look distressed, and his voice shook. 'I'll be twenty-three in January.'

'Oh.' I heard the click of high heels coming down the corridor and Mrs Tennant appeared, holding a clipboard.

'Ah, Mrs Smugge, I see you've met Mr Rycroft. Don't let me interrupt you.' And she was gone.

I found myself in a rather awkward situation. Issy Smugge is not in the first flush of youth, but nowhere near the age where policemen start to look like children. I smiled, I hoped in a charming and conciliatory fashion.

'My apologies, Mr Rycroft. Shall we?' I took a seat, folded my hands and tried to look natural. Mr Rycroft (for it was he) sat opposite me and produced a folder.

'It's only my first day, but I've already formed a very good opinion of your daughter, Mrs Smugge. We talked about poetry and acting and different ways of expressing ourselves as an icebreaker and she impressed me with her natural confidence.'

I was puzzled. 'Are we talking about the same person? Chloë Smugge? Reddish hair? Bites her nails?'

A faint note of acerbity crept into the teacher's voice. 'We certainly are. She lit up when I started talking about performance. I expect you've seen it at home. Does she put on little plays? Go to a dance class?'

I frowned. 'Well, she's a bit of a drama queen. Rather given to meltdowns and bad dreams, if that's what you mean.'

Mr Rycroft cleared his throat. 'Is there anything you'd like to ask me, Mrs Smugge? I'm aware that my 3.30 is waiting.'

The obvious question – 'How can this be? You're a child!'– was on the tip of my tongue, but I contented myself with smiling graciously, thanking him for his time and backing out, face aflame. I power-walked down the corridor to meet Mr Cresswell, the Year Six teacher. After my experience with Mr Rycroft, my son's new teacher could be a knife thrower who travelled to school on a unicycle for all I cared. **#embarrassing**

The story of Mrs Smugge and Mr Rycroft provided entertainment for my friends for several days. Lauren doubled up with laughter when I told her, and Kate admitted that she thought he looked far too young to be out without a responsible adult. Honestly!

Somehow, the Smugge household limped through the rest of September. I lived day to day, scanning my emails for directives from the school and relying heavily on Lauren. By the end of the month, I was starting to notice that my waistbands were getting tight and the comments about how tired I looked were becoming too frequent for comfort. Soon, I'd have to brace myself and talk to Johnnie. But before that, I wanted to tell Suze.

On Wednesday, everyone came out of school in an annoying mood. Finn was sulky, Chloë was excitable and kept winding him up and Elsie was whiney and irritating. We trudged up the hill to our house, me struggling with wicked acid heartburn and impatience, them complaining bitterly about the various injustices meted out at school. I was so exhausted that the *Pappardelle Pomodoro* I'd been planning seemed like a bridge too far. I went against my own excellent advice from *Issy Smugge Says: Let's Cook from Scratch*, picked up the phone and ordered in vast amounts of pizza and garlic bread. Goodness me, it was delicious. In half an hour, I ate more carbs than I normally would in a week, and I found that I didn't give a single solitary hoot.

Forgetting myself for a minute, I leaned back and stretched. I was holding on to the last few weeks of warm weather and rocking an on-trend one-shoulder ruched jersey bodysuit underneath my French blue, cable-knit cardigan. It looked great, as long as I kept the cardigan buttoned up and my tummy sucked in. Relaxing at home, I'd forgotten this. Three pairs of eyes bored holes in my abdomen.

'Mummy, you look all cuddly!' Elsie leaned forward and poked me in the stomach. Some deeply buried instinct came to the fore and I put my arm protectively across my belly. There was a silence, broken by me laughing shrilly and suggesting we found some homemade ice cream and made banana splits for pudding.

How much longer could I hide this pregnancy, and how would the children react when I broke the news? To my horror, I suddenly felt emotion wash over me, and when I dropped one of my favourite Mosaique tumblers on the floor, smashing it into a million pieces, I burst into loud and extravagant tears.

Often, I think I must be the worst mother in the world. My children have had their father and Sofija snatched away from them and are left with a snappy, overstretched Isabella M Smugge trying to do a job at which she is constantly failing. And yet, in spite of my many shortcomings, I found myself being patted gently on the back by Elsie, steered over to the sofa in the family room by Chloë and comforted by Finn, who got the dustpan and brush out of the utility cupboard and started sweeping up the broken glass. This made me cry even more.

'Would you like a nice cup of tea, Mummy?' Elsie enquired. 'That always makes people feel better.' I nodded weakly and sank back on the sofa, closing my eyes and sucking my stomach in (not easy, I can tell you). Five minutes later, the girls brought me a cup of tea – weak, milky and with bits floating in it – which was one of the most ambrosial things I have ever had the pleasure to be served. I blew my nose, wiped my eyes and cuddled up to them on the sofa.

'You're so sweet. Mummy is very tired and a bit sad. I'm missing Daddy, but I'm so lucky to have you three.'

At this point, Finn joined us.

'It's all tidied up, Mum. Don't worry.' He smiled at me. 'Are you OK? You look really tired.'

'I'm fine, honestly. I probably need an early night.'

Elsie nestled her little head into my shoulder. 'Mrs Jenkins is super nice. Today, she was telling us about being positive and focusing on happy things. She told us to think of five good things in our lives. I said you, Mummy; and Becky, and our house, and my teddy and our cousin Lily.'

I very nearly burst into tears all over again but managed to restrain myself. 'That's a lovely thought, darling. Why don't we all think of three good things about our lives? Who wants to start?'

Chloë volunteered me, Hannah and Mr Rycroft (a huge hit, it seems, in spite of, or perhaps because of, his extreme youth). Finn, clearly keen to stop me crying again, also name-checked me and added in Jake and football.

'Mummy, I nearly forgot!' Elsie was jiggling with excitement. 'I know it's your turn, but can I have one more? The best thing ever is that Hannah and Becky's mummy didn't die. That's good, isn't it?'

It *was* the best thing ever, as far as I was concerned. Claire was still very poorly and likely to remain in hospital for quite some time, but she was alive and that was the main thing. My prayer, if that's what you wanted to call it, had been answered. I gave everyone a big hug (even Finn), told them that I loved them (because I do), drank my tea and took them all up to bed. #answeredprayer #lovemyfriend #attitudeofgratitude

October

For some reason, the news of my accidental pregnancy was one that I felt terrified about sharing. Curled up on the sofa in the family room with a mug of hot water and grated root ginger (so cleansing), I contemplated my current situation. I do love a list, and in fact have been toying with the idea of writing a new *Issy Smugge Says* book of lists. Sensible and proactive ones, naturally, not those silly space-fillers you find cluttering up the shelves in the self-help section. Every Thomas, Richard and Harold seems to be churning them out. I don't mean those. Aspirational, encouraging, uplifting lists, the kind of thing my followers absolutely eat up, God bless them. **#lovemyfollowers**

There's no time like the present, so I put down my mug and picked up my current favourite notebook (a birthday gift from Silvia, my lovely Swiss mother-in-law). I find the very act of writing down a list of jobs extremely cathartic.

1. Get Johnnie back
2. Sell flat and insist we invest the money in new one of my choosing
3. ~~Find new au pair~~
4. Tell Johnnie about you know what
5. Make Johnnie see sense about Finn's new school
6. Invite Silvia up for the week
7. Ring Mummy
8. Draft next few Open Brackets
9. Talk to Mimi about you know what

10. Ring my consultant, Mr Aggarwal, about you know what and book in consultation

I laid down my pen and let out a deep sigh. With everything committed to paper (I must make sure the children don't find it), my mind was immediately calmed. After a few minutes' thought, I crossed off point 7. I'm too busy for Mummy at the moment and hearing her acidulous tones would only exacerbate my heartburn. She can wait.

On Friday afternoon, I cut myself some slack and went for coffee and cake with Lauren, Kate, Maddie, Lovely Lou and some of the other Year One mums at a local café just outside the village. To my surprise, I seem to be a lot more productive when I take regular breaks, especially if those breaks are in the company of my friends.

I'd laid my bodysuit aside for the time being and had gone with a rather fab layered look with on-trend over-the-knee black suede platform boots and a pair of statement pearl block hoop earrings. The French blue, cable-knit cardie is a great piece and has the advantage of hiding my ever-increasing midriff.

Over carrot cake and hot chocolate, I eagerly drank in the latest playground gossip. It seems that Hayley is driving everyone crazy with her constant complaints about the school's inability to support her son, her non-stop droning about the work she's having done to her house and her overriding belief that she is slightly better than everyone else in the village. It made me cringe, inwardly, to think that only a few months ago, I was just like her. Minus the eyebrows, of course. I'd be ashamed to step outside the front door with such a wild and untamed pair.

Kate was in full flow.

'Honestly, girls, if I have to listen to one more anecdote about her polished concrete floor, or what she said to Christopher about the track lighting, or her theories about hothousing children, I'll scream or hit her. One or the other. If you see her talking to me in the playground, please, I'm begging you, come over and change the subject. I can't take much more.'

'Where's she got all the money from? That's what I want to know.' Maddie was leaning forward eagerly, her lemon drizzle untouched and her mocha rapidly cooling in front of her. 'Can't be cheap. Laura told me that Carly told her that they've extended out into the garden, and apparently they're having underfloor heating put in. Carly's sister lives in one of the houses behind her and her brother works for the firm that's doing the heating. That's how she knows.'

I was intrigued. Hayley didn't strike me as the kind of person who knew much about interiors. Call me judgemental, but I would be very surprised if she had the wide-ranging knowledge and taste to pull off a truly statement kitchen.

'Do you know who she's using?' I asked. I couldn't imagine that Hayley would have the imagination or knowhow to source the right kind of cabinetry.

Kate frowned and tapped her head with her fingers. '*What* are they called? I want to say Villiers. No. Violent? No, not that either. They're out towards the coast, near Aldeburgh.'

I gasped. 'You don't mean Vainqueur Designs, surely?'

Kate exhaled. 'Vainqueur! That's the one. I knew it sounded foreign. Cost a small fortune, she tells me. All hand-made and hand-painted.'

I fell back in my seat, breathless with shock. My own beautiful dove-grey kitchen, and my utility room, and the pantry and boot room had all been designed and fitted by Vainqueur. My kitchen stories and highlights on Instagram alone had harvested at least 20,000 new followers. You can't get better than Vainqueur. And now some strident woman with out-of-control eyebrows and an incontinent son was stealing my thunder. Well! #shockhorror #copycat

I was so taken aback that I beckoned over the waitress and ordered myself an organic flax seed and apricot flapjack before I could stop myself. This brought on a flurry of coffee refills, and in the ensuing vortex of re-caffeination, I seized the opportunity to go to the toilet (why, baby, why?) and take some deep breaths.

The Isabella M Smugge who finds herself talking and laughing with a bunch of school mums while nibbling elegantly on carrot cake is not the same woman who strode so confidently on to the school playground a year ago. But she still has standards, and she is still one of the UK's premier influencers, thank you very much! I needed to find out more about this Hayley, not that it was really any of my business. I felt rather put out, for reasons I was struggling to comprehend. If only Claire was here. She would understand.

The rest of the conversation was about the shocking news that neither Lauren nor I had been picked out of the hat to go and gaze at firemen. Oh well. There's always next year.

At 3pm, we all pushed back our chairs and reluctantly poured ourselves into our cars for the school run. I'd offered Lauren a lift and was starting to regret it. The flapjack had been a mistake. I caught her looking sideways at me as I got up, and almost as soon as we'd pulled on to the A12, she was interrogating me.

'Are you all right, babes? You don't seem yourself since term started.'

I flashed one of my most dazzling smiles at her and sucked my stomach in.

'I'm fine! Really! Couldn't be better.'

Lauren was evidently not convinced. 'Cos no offence, but you never have seconds of anything. And you used to drink coffee like it was going out of fashion. And you always look great, but it's like – well, you've rounded out a bit. I won't say anything, you know I won't. You can trust me.'

Thank heavens for tractors! Suffolk is full of them. I pretended to concentrate on overtaking one, heavily laden with strangely misshapen mud-covered items and driven by a man rejoicing in the name of Baz.

'I've been meaning to ask you, Lauren, what *are* those weird things that everyone's digging up at the moment? We found some in the hedge outside the house the other day. They're too big for potatoes.'

'Sugar beet. Everyone's lifting it at the moment round our way. Bill at Church Farm got the beet contract this year, that's why they keep hammering up and down your lane. But never mind about that. Seriously, babes, is everything OK?'

Issy Smugge is known for her lightning-quick reflexes and razor-sharp mind. Should I confide in my friend? I'd be telling her the news before too long anyway. I decided against it. I needed to chat to Suze first, then break the news to Johnnie. Next week would be time enough to tell Lauren.

I indicated off the A12 and swept round the roundabout at the bottom of the village. 'Of course it is. I've been so naughty, eating far too many carbs and I've cut right back on coffee because I'm not sleeping very well. It's a combination of Johnnie and what happened to Claire. You know, the shock.'

My explanation had done enough to convince Lauren, it seemed. As I parked on my drive, though, ready to walk down the lane to school with her, she laid her hand on my arm. 'Carbs, coffee – whatever it is, I want you to know you can always talk to me if you need to. End of.'

Thank goodness for the escaped sugar beet which had somehow become wedged under the gate. Chit-chat about root vegetables and suchlike kept us going until we reached the playground. It's the weekend! Hooray.

I've never had much truck with the subconscious, but as I served dinner (seared loin of tuna with rocket, spinach and quinoa – I had some making up to do after my carb-filled week), I began to wonder if my sudden urge for cake and chocolate was something to do with the two conversations with Johnnie and Suze I was planning this weekend. After some to-ing and fro-ing, I'd agreed to meet Johnnie (not *her*, obviously) on Saturday morning at a garden centre half an hour south of the village. The plan was for us to have a civilised exchange, model adult behaviour to the children, allow them to eat cake and then for him to take them off for the weekend to a hotel in London. Clearly, the flat is completely unsuitable.

There was a strange atmosphere in the kitchen as we all cleared up and loaded the dishwasher. I'd been trying (and succeeding, I flatter myself) to present a calm and confident face to the children (apart from the disastrous evening with the broken glass), so I was surprised when Finn said, 'Mum, can we have a chat?'

We sat down in the family room, me wondering what was coming, Elsie furiously sucking her thumb, Chloë chewing her nails and Finn looking serious. I smiled, encouragingly, ready to listen to whatever they had to say.

'Mum, we don't want to upset you, but is Dad ever coming back to live with us? And what about Sofija?'

I was flummoxed, and that's not something you'll hear me say very often. I racked my brains for something inspirational and encouraging, but all I could think of was a rather splendid affirmation I'd posted on Insta that afternoon.

'Not all storms come to disrupt your life; some come to clear your path.'

Quite true, of course, and I'd accompanied it with a beautiful photo of a ragged autumn sky over the village green, but it wasn't what my children wanted to hear. Honesty and transparency had turned out to be useful tools in my struggle to become a better parent, so I decided to employ them in this slightly sticky situation.

'Well, I'm glad you asked me that. Dad and I are talking regularly, and I am very much working towards him coming back home. As for Sofija, we've decided it's best that she pursues other career opportunities, so you can see her when you visit Dad at the hotel tomorrow, but she won't be coming back. I know you miss her, and I am sorry about that. Let's keep talking and see if we can find a path through.'

Rather good, I thought. Honest, direct and open. If only Mummy had had my superior parenting skills back in the day.

Elsie and Chloë shot quick, sideways glances at their brother, who had clearly been elected spokesperson.

'But Mum, we love Sofija. It's like she's our sister, or best friend or something. Even when Dad comes home, we still want to see her.'

The girls nodded vigorously, gazing at me with wide, watchful eyes. Why do I feel that I'm always on the back foot recently? What happened to those long-gone halcyon days when I was in complete control of every aspect of my life? I thought quickly. Maybe honesty was the best policy. What was the worst that could happen?

'I miss her too. She was my friend. I promise I'll think about this and we will work something out. I'm afraid I can never have her back here in the house, but of course you can see her in London. Now, it's getting late, and we all need to be up early tomorrow! Bed!'

I chased them up the stairs, stopping on the first landing to catch my breath. What happened to that lithe woman with a BMI of just over 23? At this rate, I'll have to install a stairlift! #fallingapart #wibblywobbly

Just before I fell into bed, exhausted, and with my rapidly expanding stomach in knots about seeing Johnnie the next day, I WhatsApped Suze.

'Hi Suze. How are you all? I've got news. Can we chat tomorrow? Dropping kids off with Johnnie at 10 our time xxx'

I was asleep before my head hit the pillow.

I wonder if I'll ever get used to seeing my husband's car departing down the road with my children in it, waving goodbye to me. The handover went as smoothly as these things possibly can. Johnnie kissed me on the cheek and spent some time sitting at a table with us all listening to the children chatter. I was grateful to him for not rushing straight off.

In a lull in conversation, he turned to me and said, 'Iss, I don't want to pressure you, but have you had a chance to look over those papers about the flat? I've had a very attractive offer and I'd really like to start the ball rolling.'

He smiled his dazzling smile at me. My man. My Johnnie. I could smell his aftershave and my knees felt weak. However, Issy Smugge is no pushover, and I certainly wasn't going to roll over and give him what he wanted straight away. I said I'd consider it and told him I needed to have a chat when he dropped the children back. #didntcomedownwiththelastshower

It had just gone 10.30 when Johnnie pulled out of the car park and sped back towards London with my precious children to meet *her*. Suze had replied to my message earlier.

'Hi Bella. I've got news too! Call me when you're free, no plans today xxx'

I calculated it was teatime in Hong Kong. My early breakfast of porridge with bananas and cinnamon had hit the spot, but now my tummy was rumbling. The baby was eating its own weight in carbs, so I decided to amble back into the garden-centre café and have my chat with Suze sitting comfortably on a sofa. I ordered a hot chocolate and a fruit scone with jam and settled myself down for a good old girlie natter.

Hearing my sister's voice made everything better. Wiping some rogue crumbs off my lime-green, cropped, quilted jacket (so now), I prepared myself to tell her the news about the unexpected new family member. I was a little concerned. Even though our relationship was back on track, still, I was sharing news about a baby who had been conceived in a drunken night of passion with my cheating husband, her ex-boyfriend. I very rarely watch the type of televisual programming which covers such Byzantine issues, but even for a woman as tactful as I, it was going to be a tough subject to broach.

Fortunately, Suze was bubbling over with her own news.

'I hope you're sitting down, Bella. I'm so excited. Jeremy and I have been thinking about this for a while, and we've just had confirmation. We're moving back to the UK!'

Well, you could have knocked me down with a feather. I was delighted. My dear Suze back in the country just as I needed her more than ever! I expressed my joy and asked for further details.

'We've been talking about moving back for a while. Jeremy's transferring to the London office and I've decided to take a career break. Lily won't be little forever, and I want to devote my time to her while I've got the chance. And Bella, you know how much I want to spend more time with you and the children. What do you think?'

I took a deep breath in to reply and choked on a fragment of the scone. Wheezing, coughing and with my eyes streaming, I was making a complete show of myself, as Mummy would say. Concerned fellow diners turned round to see what the noise was and, to my utter shame, an elderly woman in an unfortunate floral ensemble came over to assist.

'Gone down the wrong hole, chicken? Happens to the best of us. Here, let me give you a bang on the back.'

This she proceeded to do, violently and repeatedly, until the coughing abated. I thanked her, blew my nose discreetly on my napkin and assured Suze that I was fine. I drained my cup of chocolate, arose and marched off to my car. Honestly!

Safely ensconced, I questioned Suze about her move.

'We think between Christmas and Easter. Jeremy needs to finish up in the Hong Kong office and do the handover and we've got to find a house. We found a couple of nice places in Amersham, big gardens, close to the station, so ideal for work.

The schools are good around there too. I would have loved to come to Suffolk, but Jeremy's parents are in Chalfont and he wants to be close to them. His dad's not too good, as you know. We worked out it's just over two hours to yours. You can come and stay with us at weekends and in the holidays. Just imagine how much fun it'll be, Bella! And not too close to Mummy.'

We both laughed. Our mother lives in a village just north of Tunbridge Wells ('*Royal* Tunbridge Wells, girls, I'll thank you to remember'), and while the train connections to London are good, travelling further afield is time-consuming. Neither of us wished to spend any more time with our parent than we absolutely had to.

I was overcome with joy at the thought of having Suze back in the country. We chatted for a bit longer while I braced myself to tell her my news.

'I hope *you're* sitting down, Suze. I've got something to tell you that you won't have been expecting. I'm pregnant.'

There was a short silence followed by a gasp. 'Pregnant? But – I thought – who – I mean, *what*, Bella?'

I could feel my face reddening. 'It came as a huge shock. You're the first person I've told. Johnnie and I had a massive fight when he came up to the house in July. Things got a bit out of hand, we both had far too much to drink, and we had a screaming row. Finn saw, and it was – well, it was awful. You remember how we swore we'd never do to anyone what Mummy and Daddy did to us? I felt so bad that he saw us fighting like that. Once Johnnie had calmed Finn down and put him back to bed, we had some port and got chatting about the good old days. We went upstairs and – well, it just happened. I thought it meant he was back, but the next morning he left and went back to *her*. Obviously, I'd stopped taking the pill and it was the last thing on my mind.'

There was silence.

'Are you there, Suze?'

'Yes, still here. Just trying to take it in. Goodness. I don't know what to say.'

I felt more awkward than I had for a very long time. What if this news damaged my newly restored relationship with Suze? What if she changed her mind about moving? What if… but I couldn't even begin to give such a terrible thought house room. I felt tears begin to fill my eyes.

As I tried to think of something to say, I became aware that the scone and hot chocolate had made their way far enough south to meet the porridge and bananas sitting, leaden, in my stomach, with catastrophic results. The familiar acidic burning sensation kicked in as I opened my mouth to speak. To my utter horror, an extremely loud and very impolite noise emerged, right down the phone into my unsuspecting sister's ear.

I blushed. 'Oh gosh, sorry, Suze! I do beg your pardon. I've got the most terrible heartburn…'

My apologies were met with howls of laughter. The sound of my sister's mirth set me off and I found myself with tears pouring down my cheeks, my nose running and the most unladylike sounds filling the car. It's true what they say. Laughter really is the best medicine. I blew my nose loudly and wiped my eyes for the second time in half an hour. My stomach rumbled loudly, and I let out another discreet burp.

'Looks like my timing's spot on, Bella.' Suze had calmed down and I could hear nose blowing at her end. 'When are you telling Johnnie?'

'Tomorrow when he brings the children back. I haven't really got my head around it yet, but I do know he'll stop all this nonsense with Sofija and come back home when he hears. Silver lining and all that.'

'Hmm.' Suze was thoughtful. 'I suppose. Is that what you really want?'

I was surprised. 'Of course! That's all I'm thinking about at the moment, how to get him back home and get everything back to normal. I'm managing somehow, but it's such a struggle. I can't carry on like this much longer.'

'OK. You know we'll support you whatever happens, don't you, Bella?'

What would I do without my lovely Suze? We bade each other a fond farewell and I glanced in the mirror. I had panda eyes from the mascara and eyeliner, smeared lipstick up one cheek and some kind of viscous substance in my hair. I looked up and saw the elderly woman from the café walking towards me, en route to her car. She glanced sideways and caught my eye. Isabella M Smugge is not used to being the recipient of sympathetic looks. I gunned the engine and roared out of the car park, homeward bound. **#nomorescones**

Back home, I felt at a loose end. The house seemed empty and quiet without the children and I couldn't settle to anything. I texted Lauren.

'*Hi. Got any plans? I'm home alone xx*'

Back came her reply.

'*Taking kids to park for a run-around in half an hour. Want to meet us? Market on today xx*'

A market! I used to love mooching around markets in town, not that a small Suffolk village was likely to offer those kinds of delights. I removed the smudged mascara and eyeliner, reapplied lipstick and touched up my brows. Sucking in my stomach, I grabbed my phone and keys and sashayed out into the crisp autumn air.

Back in London, we had the world on our doorstep. When Johnnie and I were first married, we used to sleep in on the weekend, then go out for a leisurely breakfast and a bit of ambling around the markets. Borough and Greenwich were our favourites (Johnnie would never let me go to Camden), we'd often pop down to Brick Lane and have a bagel and we even ventured as far south as Brixton from time to time. Those were the days! It was a foodie's paradise, and I have to admit that buying food yourself is rather fun. These days, of course, I have everything delivered. Who's got time to shop? What a time suck.

I walked briskly down our lane, past the school and turned left on to the square surrounded by shops, where a collection of traders had set up their stalls. I was expecting some cheap mass-produced clothing and perhaps a fruit and veg stall, but to my surprise, there were a number of purveyors who wouldn't have looked that out of place in Covent Garden.

I perused with interest. There was a cheese provider, two ladies with homemade quiches and cakes and a cheerful-looking woman under a gazebo selling jams and various tracklements. I purchased a jar of reasonably priced Lebanese fig chutney and some salted almonds. A loud man in red trousers and a ludicrous hat was marching round braying at the stall holders (clearly not from round here), but otherwise it was mostly middle-aged people wandering around with bags made from jute.

To my delight, the woman on the cheese van really knew her stuff. We had a long and fascinating conversation about the merits of Cornish Camembert versus French while, to my surprise, she disinterred a piece of Sage Derby (my absolute favourite) from beneath a stack of smoked Bavarian cheeses. My bag packed with delicious goodies, I headed over to the park, while mentally noting up the delights of the market to help to lure Johnnie back to my side. He's a sucker for all things artisan.

Lauren was sitting on a bench in the playpark knocking back an energy drink. I sank down beside her with a sigh and sucked my stomach in. She laid a kindly hand on my arm.

'How was it? Grim?'

'It isn't getting any better. But I chatted to Suze and she's got some great news. They're coming back to England!'

Lauren beamed. 'Oh, babes, that's amazing! And what excellent timing with the baby coming.'

I nodded. 'I know. That's what I thought. I wasn't sure how I was going to manage without…'

I broke off. Lauren was grinning at me.

'Honestly, darling, if you'd pinned a sign to your back saying "I'm up the duff" it couldn't have been more obvious. Knocking off coffee, eating carbs like they're going out of fashion, buying up all the sardines at the shop. That means Maddie owes me a fiver. Do you want to tell the girls, or shall I?'

I sighed and let my stomach do its thing. The French blue, cable-knit cardigan parted to reveal the incipient young Smugge, stretching my skin and causing such inconvenient symptoms. Lauren gasped.

'Look at that. How far along are you?'

I counted up on my fingers. 'Must be about ten weeks.'

'And you haven't told anyone? Babes, you need to get yourself booked in at the surgery. You should be having your twelve-week scan soon.'

I shifted uncomfortably in my seat. This was one of the reasons I'd been putting off sharing the news. Talking about it made it all too horribly real. I tried to convey this to Lauren in a few well-chosen words. All I had to do was ring Mr Aggarwal and book myself in, but by doing that, I would confirm that child number four was on the way and that technically, in the eyes of the law, I was a single parent. Although, of course, Johnnie would be dumping Sofija and returning to the marital home as soon as he heard the news.

Lauren swung into action. 'Seriously, this is not good. You're nearly three months gone, and you haven't seen anyone yet. There is a baby in there and it's going to be coming out in six months! I know I'm poking my nose in, but I'm coming back to yours straight after drop-off on Monday to make sure you ring your consultant bloke, all right?'

Reluctantly, I agreed. Three months is the standard time for the big reveal in the world of bloggers and it was testament to my inner turmoil that I hadn't even thought of how I would tell my followers the good news. Because, of course, I would have to pretend that good news it was. Isabella M Smugge doesn't make mistakes and stop taking her pill and sleep with her cheating husband in a drunken haze. Or at least, if she does, she doesn't trumpet it all over social media.

Sitting in the park with my friend was bringing up lots of uncomfortable thoughts I'd been assiduously repressing. Mummy would be horrified, of course, and Mimi would be over the moon. What if I had damaged the baby by not getting myself booked in for antenatal care? How would the children take the news? And worst of all, how on earth was I going to manage with four children and hardly any help?

My reverie was interrupted by Lauren's youngest daughter, Pearl, in dire need of both a number two and a long chat about what Connor had said to Ethan in the bushes and what she thought about it. I promised to keep an eye on Ruby and Crystal while Lauren headed off over the playing field to the public toilets.

I sat gazing into the middle distance, trying to work out how I was going to couch the good news to Johnnie tomorrow afternoon. While writing my speech in my head, I noticed one of the children hanging from an alarmingly high branch with only one limb (theirs) attached. I trotted over to save whoever it was, only to be confronted by a howling person to whom I had not been introduced and a circle of short people shouting advice up at him.

'Let go! We'll catch you.'

'Hold on! You'll break your leg.'

'It's OK, Chloë's mum's here.'

The child, a grimy individual who looked vaguely familiar, had got himself stuck on a high branch and was clearly frozen with fear. What was really needed was:

a) A ladder

Or

b) A person taller than myself

Sadly, neither appeared to be available. I instructed the children to stop yelling and deployed my calmest, most soothing tones.

'You're going to be absolutely fine. Stop crying and try to relax. If you can get yourself back to the trunk, you can drop down and I'll catch you. Come on, now.'

This, if anything, made the situation worse. More cries of fear drifted down from the tree. I decided to call in the big guns. Thank heavens there's no need to drop to your knees, put your hands together and close your eyes when you wish to address the Almighty, or so Lauren tells me.

'Dear God. Isabella M Smugge here. I wonder if You would be so kind as to send a tall person along to help me out in this difficult situation. I'm all for equality, but as You decided to stop me growing any taller than five foot five, I think we can both see that there isn't much I can achieve in this situation. Anyone would do. Preferably someone who knows this child. Many thanks. Amen.'

The good Lord had answered my prayer about Claire, and it seemed that He was smiling upon me yet again. Without further ado, Claire's husband, Tom, appeared with Joel on a buggy board and the baby fast asleep in his pram. Even with circles under his eyes and wearing what appeared to be combat trousers, he was still startlingly good-looking. And tall. Reassuringly tall.

After the briefest of greetings, I apprised him of the situation. He held out his arms.

'Down you come, then, Max. I've got you.'

Without a murmur, the child was returned to *terra firma*. I made a mental note to thank God for His very efficient answer to my request and to reinforce my gratitude to Him for saving Claire, as per my entreaty. I don't know how the stats normally stack up, but a 100 per cent success rate is most pleasing.

Tom, Lauren and I sank back on to the bench. The baby slept on and Joel pottered over to the play equipment and amused himself by running around in circles.

'How's Claire doing?' asked Lauren, lighting a roll-up. 'Any idea when we might be allowed in to see her for a proper visit? We all miss her so much.'

Tom took out his phone. 'I've got a picture for you. She asked me to take one of her and Ben and show it to you. She sends her love. She's still very weak, asleep a lot of the time. The surgery really took it out of her, and of course the sepsis made it all so much worse.'

He showed us a photo of poor Claire lying back against her pillows with the baby in her arms. Her face was drawn, and she looked bone tired. I barely recognised my round-faced, cheerful friend. The last time we'd been allowed in to see her, she was hooked up to drips and tubes and half-asleep.

'My parents keep threatening to come to stay. I've told them we're managing with everyone's help, but they won't take no for an answer.'

'Oh dear. I can pop over if you like, you know, to lighten the load.' Lauren was looking concerned. 'Maybe we could have a safe word on the WhatsApp group if it gets really desperate. No offence, Tom. I know your mum and dad mean to be kind.'

I was intrigued. I wanted to find out more but didn't like to appear nosey. Claire hadn't really said much about her in-laws. All I knew about them was that they didn't approve of her, which was reason enough to dislike them.

On our way home, I quizzed Lauren. 'Tell me about Tom's parents. Aren't they very nice?'

She grimaced. 'I can't lie to you. They're not. I've met them a couple of times and they look at me as if I was something that had been trodden through the house. They're minted, always bring flowers and chocolates and expensive toys for the kids. I don't know what it is about them. Whenever they're in the room, there's a bad atmosphere.'

'Maybe we'd better pop round a few times, then. Give Tom a break.'

Lauren nodded in agreement. 'Yeah, let's. They'll love you. You're right up their street!' She gave me a big hug. 'Love ya! Good luck with Johnnie.'

Without the children, the house seemed empty and echoing. I ambled about aimlessly, took a few shots and posted some fashion content. Sometimes I wonder what it would be like to be a homemaker. A lot more scrubbing and a lot less snapping, probably. I've noticed that I'm one of the very few school mums who has regular manicures. Even though Johnnie's not here, I'm keeping up with my self-care. I owe it to myself.

One good thing about having my bedroom to myself is that I can really ramp up my moisturising routine. You'll never see Issy Smugge in any of those tacky magazines with a red circle around a body part. My heels aren't cracked, my toes are straight and my neck is as smooth as a pair of organic French silk lounging pyjamas. By nine that night, I was in bed, with my Pro Vitamin Tea Tree Oil Infused moisturising socks pulled up over my ankles and my hands encased in my Stroke Me! deeply hydrating hand gloves.

In my relationship enrichment bestseller, *Issy Smugge Says: Turn the Lights Down Low*, I advise my readers to keep the mystique alive in long-term relationships:

> Don't let your partner see you applying spot cream, touching up your roots or donning moisturising socks and gloves. Beauty routines, for him and her, need to be carried out with the bathroom door firmly closed. Take advantage of trips abroad or short absences to double down on your intense self-care regimen. Hard work in the bathroom pays off in the bedroom!

I settled myself back on my award-winning self-plumping, lavender-infused, goose-down pillows and took some deep, cleansing breaths. Why people don't invest more in their sleep accessories I simply don't know. And I'm not just saying that because I'm the face of Plump No More Pillows. I only endorse products that I am entirely happy with. Everyone in the Smugge household takes their nightly rest on a pair of Plump No Mores. Even *she* had them in her bedroom, and I could have just as easily fobbed her off with bog-standard cotton ones. #neverthinkingofmyself #generoustoafault

My mind was racing, so I sprinkled some extra lavender oil on my pillow and thought calming thoughts. They didn't work. All night long I dreamed of Johnnie, and when I woke up, my award-winning pillow was wet with tears.

Considering that God answered both of my prayers very quickly and efficiently, I should really be paying Him back by going to church on a Sunday. I will, too, just not yet. I slept in on Sunday morning and by the time I got up and had my shower, it was gone half past ten. I contented myself with having an informal chat with Him while I exfoliated and patted in my eye cream.

'Dear God. Isabella M Smugge again. I wanted to express my sincere thanks for Your kindness in sending Tom to rescue that grubby little boy from the tree yesterday. And again, thank You so much for Claire not dying. I absolutely promise that I will keep my word and not look down my nose at anyone or think horrible things. Please forgive me for thinking snobbish things about Hayley's kitchen. Amen.'

Prayers don't come much more sincere than that. Plus, I had contributed lavishly to the repair of the roof at church, so surely I was still in credit. I decided to spend some time on household activities which could be repurposed for my followers. They love it when I make bread or bake, so I duly made three loaves of sourdough and a batch of scones. I posed my shots artfully, with the autumn light slanting in through the kitchen window, illuminating the jar of homemade jam, the clotted cream and the splash of flour on the rose quartz granite. **#bakinginspo**

Once I'd done that and posted the images across my socials, it seemed a wicked waste not to try some of it. I toasted a couple of slices of the sourdough and spread them with butter and some of Wendy the church jam-maker's delectable blackcurrant preserve. Posed prettily on my charcoal speckle glaze Insta-friendly plate with a steaming mug of Lapsang Souchong by its side, they made a pretty picture. The likes and shares would soon come flooding in.

I spent the rest of my time wandering round the garden taking pictures. I love autumn. And it's a season that lends itself particularly well to the lifestyle blogger's Insta grid. Rich, ruby leaves with sunlight shining through them, blue autumnal skies, trees reaching up to the heavens and so on. I became so engrossed that it was two o'clock before I knew it and I only had an hour left before Johnnie was due.

I needed to focus my mind. I did some deep-breathing exercises and scrambled myself a couple of eggs.

My hope was that Johnnie would leave Sofija immediately and that we could start to rebuild our life together without further ado. However, I had to be prepared for the faintest of chances that he would take a little more persuading. Should I be businesslike, pointing out that we shared a very successful and profitable life together, or tug on his heartstrings? I got out the children's baby books from upstairs and arranged them on the dresser, just in case. I also had to talk him into agreeing to send Finn to the local state school. The deadline for the application was fast approaching and I needed to nail it down today.

Bang on three o'clock, I heard the crunch of wheels on the gravel. I opened the front door, and there he was, climbing out of the car, tall, handsome and smiling as ever. I'd chosen my outfit with care, wearing his favourite colour (duck-egg blue), putting in the aquamarine earrings he'd given me for our last anniversary and spraying his favourite perfume lavishly on my wrists and on the back of my neck. The girls came running towards me, shouting, 'Mummy! Mummy!' which was heartening. Finn got out of the car more slowly, his head down. My heart sank.

But there was no time to worry about whatever pre-teen grumps my son was in. I smiled radiantly and stood on tiptoe to kiss my husband. 'I've made scones and there's clotted cream. Come on, you lot! They won't eat themselves.'

I sounded like a housewife from a 1970s advert for carpet cleaner, but sometimes we must wear the mask. After everyone was sated with hot chocolate and baked goods, I chased the girls upstairs to unpack, patted Finn's head and beckoned Johnnie into the snug, where I'd lit the fire.

I smiled, I hoped in a loving and non-threatening way. 'So. How was the weekend? What did you get up to?'

'We had a lovely time, Iss. The hotel was fantastic, great pool and spa, we took the kids to a couple of museums, went down the Thames on a boat, let them have far too many chips – you know the kind of thing. I think our arrangement's working out incredibly well.'

'Finn looks a bit down in the dumps,' I remarked.

Johnnie frowned a little and shifted in his seat. 'We had a bit of a row about school. He knows he's off to my alma mater, but he kept insisting he was going to the local high school. I'm afraid I had to be a bit sharp. I'll make it up with him before I go.'

I took a deep breath. When you've been married to a man as long as I have, you know all the little tips and tricks for getting your own way, although of course it helps if you're sharing the same bedroom. Never mind. I would simply have to do my best.

'Johnnie, there's something I have to tell you. It's good news, but it might come as a bit of a shock to you. I'm expecting a baby.'

I smiled into his eyes and reached for his hand. I waited for him to tell me that this changed everything, and that he was sorry and would be dumping Sofija in short order. After a minute or so, still waiting, I gave his hand an impatient little shake.

'Did you hear me? I'm having your baby. I'm nearly three months along. I haven't said anything up to now because I was a bit nervous, but you always said you wanted four and so...'

My speech was interrupted by Johnnie jerking back in his seat. His face had gone white, his nostrils were flaring and his fists were clenched.

'What do you mean, pregnant? By whom? If this is some kind of trap to get me back – well, I'd have thought more of you than this.'

I was speechless. I'd never heard my husband speak in such a cold, angry voice. He was looking at me almost as if he hated me. I shivered and put my hand on my stomach.

'I wasn't going to say anything about your weight gain. I thought you were hammering the carbs to compensate for me not being here. You've certainly filled out in the last couple of weeks.'

I looked him dead in the eye. 'How dare you! Of course it's your baby! Remember that night we had the fight and then you kissed me outside our room?'

He had the grace to colour slightly and look at his feet.

'Well, this is the result. I'm at home, looking after *your* children round the clock, having to pick up the slack because *she's* run off and you dare, you *dare* to accuse me of trying to trap you? You scumbag. You've got me pregnant, and you honestly think I'm going to let you carry on gallivanting around town doing whatever you please while I'm stuck in the country? I don't think so.'

'All right, Iss. You've made your point. And what do you want me to do about it?'

My voice came out rather more screechy than I'd planned. 'Do? Come back home, of course! Leave her and start behaving like a decent husband and father again. You've had your little fling, and I think I've been very good about it.'

Johnnie shook his head. 'No. I can't do that, Iss. I told you before. I still love you, but I'm not *in* love with you any more. Sofija's the one for me. I can't just dump her and leave her all by herself. I'll support you, of course, and be here for the baby as much as I can, but you can't seriously expect me to agree to come back, just because you got yourself pregnant.'

Isabella M Smugge is a woman with deep reserves of patience, and she rarely loses her temper. However, this was too much. I seized his forearms and dug my nails in hard. 'Got *myself* pregnant? You miserable, cowardly, two-faced pig!' Ignoring his yelps of pain, I kicked him hard in the shins. 'I am not being left here in this house as a single parent. You made vows to me, to love me and honour me and all that stuff, in a church! I've got witnesses. This is just a temporary fling – we both know that. The sooner you finish things with that little slut, the better!'

I was breathing heavily, and I could feel my heart beating at 100 miles an hour. We stared at each other for a long moment. Johnnie let out a deep sigh.

'OK. I can see we've got a situation here. Losing our tempers isn't going to do any good. Now, my issue is that Sofija can't know we slept together after we broke up. So you'll have to pretend that you got pregnant just before that, in June. All right? And then we can say that the baby was late. When is it due, anyway?'

'April.'

'Right. That's sorted, then. Naturally, I'll sort out the money side of things and we'll arrange plenty of visits so I can bond with it.'

My heart was sinking into my boots. What had *she* done to my lovely Johnnie? My loving, funny, adorable man had morphed into this hard-faced stranger.

Difficult and tangled though the situation undoubtedly was, I didn't feel that lying was the way forward. I'd blocked Sofija as soon as I found out about her betrayal, so she certainly wasn't following me on the socials any more so wouldn't see me posting about the baby to my followers.

'You can tell her whatever you like. I don't care. I know the truth and unless I have it early, it's coming out in April and that's all there is to it. I've got my followers to think of. A couple more weeks and I'll have to start posting about it.'

Johnnie's face darkened and his eyes narrowed. 'I should have known your followers would have something to do with it. I wouldn't put it past you to have done this on purpose to get your numbers up. What do you think's going to happen when that toxic harpy Lavinia Harcourt finds out? Honestly, Iss, listen to yourself. I can't believe what I'm hearing.'

'And I can't believe what *I'm* hearing, Johnnie Smugge!' I could feel my voice getting louder and I clenched my fists hard. 'We got drunk, and you made me think you were coming back. You hurt me so badly by going behind my back with her in the first place and then leaving on Sunday morning when we'd slept together. Did it ever occur to you what that felt like? I wouldn't dream of getting pregnant just to advance my brand. And let Lavinia say what she likes. I've got Mimi on my side, even if I haven't got you.'

My voice broke and my eyes filled with tears. I looked down at my hands, still balled into fists. There was a silence. My mind was racing but time was also running out for Finn's school application, and suddenly I saw the way ahead.

'We made a child together, even if we didn't mean to, and I am not going to start that child's life off with lies. I'll sign the papers for the flat, even though I don't see why I should. You pay the fees, I get half the profit. In return, you agree that Finn goes to the local high school. He's wretched, thinking about being sent away to your old boarding school, and we've talked about it a lot. I won't inflict any extra misery on our child – he's unhappy enough about the situation as it is. Deal?'

I gave him the special look. He quailed slightly, as well he might, and frowned.

50

'I can't believe you would sink so low. You know how much it means to me that my boy goes to my old school. Three generations of Smugges…'

I interrupted. 'I know, I know. School makes a Smugge, meeting the right people, best start in life, blah blah blah. Well, too bad. This past year has changed me. It's not all about money and how things look. What about feelings? What about emotional intelligence? You're not stuck in the house every day having to struggle with three children and their needs. You'd be singing a different tune if you were.'

Johnnie snorted. 'It's not all about how things look? Don't let Mimi hear you saying that. *You've* changed. You were never like this when we lived in London.'

I stood up. 'Are we all done here? Finn goes to state school, agreed? Give me those papers to sign before I change my mind.'

My husband banged his hands down on the sofa. 'You haven't given me much of a choice, have you? I never thought I'd see the day I was being blackmailed by my own wife.'

'Tough. I never thought I'd see the day I was having to persuade my own husband to do the right thing. Your actions have consequences. I'll be ringing Mr Aggarwal tomorrow to book myself in, not that you care.'

We marched out of the snug, leaving the fire dying in the grate. I plastered on a big fake smile and engaged in inconsequential chatter for the sake of the children, who had come back downstairs and were eyeing up the remains of the scones. Johnnie looked at his watch. 'Better hit the road. Early start tomorrow. Bye, kids, see you soon. Iss, take care of yourself. And lay off the carbs.'

And with that he was gone, roaring off down the road, London-bound, leaving me trembling inside and feeling as though I had been punched in the stomach. #fightingformyboy

I didn't have the energy left to break the baby news to the children. I listened to them chat about their weekend. Finn was quiet. Once the girls were in bed, I told him the good news about his future education.

'Thanks, Mum.' He smiled for the first time since he'd come home. 'How did you talk Dad round?'

I grinned. 'I've got my ways. I'll fill in the form tomorrow and then you're all sorted. Come on now, it's late and you've got school in the morning. Love you.'

'Love you too.' He smiled over his shoulder as he walked into his bedroom and shut the door. Maybe I'm not such a terrible mother after all.

I slept badly, my rest punctuated by dreams where I was running down a long, dark corridor trying to find something very precious which was just out of reach. I woke with my eyes wet with tears to find Elsie curled up beside me, fast asleep. I lay gazing at her face, the long lashes quivering as she slept, and her thumb plugged into her mouth. When she's asleep, I can still see traces of the baby she once was. I leaned over to kiss her gently and smelt an all-too-familiar aroma. I'd have to strip the bed and ask Ali to air the mattress again. Sighing, I swung my feet out of bed, and the day began.

Lauren was as good as her word. Straight after drop-off, I found myself marching back up the lane with her by my side, questioning me about the weekend. The old Issy Smugge would have covered it all up and pretended that everything was fine. The new one couldn't really see the point.

'Obviously, she's influenced him. He didn't mean any of those things. I know he'll be back once the news has sunk in. And to be fair, I *have* been overeating. Johnnie always kept me on the straight and narrow as far as food's concerned.'

'Hmm.' Lauren didn't look convinced. 'If Scott had even mentioned my weight when I was carrying the girls, he'd have had a smack. It's the one time you can stuff your face, and no one can tell you not to. Everyone knows that.'

Back at home, I rang Mr Aggarwal's secretary. I don't care what anyone says, private health care is worth every penny. Everything was going along beautifully when she suddenly said, 'Hang on a minute, Mrs Smugge. There's a note on your file. Let me just have a look.'

There was silence for a minute or two. 'I'm going to have to speak to Mr Aggarwal and come straight back to you. I don't know if you recall, but there was quite significant scar tissue when you had your six-week check-up after Elsie was born. You weren't planning to have another baby at the time, and we did discuss the issues you might have with a fourth C-section.'

I sat at the island listening to some delightfully soothing holding music (a Scarlatti sonata, if I wasn't very much mistaken). Lauren raised her eyebrows and mouthed, 'All OK, babes?' I nodded and sipped my tea.

There was a click and the Scarlatti stopped, mid-arpeggio, to be replaced by the mellifluous tones of my consultant.

'Mrs Smugge! How lovely to hear from you. Let me pass on my congratulations to you and Mr Smugge on your happy news. Now, Stephanie I think has already mentioned the issue we had with scar tissue after Elsie's birth. My notes also refer to a couple of adhesions. I know you experienced quite a lot of discomfort from those. I would suggest that you make an appointment, and we'll have a look and see where we are. How does that sound? Are you still in West Brompton?'

I explained that we had moved out to the country. 'Ah. Can I perhaps suggest that you consult one of my colleagues at The Friary? While I'd be delighted to be in charge of your care, that would be a very long journey for you, and in case of emergencies, I'd be easier in my mind if you were closer to home.'

Reluctantly, I agreed that this was probably sensible, said goodbye to Stephanie ('I loved your last *Issy Smugge Says*! Keep it up!') and rang off. Great! Now I'd have to break in a new consultant at a hospital with which I was not familiar. The Friary was on the other side of Ipswich, probably a half-hour drive. I certainly wouldn't be having a natural birth, so once my Caesarean was all booked in, I could relax.

I passed on the news to Lauren, who looked puzzled. 'No offence, babes, but why are you jumping through all these hoops? We've got the doctor's five minutes' walk away and the hospital maternity unit is brilliant. I had the girls there and I couldn't have asked for better care. It's not even twenty minutes if you hammer it a bit.'

'You mean – use the NHS?'

'Yes. You pay your taxes, don't you? Might as well get the benefit.'

I considered her suggestion. Johnnie would be horrified at the very notion, which almost made it worth doing. We've got private health care, because why wouldn't you, but to be fair, the children were all registered at the local surgery and they did seem very pleasant. I promised Lauren I'd think about it and settled down to another day's work. **#awomanswork #whattodo**

After much pondering, I decided to ring the doctors' and see what they had to say, although of course I would also be visiting the elegant confines of The Friary.

I must confess that I was keeping a weather eye on how my health and well-being decisions would affect my followers. You don't get as far as I have without tailoring your content to the people who support you. I've always been fortunate enough to have private care and plenty of disposable income, but my first year in Suffolk had shown me that I was very much in the minority. What if I took the burgeoning young Smugge and plugged him or her into the velvet embrace of the private health sector and it turned people against me?

On a crisp autumn morning, I betook myself to the surgery (red brick, plenty of parking, nice perennial borders) and sat myself down in the waiting room.

Our old surgery at home was delightful, a muted earthy palette, fresh flowers, charming staff and, of course, no waiting. Here, there were sad-looking chairs in clashing colours, a small table covered in dog-eared periodicals and a distressingly high number of patients with deep, chest-rattling coughs. To my horror, I spied hirsute Hayley, sitting at the other end of the waiting room gazing at her phone. Before I could decide whether to make myself known, a voice from a box on the wall squawked, 'Smudge. Isabella Smudge to Room 3.' Hayley's head snapped back, and I was enveloped in her gaze, more eyebrows than eyeballs. I smiled insincerely and scuttled down to Room 3.

I am leaving October more rotund and curvaceous than I entered it. I have a due date – 5th April. Nearly everyone knows I'm expecting. I've applied for Finn's high school place, signed off the papers for the sale of the flat, allowed Johnnie to have the children for three days of half term and cried so much my eyelashes are starting to look positively threadbare. I've baked, I've inspired, I've filtered, I've won new followers, but nothing is filling up the aching void within. Once upon a time, a new baby would have heralded a season of joy, but now I simply feel terrified. No help to speak of (unless you count all the cooking, cleaning and gardening being done for me) and yet another barrier between me and Mummy.

The only bright spots are that Finn is far happier now that the threat of being the fourth generation of Smugge men to be sent away to school has been lifted, my skin is starting to clear up (hooray) and Silvia is coming to stay soon. Davina is texting daily as she's now a week overdue with her first baby. I may ring her tonight to tell her the good news. I must try to sound happy. **#wearingthemask #whatliesahead**

November

I've often heard other women talking about feeling overwhelmed. I hope you won't judge me when I tell you that I used to think it was all down to their lack of planning. I've always been known for my incredible efficiency, but now I come to think about it, I always had Sofija to rely on. I think I could have forgiven nearly anything, but stealing my husband is the ultimate in betrayal. There are some people in my old social circle (two-faced Meredith, my so-called friend from my London days, for example) who would simply laugh and say something like, 'But darling, you can always get another husband! Good au pairs are *so* hard to find.' But that's Meredith for you. So shallow.

However, here I am, stuck in the country, rain lashing against the windows, abdomen swelling apace and jobs piling up – and I have to confess, I feel overwhelmed. I hadn't realised how much paperwork three children generated. *She* used to do it all. And while Ali is absolutely marvellous, still I have to keep the whole household running, and that's not easy. I'm so tired all the time, too, and my ankles are swollen, and I keep wanting to cry. All I want is for Johnnie to come back and say he made a mistake. That's all. Having a nice kind mother who understood rather than judged couldn't hurt either.

Sitting on the sofa under a cosy cashmere throw in the family room, I winced as I recalled my conversation with the woman who gave me life.

'Pregnant? By that worthless snake in the grass? Good heavens, darling, what were you thinking? No wonder you were looking so wan when I visited. Well, I hope you've jolly well told him what's what!'

I murmured that while I had jolly well told him, he hadn't taken much notice.

'What nonsense!' Mummy tutted. I heard the impatient click of her lighter and the chink of ice cubes in her glass, the soundtrack of my childhood. 'If he can't control his animal lust, he'll have to face up to the consequences. I never heard of such a thing. What does that mother of his have to say about it?'

Silvia had been her usual supportive self, promising me that she would have a word with Johnnie and reassuring me that while this was not ideal, men of his age often had little flings and always came back to their wives in the end. To the best of my knowledge, my late father-in-law Bishop Smugge had never done any such thing, but in her career as the helpmeet of a career clergyman, dear Silvia must have done her fair share of reassuring and consoling betrayed spouses.

Mummy snorted. 'Four children! I don't know what they're going to say at the club. Two is perfectly adequate, if you ask me (I hadn't), unless you're trying for a boy, of course. Four is rather common unless you're the Queen. Which you very much are not, darling.'

I spent much of half term ringing up my social circle and breaking the news. I was selling it as 'one of those things'. 'Johnnie and I are taking a break at the moment, but he's fully on board, of course. Just one of those things.' True friends, like Nicki Hartington, my old second-in-command on the PTA at Beech Grove, the children's primary school in London, had been delightful. Two-faced schemers, such as Meredith, not so much. But no need to bore you with what *she* had to say.

Mimi was radiant with joy. 'Well done, sweetheart! Keep going at this rate and we might hit four million by next spring. No one does mood photography like you – I'm seeing tiny feet, silver trinkets, knitted hats, hands clasped around thumbs – newborns really sell! And never mind about Johnnie. He'll come back with his tail between his legs soon enough.'

That was my hope. For now, I was bracing myself for the next outburst of venom from Lavinia. She'd gone worryingly quiet, contenting herself with a series of generic attacks on women: working women, women who chose to stay at home, foreign women and women in power. Like a cat with a mouse in its sights, lashing her tail and showing her teeth, my old adversary was sure to strike before too long.

Davina's due date had come and gone, and I was beginning to wonder if she would ever be brought to bed, when a text came in.

'So excited! My waters have broken, all over the pantry floor. What should I expect next? xx'

I stopped myself from replying, *'A baby, I should imagine xx'*, and replied in a kindly and supportive fashion. Having never given birth via the traditional route, I was a little flummoxed by the terms my sister-in-law was using. What on earth was a show? How was I supposed to know how many minutes there should be between contractions?

I had always presented myself at Mr Aggarwal's establishment, bag neatly packed, phone fully charged, and allowed him to work his magic. There was no grunting and sweating for Isabella M Smugge, thank you very much! My job was to lie still and wait for the baby to be removed, then to share my joy all over the socials.

Texts continued to fly between Suffolk and Stoke Poges with ever more indelicate revelations. By the time the show (whatever that was) had made its appearance, Toby had joined in. I was now receiving two lots of texts from two very excited parents-to-be. The tone of the two conversations was subtly different. Whereas Davina was sharing every revolting detail of her experience, Toby was being his usual reserved self.

'Davina being such a brave girl. So proud. Lots of fluid from the nether regions. Should I be concerned?'

To which I replied, *'Fluid very much part of the whole business, so I am given to understand. Have you rung the hospital yet? I would if I were you.'*

I texted Silvia.

'Have you heard from Davina and Toby? Things seem to be progressing xxxx'

'Hello darling, how are you? Yes, we've been texting since 5. I told Toby to ring the hospital at once and get her up there, but they say not until the contractions are closer together. The minute that baby's safely born, I'm going down to stay and help look after them all xxxx'

I wondered who Davina and Toby *hadn't* texted. While my two other sisters-in-law Amanda and Xenia and I are on cordial terms, I couldn't imagine contacting them about cervical progress, contractions and so on. I hadn't even got round to telling Amanda about Baby Smugge number four. An embarrassment of riches, as it very much were. I thought I'd let Davina produce this niece or nephew before I shared my news.

There was a short cessation in communication then a text from Davina.

'Driving to the hospital. Contractions ten minutes apart. So excited!!! xx'

I was starting to feel quite tired. Vicarious contractions really take it out of a girl.

I put my phone down, served dinner and told the children that Aunty Davina was in labour. The girls were terribly excited, firing questions at me, which was very sweet. Finn grunted and occupied himself by shovelling in mouthfuls of *tagliatelle salmoriglio* lavishly sprinkled with organic Parmesan and cracked black pepper.

Elsie was bouncing up and down on her stool with excitement. 'Do you think it's going to be a boy or a girl, Mummy? I want it to be a girl. How many cousins will we have then?' She started counting up on her fingers. 'Lily, one. Will, Xander, Natasha and Kitty, five. Aunty Davina's baby, six. Do you think Aunty Xenia will have a baby, Mummy?'

I wasn't sure that the vagaries of reproduction were on Rafe and Xenia's to-do list. They had both been working super hard since the wedding last year and we'd hardly been in touch. They'd been very sweet about the new little Smugge, promising that they would be there for me whatever happened. Although, of course, being there for someone when you live in Kent and work round the clock is fairly difficult. Still, it's the thought that counts.

'Do you think you've got a boy or a girl in your tummy, Mummy?' Elsie was still going strong and letting her pasta go cold. 'I want it to be a little girl so we can play dollies with it. I want it to be called Holly, like *Ben & Holly's Little Kingdom*, or Dora, like *Dora the Explorer*, or Miranda like in *Miranda...*'

Her excitable babblings were interrupted by her brother banging his fork down on the island and telling her to shut up.

'I don't want a baby in the house. It's so embarrassing. Everyone's going to stare at you in the playground again and Sofija isn't here to do all the work for you and people are going to laugh at me. You are so lame!'

With that he slammed out of the kitchen, ran up the stairs and banged his door, leaving poor little Elsie in tears and Chloë shredding her nails. Great.

I cuddled Elsie and tried to explain that Finn was of an age where his mother's fertility was a source of huge embarrassment. I don't know that it got through, but when I said I'd serve some of Ali's chocolate brownies warm with clotted cream, she soon stopped crying. What has health-conscious Isabella M Smugge become? Comforting with food can lead to all kinds of unfortunate consequences, but I cannot deny that a huge mouthful of rich, silky chocolate and melting clotted cream really hit the spot.

The chocolate brownies were just a memory by the time we finished our conversation. I promised Elsie that everything would be OK and that if it was a girl she could play dollies with it, and that if it was a boy, we wouldn't be imposing gender stereotypes on it and she could also play dollies with it. This seemed to reassure her. Chloë took a bit more work. It turns out that she's been bottling up her feelings and is convinced that Johnnie is never coming back. She's also terrified that I'm going to die.

'Why on earth would you think that?'

We'd moved to the family room and I put my arm around my sad little girl and gave her a cuddle. 'Well, Hannah and Becky's mum nearly died, and she's been in hospital for ages. Hannah says she cries a lot when they go to see her, and it makes her feel really bad. What if that happens to you? I don't want you to die.'

I assured her that I would be having the best care that money could buy and that I had no intention of dying. I may be in my late thirties, but I'm in great shape (considering), eat healthily (most of the time) and have had three babies already. I was just pointing out that Auntie Amanda had had four children and was in the best of health when Elsie, returning from the loo, flagged up that my phone, which had fallen down the side of my statement teal suede ottoman, was going mad. I picked it up and found I had four missed calls and any number of texts from Toby and Davina.

Scrolling through them ('*8cm! So excited!! xx' 'Davina doing so well and being such a brave girl, midwife jolly pleased with her*'), I reached the one that really mattered.

'*Davina and I have a beautiful, healthy little boy. He weighs 7lb 5oz and we are calling him Matthew James Lawrence, after his two grandfathers. Davina doing marvellously.*' A picture was attached of what appeared to be a small beetroot wearing a knitted pale-blue hat.

To my amazement, my eyes filled with tears. The thought of Davina and Toby being parents at last, after all the heartbreak of so many miscarriages, had touched me deeply. I vowed to be a good sister-in-law, to offer my advice and support when required and to make sure my children had a close relationship with their new cousin. Through a combination of geographical and emotional factors, this had never been the case in the past.

I shared the good news with the girls, who were delighted. It was gone nine by now and I really needed some headspace. Plus, it was a school night. I chased them up the stairs, read them both a bedtime story then knocked on Finn's door.

'What?'

'May I come in?'

Grudging acceptance was given in the form of a grunt. Honestly.

I shared the glad tidings of Baby Matthew's arrival. I could see that my son was brewing up another grunt, but at the last minute it turned into actual words. Not many, admittedly, but at least expressing a modicum of happiness.

I sat down on his bed. 'Look, I know all this has been really hard for you and I am so sorry. I never meant for any of it to happen. I want you to know that I'm doing my very best to get everything back to normal and I promise to try not to embarrass you. That's the last thing I want to do.'

Finn looked at the floor. 'I've been trying really hard not to be the weird one at school and not talk posh and keep my head down. Now you're having this baby, everyone's going to take the pee out of me and say stuff. I just want to fit in. Jake does too, but people in my class just laugh at us and say mean things. And don't tell me to talk to the teacher. That makes me a snitch, and no one likes a snitch.'

I genuinely didn't know what to say to him. Being a mother is jolly hard, it turns out. I'd thought I was doing quite well, but obviously not. While I fumbled for the right words, Finn continued.

'And Mum, no offence, but can I have normal food in my packed lunch, or can I have hot? Everyone else has sandwiches and crisps and sausage rolls and things like that. No one has salad, or bulgur wheat and couscous and all that stuff we eat at home. It's another reason for people to be mean to me.'

She used to make all the packed lunches, but now Ali does them and puts them in the fridge just before she leaves for the day. I thought I was doing so well, giving my children a delicious, healthy lunch. Apparently not. My face must have betrayed my feelings. Finn let out a deep sigh.

'I don't want to you upset you, Mum. I know you're missing Dad and Sofija, but we are too and it's really hard. I just want to fit in. Maybe it won't be so bad at high school. Jake and I can't wait for Year Six to be over.'

I was confused. 'But I thought you liked your new teacher. He seems delightful.'

'He is really nice, and I like his lessons. But you don't understand what it's like at school. Zach leaves us alone most of the time now, but some of the girls laugh at us and try to kiss us, which is gross, and when we go off together to get away from them they call us gay.'

I was completely flummoxed. My son seemed to have handed me a whole slew of new problems with which to deal. Zach's mother, the terrifying Liane Bloomfield, seemed to loathe Isabella M Smugge a little less, and her attitude was clearly rubbing off on her son.

The packed lunches I could sort, at least. Although tomorrow's offering was sitting in the fridge already, I suggested hot lunch instead, which was met with great relief. I made a mental note to go online and pay for it. So much to remember. I gave Finn a hug and wished him a good night, before returning downstairs to load the dishwasher and text Davina and Toby. The rest of the evening was spent in messages of congratulations, a chat with Silvia ('Isn't he beautiful? I see a look of the Bishop about him'), a quick voice call with the proud parents ('Oh Isabella, we couldn't be happier. Look at him!') and a veritable outburst of texts between myself and various family members.

The baby was hardly out before Toby had set up a Matthew James Lawrence Smugge WhatsApp group. Amanda, Charlie, Xenia, Rafe, Silvia, myself and, of course, Johnnie were all treated to a selection of pictures of the hat-clad beetroot nestling up to Davina's ample bosom, gazing drunkenly at the camera with one eye shut and lying on Toby's chest – *'Baby Matthew's first skin-to-skin with Daddy'*. At eleven, I fell into bed, donned my moisturising socks (no cracked heels for Issy Smugge, thank you very much), changed the notification for the baby WhatsApp group so I could differentiate between DMs, likes and shares and postnatal ravings, and fell into an exhausted slumber. **#imanauntyagain #OTT #babylove**

November is going to be an absolute whirl, and probably not in a good way. After school on Monday, the girls set to with the craft box and produced a large, jewel-encrusted card for Baby Matthew. Finn deigned to sign his name underneath theirs, I wrote the address on a large envelope in my best calligraphy and packed up a box of gorgeous, on-trend, gender-neutral baby clothes. **#buyoncebuywell** I took some beautiful photos of the girls embellishing their card, and once I'd tagged the clothes label across my socials, off they went, first-class post.

My first duty as an aunt to Baby Matthew done, I moved on to Chloë's birthday party. Isabella M Smugge is a planner, not a pantser, but recent events had severely eroded my renowned organisational abilities. Leaving the party planning so late filled me with panic, and I was relieved when my daughter informed me that another pool party would be perfectly fine. I hurled out a handful of hashtags on my socials (**#partytime #kidsofinstagram #birthdaygirl #partyinspiration**) and waited for them to start trending.

Sometimes I wish I could lock myself away in my beautiful house and spend the rest of my life taking photographs and writing content, while someone else does all the things I'm no good at. I've worked so hard to get to where I am today and, as

Johnnie used to tell me, once you're at the top, there's only one place to go unless you work around the clock. He's been such a huge part of my life for so long, and often I lie awake at night wondering how much longer it will be before he's back. It's been the Johnnie and Isabella show for twenty years and without him by my side to keep me focused, I don't know how I'm going to carry on.

Another thing disturbing my slumbers is the inevitable fallout from my pregnancy announcement. Everybody at school knows now, and while nearly everyone has been lovely, giving me big hugs and promising me they'll be there for me, Hayley and her bristling eyebrows have been hovering just out of my peripheral vision for a while. She makes me feel uneasy. I can't put my finger exactly on why that should be, but there it is.

Liane Bloomfield, clad in the shocking pink smock she wears for work, hailed me loudly across the playground at pick-up time today.

'Oi! Smug!'

I turned round to see her jerk her head at me in what I could only assume was an invitation to join her. With Lauren by my side, I trotted over to where she was standing, hand on hip, terrifying as always.

'So, you're one of us now. A single parent. Bet you didn't see that one coming.'

I took a deep breath and summoned up all my courage. 'My husband and I are on a break, that's all. He'll be back soon. We're rock solid.'

Even to my ears, it didn't sound terribly convincing, and my voice cracked embarrassingly halfway through. Liane Bloomfield sucked her teeth in a menacing manner.

'Newsflash, Smug. Your man's run off with another woman. That makes you a single parent. Not so high and mighty now, are you?'

Lauren spoke up for me, God bless her. 'No need to be mean, Liane. Issy's having a rough time at the moment. We need to stick together, not tear each other down.'

'No offence, Smug. Just reaching out.' She laughed, not unpleasantly. 'And you've got yourself in a fix too, I see. Dear oh dear. My last two weren't planned either. Should have got him done.'

I tried to think of a clever retort, but my mind was blank. After a minute or too, she bade us farewell and marched off down the playground, leaving me feeling anything but confident. I asked Lauren about the pink smock, which now I thought about it was being modelled by several other mums in the playground.

'Liane got a new job. There's a new care agency moved into the village, down the bottom of the high street. Run by a really nice woman. Liane says she treats everyone fairly, pays well, and they wear the pink because it doesn't look all medical and bland. Loads of the girls have gone to work for her.'

That explained that. We ambled out of the playground and I showed her the latest pictures of my nephew. The resemblance to a root vegetable was wearing off and he now looked almost human. Davina had sent me a very sweet text about my own baby news.

'So exciting! Baby Matthew will love having a cousin so close to his own age. We must make sure that we see an awful lot more of each other xx'

Toby too had been supportive, in a long and rather baffling phone conversation which kept returning to his firstborn. His paternal instincts seem extremely strong. I confess that I may have misjudged him. Johnnie always teased his brother and called him a stuffed shirt, and I thought he didn't mind. Since my husband left, however, Toby, it seems, has been trying to persuade him to come back.

'It's just not the done thing to leave your wife and children, Isabella. I've spoken to him several times about it. Davina and I both hope he'll see sense and come home.'

At this point he broke off to attend to young Matthew's needs. I could hear wailing and snuffling in the background. All the hairs on the back of my neck stood up. Newborns terrify me. I've always kept that particular secret to myself, but there is something about their vulnerability and their complete reliance on a flawed, sleep-deprived person which fills me with fear.

Toby returned. 'How are you managing? I know Ma said she's coming to stay when she leaves us. Give you a bit of moral support. Davina and I are always here for you. My brother has been a big disappointment to me. He had everything, a super wife like you, three smashing children, and he's gone and ruined it all.'

This was the longest speech I'd ever heard Toby make. I was rather taken aback but oddly touched by his kind words. After some more chit-chat about Baby Matthew (exceptionally gifted already, apparently), we rang off. Well. Funny how wrong you can be about someone. Johnnie always said that Toby was emotionally constipated and never talked about anything except work. Apparently not. **#liveandlearn**

The rest of the month shot by. Chloë's party went well, although I had to manage it all by myself. Mummy offered to come and help me (as if!), but I pretended that the south wing wasn't ready yet. To be honest, I could have put her up, but I'd rather run a party alone than have my hyper-critical mother at my shoulder, dragging me down.

Ali was marvellous and cooked some party food ahead of time to help me. She is a treasure. Fortunately, it was a beautiful, crisp day so I was able to capture some landscapes to mix in with the photos of the girls enjoying themselves (tastefully, in soft focus. One has to be so careful). **#livingthesuffolkdream #perfectlyperfect**

Things have not worked out as I planned regarding the emergence of Baby Smugge Number Four. Having met with my local GP, Dr Moira Gallacher, a Scottish person who seemed very well up on all things gynaecological (even if she did think I was called Mrs Smudge), naturally I'd spread my nets and paid a visit to the well-appointed corridors of The Friary as well.

Pulling into the large, tree-shaded car park, I took a moment to drink in the scene before me. Neatly tended trees and shrubs framed the pretty, two-storey building with its extremely clean automatic doors. Even the birds seemed to be singing in a better class of accent. Surely, this was the place in which Isabella M Smugge would be delivered of her fourth child. Walking in, I savoured the clean lines, the freshly painted walls, the scent of really good coffee. I was home!

Funny, isn't it, how you have everything sorted in your mind and then one tiny thing happens and it all shifts. That's what happened to me at The Friary. I was booked in by the smiling receptionist, and as I leafed through some brand-new glossy magazines I was offered a bewildering variety of complimentary drinks.

After a few minutes' wait, I was ushered in to see a consultant. We moved briskly through my reproductive history and chatted about vaguely indelicate matters. As I was lying on the couch, the gentle incline of my abdomen being massaged by the well-shaped hands of the consultant, he asked me about my domestic situation. I gave him the 'trial separation' line and he flicked his eyes sideways to the nurse, just for a second. That was all it took.

Suddenly, the smell of coffee was cloying, and the glossiness and perfection seemed fake. I could have all this ease and comfort if I wished, but I'd have to pay for it.

Back in the village, although the surgery was shabby and the waiting room was full of coughing people and wailing babies, everyone smiled at everyone else. An old lady held the door open for me and called me 'dear'. Back in London, I would sooner have let my brows go *au naturel* than be seen dead at an establishment run by the NHS. I mean, they are wonderful and selfless and the backbone of our country, of course, but for a person like me, just not an option.

Moving to Suffolk seems to have changed something fundamental in me. Suddenly, sitting on a chair that was not properly sprung and having to wait for an appointment didn't seem so bad.

The consultant indicated that I could adjust my clothing and sit back down again.

'I'm afraid that I agree with your London consultant, Mrs Smugge. There is a significant amount of scar tissue and, at your age (here he smiled, in a conciliatory fashion), we would prefer not to take any risks. May I ask why you opted for C-sections with your other children?'

Well, of course, the reason was that Johnnie couldn't bear the thought of me being in pain. We talked about it extensively when I was first expecting Finn.

'Darling, I can't have you lying there in agony for hours, pushing and pushing, bursting blood vessels and perhaps having to have a C-section in the end. Surely it would be better for you and the baby to have a date booked. So much simpler all round.'

The net result is that Issy Smugge is in tip-top condition, inside and out. No internal stitches, ruptures, sagging or drooping for *me*, thank you very much! The thought of giving birth naturally did not appeal, but both Dr Gallacher and the charming consultant at The Friary had said the same thing.

Sitting outside in the car park listening to the upper middle-class birds tweeting, I texted Lauren.

Be honest. How much does giving birth hurt? Do they give you painkillers? xx'

Back came her reply.

'A bit like pooing out a bowling ball, tbh, babes, but not that bad as it goes. And they give you drugs. No scar afterwards and you can drive and stuff. Are you going for it?? xx'

It seemed that I was.

#issysmuggesayschallengeaccepted

Before I knew where I was, there was only one week of November left. I had a Zoom booked with Mimi on Monday morning to discuss the next *Issy Smugge Says* book, put the final touches to the Christmas campaign and talk about family matters. My agent's familiar features leapt on to the screen.

'Sweetheart! How *are* you? Looking marvellous.'

I wasn't sure that I could say the same about her. Her face seemed strangely immobile. We ran through the weekly figures and I asked her what she'd thought of the party.

'Darling, I am simply over the moon! We all are! Trending hashtags, retweets, all your Pins being shared – I couldn't be happier.'

I peered at the screen. 'Are you sure, Mimi? You don't look very happy from here.'

I detected a slight twitch of one eyebrow. 'I'm beaming all over my face! Delighted about how Open Brackets is going. You were so right to dump From Tramp to Vamp.'

I could see no evidence of beaming, grinning, smiling or even smirking. A terrible suspicion came to mind.

'Have you had surgery, Mimi? You look *different*, somehow.'

She leaned in towards the screen. 'No flies on you, sweetie. A drive-through Botox bar opened up next door last week. I booked the whole team in. It's fabulous! I feel ten years younger. You should try it.'

I didn't know whether to laugh or cry, actions with which my agent would clearly be struggling for some time. The notion of having toxins injected into my face did not appeal. A good diet, plenty of sleep and the very best products keep *me* looking dewy and fresh-faced.

We discussed Christmas.

'I'm loving your Nordic Luxe mood board, darling! No one does Christmas like you. Can I ask who you're spending the festive season with? I think we're both hoping for scenes of family togetherness.'

She blew a huge cloud of smoke from her scarlet lips and twitched the edge of her eyebrow at me. It was quite sinister.

Normally, I have Christmas nailed down by the time the candy-striped pink camellia at the boot room door is in bud, but this year was different.

'I'm staying light on my feet,' I trilled, sipping my peppermint tea. 'I expect Johnnie will be back by then, but I've got plenty of ideas up my sleeve.'

This was a lie. I had no way of knowing if Mimi believed me or not, since her frozen features remained unchanged. Christmas sorted (and I genuinely have no idea if anyone is even coming to stay), we moved on to the next *Issy Smugge Says* book.

Now, I wouldn't want you to think that I am some kind of literary genius. Nothing could be further from the truth. Yes, I do publish between four and six *Issy Smugge Says* books each year, yes my publisher has had to double the print run to keep up with demand, and yes, I have hit the giddy heights of the top spot on of the *Sunday Times* Bestseller List more times than I can remember. That said, I'm not writing novels, or fat biographies of nineteenth-century worthies. They're manuals, advice books, something inspirational yet comforting which my followers can use to replicate elements of my gorgeous lifestyle.

Right from the start, I've always insisted that they are beautifully presented and packaged. The first editions sell on eBay for more than £200, they tell me. My first-ever title, *Issy Smugge Says: Let's Refresh Our Home*, was written at top speed when we were just about to sell the flat in Highgate. When we moved in, it was shocking, all blocks of lurid colour and poor-quality carpet. From necessity, we painted it all white, but it was in desperate need of some zhuzhing.

I don't want to give you the impression that I was making it up as I went along, but I think the timing of that first book was spot on. I already knew all there was to know about accent colours and lighting and perspective, thanks to Mummy. She and her best friend, Arabella Pryke-Darby, founded Carobella, the interior design company. I expect you've heard of it. I flatter myself that I've got a natural eye for interiors. No one else was writing easy-to-read manuals or sharing their mood boards, and a mixture of chatty advice and great photos, plus the authenticity of featuring my own abode was irresistible to my followers. It only took a couple of statement lamps, a feature wall and some on-trend colour blocks and I was there. I never looked back.

'Now, darling. I know you're having issues with the thought of having another baby, but I'd be drummed out of the Agents' Union (*note to self – is there such a thing?*) if I didn't suggest it.'

Mimi was leaning forward and exhaling smoke from her elegantly flared nostrils. I have never met a woman who is able to speak so fluently while conveying nicotine in and out of her respiratory system with ease.

'You've done your baby reveal, and the socials have gone crazy. I'm delighted. I am literally aglow with joy.'

I had to take her word for it.

'To capitalise on this, I'm thinking cots, I'm thinking sustainable, organic baby blankets, I'm thinking prams made by well-paid indigenous workers. How quickly could you knock out *Issy Smugge Says: We're Having a Baby*, do you think, my darling? This one's going to run and run.'

I put my hand up. 'Hang on just a sec, Mimi. I don't know. I've covered that ground before with *Issy Smugge Says: We're Adding to the Family.*'

Mimi ground out her cigarette with savage force and lit another one. 'Yes, yes, but that was ages ago. Which one was it? The middle one or the little one? People won't remember that far back. It's all about adding value, sweetie. I know you won't thank me for saying it, but you're forty next year (and looking absolutely marvellous, may I say). An older mumfluencer, juggling children and home and work, striking out on your own, tapping into real lives. I'm sure lots of those lovely followers are bringing up children on their own.'

She coughed, *basso profundo*, and took a swig of coffee.

'Johnnie may come back. If he's got any sense he will. But I wouldn't be doing my job if I didn't talk to you seriously about the possibility that he might not. If we've learned anything in the last five months, it's that your brand is strong enough to survive a catastrophic marital break-up. I thought we'd be shedding followers, but if anything, they're increasing. And that is all down to you, sweetheart, your images, your content, you.'

She leaned back and surveyed me with a beady eye.

'Thoughts?'

Mimi has never been one to call a spade a vertical digging implement, but I was taken aback by her directness. Of course Johnnie was coming back. My whole life was built around him, and without him, where would I be? The thought of writing a book about the burgeoning young Smugge didn't appeal, but deep down, I knew Mimi was right. This was most certainly my last baby, and I wouldn't want you to think I am a venal person when I say that nothing garners fresh followers and builds a family brand like mine in quite the same way as a new baby.

'Let me think about it, Mimi. It's a lot to take on board. I haven't really come to terms with it yet, if I'm honest.'

My agent drummed her vermilion-tipped nails on the desk.

'Well, don't take too long, darling. We need to get it out as soon as. Your Christmas boxset sales are going through the roof. People can't get enough of you. We need to capitalise on that. Now, one more thing and then I promise I'll let you go.'

I stifled a sigh. Our Zoom had already gone on far longer than usual and I had a whole heap of work to do.

'I know you think the sun shines from Johnnie's apertures, and you two do make a lovely looking couple. No one can deny that. But while he's off the scene, can I implore you to break that stupid promise you made to him, and do some appearances and meet and greets? All the other mummy bloggers and influencers are schlepping around doing book signings and heaven knows what. You never have, and while at first it made you look enigmatic, now it just looks weird. Sorry to be blunt, sweetie, but it's true.'

I've always known that my agent loathes Johnnie, an emotion which he heartily reciprocates. However, encouraging me to break my word to my husband was going too far.

'Mimi, you know Johnnie's only protecting me. He's always hated the idea of me being out and about, exposed to the public and perhaps being threatened or put in danger. How can I break my word to him and go out to shopping centres or wherever you want to send me?'

Had Mimi not had her entire face injected with neurotoxin proteins, no doubt it would have been alive with emotion. As it was, she leaned close to the screen and I saw one eyelid flicker, momentarily.

'Darling, break your word? Break *your* word? To him? Do I really have to remind you what he's broken? Be sensible. Think about yourself and your brand for a minute. You don't have to do what he says any more.'

I was desperate for a wee and my stomach was gurgling in an alarming manner. I gazed longingly at the pantry door, behind which reposed many, many tins of organic, sustainably caught sardines. Hastily, I promised Mimi that I would think about it and reply shortly. The connection broken (*'Love you, miss you sweetie, mwah mwah!'*), I made an emergency trip to my downstairs cloakroom (my second home these day), then trundled at top speed towards the slippery little delights and made myself a doorstep sandwich. Bliss! **#babyneedsomega3 #hungrymummy #issysmuggeownsit**

I worked hard all week, some of my old energy returning. With that tricky first trimester out of the way and my baby news out in the open, I was starting to feel a little more like my old self. All three children seemed to be building good relationships with their teachers, and their behaviour was slightly less needy.

Having felt like an ageing prize fighter, slammed back against the ropes again and again since Johnnie left, the last week of November brought only good news.

First of all, Suze messaged to tell me that they'd made an offer on a house which had been accepted and that their moving date was pencilled in for mid-March. Excellent. Then Silvia rang and asked if she could come to stay for the first week of December (having done her time with Baby Matthew and his adoring parents) and then impose herself on me for Christmas. As if she could ever be an imposition!

Finn came home from school on Wednesday actually smiling. The school football team had been playing away and scored a mammoth victory against their sworn enemies at St Mark & St Matthew's, two of the goals scored by my boy. He also shared the news that a new boy had joined Year Six, shy and restrained and quite possibly an outsider like himself and Jake. I vowed to zero in on the parents in the playground and charm them. Finn needs some more friends.

Then Chloë came home beaming, clutching a script lavishly annotated with pink highlighter. Young Mr Rycroft it seems, fresh from teacher training college and as yet unbroken by the educational system, has decided to put on a joint Year Three and Four play, for which my daughter has auditioned and won the main part. You have to believe me when I tell you that it took me half an hour to even remember to post the good news on my socials. It was such a delightful surprise to see her chatting with such animation, a light in her eyes that I had never seen before.

Finally, perhaps the best news of all. Claire is now allowed to have more regular visitors. Lauren and I have booked our slot. I am ridiculously excited and thanked the good Lord in an ungrammatical but entirely sincere fashion just before I nodded off to sleep. **#bestfriends #happydays #lightattheendofthetunnel**

Full of tinned sardines and hope, and with a new spring in my step, in spite of the appalling weather (I am beginning to understand why root vegetables thrive in this part of the country. It has rained every single day this week and my taciturn gardener, Ted, has spent more time lurking in the potting shed than actually working), I pondered Mimi's suggestion re making personal appearances. It pained me to admit that she might have a point.

Johnnie has always been very protective of me, one of the many reasons I love him so much. I used to go out clubbing a lot when I first met him (I adore dancing) but as he so rightly pointed out, clubs attract the Wrong Sort of Man, and while he would never stop me doing anything I loved, he couldn't bear the thought of men disrespecting me and undressing me with their eyes. I'd never particularly noticed anyone doing anything of the sort, but when you fall in love, you make concessions. As he said, clubbing is for teenagers with fake IDs, so I turned my back on it all without a thought.

Once Mimi talent spotted me and my online presence started to attract attention, the offers poured in. I did a couple of book signings in the very early days and people seemed to love it, but I could tell that Johnnie didn't.

'Honestly, Iss, I'm not trying to limit you. It's just that I love you so much that I can't bear the thought of anything ever happening to you. Without you, my life would be pointless. I know Mimi's thinking of your career, but I'm here to take care of you and make sure you're safe.'

It took a while to convince me (I must confess, I loved the buzz that personal appearances gave me), but then Bendy Wendy, the fitspo queen, had a crushed blueberry and kale smoothie thrown over her at a photo opp and that made my mind up. Mimi was furious, but where I felt myself to be right, I was firm.

However, that was a long time ago, before my husband broke his marriage vows and gave me a present I wasn't expecting.

Ahead of Christmas, Lavinia Harcourt started taking pot shots at me in her stupid column.

Dirty Little Secret?
What is so-called mumfluencer and aspirational lifestyle blogger Isabella M Smugge trying to hide? *Are* the rumours true? *Has* she had botched surgery? *Is* she keeping the terrible truth from her followers? While others have the common touch and are happy to sign books and actually meet the people who pay their wages, this two-faced filter obsessive hides behind her syrupy outpourings online. So, tell us the truth, Issy Smugge. What are you trying to keep from your fans?

Honestly! I hated to admit it, but maybe it was time to emerge from my beautiful house and show my face to the people who put me in it. And who cares what Johnnie says? The longer he's away, the easier I'm finding it to do things I know he'll disapprove of. I emailed Mimi the news that I would accept a selection of carefully curated personal appearances. She emailed me back a smiley face. **#ironic**

We'd arranged for Johnnie to have the children for the weekend, and I decided it was time to commit to churching myself up. I texted Lauren.

'Are you going to church this Sunday? Bit scared about walking in by myself. Do you mind if we go together? xx'

'Babes, that will be so cool! I'm coming solo. Want me to come to yours and we'll walk in together? xx'

If that doesn't build up my holy points, I don't know what will. **#fixedtheroof #hellogod**

December

Issy Smugge is not one to walk into a new experience without doing her research. On Saturday evening, having enjoyed a light supper of grilled aubergines with cascabel honey and lime couscous, I settled down to check out the C of E brand. **#thethrillofthegrill**

My original assumption that church was a weekly social club in a historic building presided over by an octogenarian had been disproved the moment I met Claire and Tom. I had no idea that churches had trends, like normal buildings. Norman, Gothic, Perpendicular. I found myself going off down internet rabbit holes as I researched hammerbeam roofs, manifest piety, naves and pillars. **#ontrendchurch #everydaysaschoolday**

Now that I was an expert on arches and windows and decoration, I felt more comfortable about my visit. No doubt Lauren would introduce me to the right people, and of course I already knew the jam-making ladies. I'm used to turning heads, and I assumed that church would be no exception.

Pleasantly nourished by a mixture of my delicious supper and my new ecclesiastical knowledge, I fell into a peaceful slumber and dreamed about lovely things all night.

At 10.30, there was a knock on the boot room door and Lauren appeared. My ensemble of black slimline trousers tucked into a pair of high boots, teamed with a slouchy cream knit jumper, was given the thumbs up. I'd added a pop of colour with a trio of chunky silver and teal bangles and a pair of hoop earrings with some sparkle.

'You always look amazing!' Lauren was gazing at my statement clutch bag with awe. 'I get all my stuff from the charity shop.'

Is it wrong of me to admit that I like getting praise? My friend's words gave me a warm glow and I found myself enveloping her in a spontaneous hug, something I would certainly have never done back in London. Shrugging on my colourful maxi-coat (so now), I locked the back door and we marched briskly up the garden to the gate through to the graveyard, Lauren briefing me on what to expect.

'It's Share Your Story Sunday. People come up and say how their prayers have been answered, or tell us something good or encouraging, or ask for help. Keith's doing the talk. He's one of the retired vicars. Oh, and I think there might be cake.'

By the time she finished, we had reached the glass entrance porch. I felt unaccountably nervous. I couldn't tell you why. Here I was, doyenne of the lifestyle blogging world (I pretty much invented the genre), generous saviour of the church roof and friend of the vicar's wife. Surely I would be hailed as a VIP. And yet I found I wanted to slip in, unnoticed, and sit quietly at the back. So not me.

As Lauren waved at people (she seemed to know everyone), I gazed around me. While there were many grey-haired people, there was a surprisingly large number of younger ones too, plus children and some teenagers. Everything I had read about the Church of England had indicated that it was a place where only the elderly and desiccated felt at home. A person with pink streaks in her hair threw her head back and laughed loudly. A toddler ambled past, picking its nose and looking quite at home.

The organ music stopped, and a person addressed us from the front. I had no interest in what he was saying, so I zoned out and scanned the hammerbeam roof above me, trying to work out which bit of it I had been responsible for fixing.

A jolly-looking chap bounced up from the seats at the front and welcomed us all. Alarmingly, we were encouraged to turn and greet our neighbours. I was importuned by a middle-aged couple in front of me ('Hello! Are you new? How lovely to see you!') and by Wendy the jam-maker who was sitting behind me. Once the chit-chat had subsided, Keith (for it was he) informed us that it was time to worship the Lord.

A group of teenagers wandered up to the front and picked up some guitars which had been left lying around. They launched into a loud intro, accompanied by frantic hammering on the drums by a spotty youth with an intense look in his eyes. I turned to Lauren in alarm.

'Contemporary worship, babes. We have this three Sundays and then a traditional service once a month for people who like that kind of thing.'

She began to sing, loudly and enthusiastically. All around me, the congregation were belting out words that made no sense to me, some with their eyes closed, others with their hands waving about in the air. I felt completely out of place.

At verse two, I pulled myself together and began mouthing the words to show willing. I wondered why people kept putting their hands up. Was this something to do with volunteering for the story sharing later? Mine were clamped firmly by my sides. I certainly wasn't going to get involved in anything like that, thank you very much! **#traditionalgirl #whatshappening #embarrassing**

By the time the third song commenced, I was starting to wish I hadn't come. Hymns written by people 300 years ago, pews, an elderly middle-class congregation and rules and regulations, surely, were what the Church was about. Not this.

Mercifully, after repeating the chorus four times, in a kind of yearning, half-witted way, the main teenager retreated from the microphone and the worship portion of the morning appeared to be over.

A youngish chap in jeans sporting an earring trotted up the aisle and took the stand. 'We're going through the book of Acts,'

Lauren whispered. I consulted my programme. It seemed we would be hearing the story of someone calling himself Simon the Wizard. I had hoped to be told a familiar story, something about sheep, or arks, or blind men.

The story unfolded, told in the most disrespectful language. No 'thees' or 'thous' or anything of a religious nature. Instead, I found myself listening to a tale about someone called Saul who was dragging people off to jail, while the followers of Jesus became missionaries.

Simon the Wizard, it seemed, had held centre stage with magic tricks and dazzling sleights of hand for many years. Presumably, this was how he made his living, and for the first time since I'd walked into the church, I had found a character I recognised. He wouldn't have been out of place doing close-up magic at a conference dinner or busking in Covent Garden.

Simon's career, however, was about to come to an abrupt end. Someone called Philip came to town ('He was one of the followers – like an evangelist. You know, telling people the good news,' Lauren whispered) and told everyone some stories, whereupon they all stopped watching Simon's magic show and were baptised. ('It's like when you get dipped in water and cleansed of all your sins.')

The story hotted up as two chaps called Peter and John appeared. When Simon saw the miracles they could do, he pulled out his wallet and asked for their secrets, understandably. I think most of us in the entertainment business would have done the same. At this point, the man doing the reading forgot himself and used some bad and unreligious language. I was shocked. Yet upon consulting my programme, where the passage in question was helpfully printed out, I read these words:

> Peter said, 'To hell with your money! And you along with it. Why, that's unthinkable – trying to buy God's gift! You'll never be part of what God is doing by striking bargains and offering bribes. Change your ways – and now! Ask the Master to forgive you for trying to use God

to make money. I can see this is an old habit with you; you reek with money-lust.[1]

Darting covert looks at the rest of the congregation, I could see that they were all listening with interest. The story ended with the wizard deciding to join the winning side.

The reading over, Keith asked us to spend a few minutes in quiet contemplation before we shared our stories. I spent the time enquiring of my friend in a discreet whisper what on earth was going on.

'That's not the Bible! It doesn't sound religious at all. I didn't know there were wizards back then and that you were allowed to say "hell".'

Lauren explained that this was a reboot, written in up-to-date language so that normal people could understand it. I was none the wiser. Where were the comforting stories about the animals going in two by two and men being lowered through roofs? #help

Keith joined us again and announced that he was handing the service over to us. He sat down and there was a long silence. I felt terribly uncomfortable. Religious people shouldn't try to do this kind of thing. It's best left to professional entertainers.

After what seemed an age, the woman with the pink hair got up and shared that she had been worried about her daughter. She had prayed and the daughter was now free of the illness she had been suffering from. Everyone clapped. Rather disrespectful in a church, I thought.

The floodgates opened. Person after person, of all ages and shapes and appearances, got up and told us tales about themselves, most of which seemed to involve coincidences. Lauren nudged me.

'That might be you one day, babes. You prayed for Claire and that was answered.'

It wasn't the same kind of thing at all, and I couldn't imagine ever standing up in a church and letting myself be that

[1] Acts 8:20-23. From *The Message* translation.

vulnerable. I smiled weakly and fiddled with my on-trend hoop earrings.

After an interminable selection of stories, Keith got up again and shared the news that we would have the prayers before his talk. Here I was back on familiar ground. A kind-faced woman with clumpy shoes prayed, in normal language, for lots of people. Claire and Tom and the children were mentioned a great deal. Very rudely, I thought, she was almost constantly interrupted by members of the congregation speaking over her. As she prayed for Claire's complete healing, the middle-aged couple in front of us shouted out, 'Yes, Lord!' and I could hear murmurings and exhortations all around the church. Quite uncalled for, if you ask me. Let the poor woman have her moment.

As she prayed for the vicar and his family, I felt tears pricking my eyes. I couldn't tell you why. I sent up a quiet prayer of my own, couched in respectful language. I'm sure God was relieved to hear someone addressing Him in the correct fashion. #honestly #poorgod

For a retired vicar, Keith seemed very cheerful. He made several jokes, which were actually funny, explained the story in interesting detail and held my attention throughout. I wondered if he had ever thought of taking on an auxiliary career as an after-dinner speaker. It's a lucrative profession and I don't suppose vicars get paid very much. At the very least, it would keep him in walking shoes and knitted pullovers.

Finally, a hymn was announced. We rose to our feet as one and I felt confident enough to turn up the volume on my singing. Five verses and a chorus with lots of archaic language and a tune I remembered from St Dymphna's. I was back on safe ground. Some large wooden plates were passed around by the teenagers from the band, into which people were placing small blue envelopes and tenners. I whipped out a fifty and hid it at the bottom of the plate.

Once Keith had received the plates and said some more prayers, he beamed, threw his arms open wide and blessed us in words which again made my eyes fill up with tears. He seemed as if he meant them, and just for a moment, I felt it might be possible that Isabella M Smugge, abandoned wife, terrible mother and bad daughter, was loved by someone she couldn't see.

We all sat down again and the organist, hidden away behind the carved screen, began tickling the ivories.

I let out a loud, involuntary sigh. Lauren patted my arm.

'How was that, babes? You look a bit overwhelmed.' Just as I was about to try to explain how I felt, Keith seized the mic again and reminded us that there was cake to celebrate Pat and Richard's Golden Wedding anniversary. Everyone clapped and there was a surge towards the hatch, whence the rich fragrance of coffee was drifting out.

Lauren grinned. 'Tell me later. Come on – baby needs cake.'

'Are you OK?' Lauren was looking concerned and took my arm as we walked out through the graveyard. 'You look a bit out of it.'

I tried to explain my feelings about church. 'I didn't realise they'd rebooted the Bible. I need to get my head around it. It's just not what I'm used to.'

My friend nodded. 'I know what you mean. I zone out a bit sometimes and I don't understand a lot of it, but I'm getting there.'

We hugged affectionately and I bent my steps back to the Old Rectory. Johnnie was bringing the children back at about four and I had plenty of time to tidy up and get myself looking presentable. I waved my friend goodbye and yawned. What harm could a little doze on the sofa do? I curled up under my cashmere throw and fell fast asleep.

I awoke with what I suspect was a loud snore to the sound of the front door banging and my husband's voice calling my name. I sat bolt upright, bleary-eyed and confused as the children came running into the room. I wiped drool from the side of my mouth and tried to look alert as Johnnie appeared.

'Are you OK, Iss? You look a bit rough.' His eyes flickered to the kitchen where mugs and plates sat, unwashed, on the island and a basket of dirty clothes squatted menacingly by the washing machine. This wasn't what I had planned at all.

I arose, letting out an involuntary grunt as I did so. I've noticed that old people do this. I could only put it down to the pregnancy. I smoothed my hair down, hugged my children and made Johnnie an espresso. Thank heavens for the Christmas decorations, which gave the whole place a delightfully on-trend and vibey air. Ali and I had spent most of one day dressing the house, and while she was marvellous, I caught myself reminiscing about the fun *she* and I had had the year before. My choice of Nordic Luxe as a theme meant that the house was alive with pinecones, dark green foliage, thousands of tiny twinkling white lights and silver baubles.

The children seemed happy, which was a relief. I excused myself and went to check on my look in the mirror in the cloakroom. My hair was fuzzy, my eyeliner smudged and my lipstick patchy. I did some emergency running repairs and emerged to talk to my husband in an adult fashion.

After the usual polite chit-chat, which never fails to pierce my heart (that we could have come to this!), Johnnie broached the subject of Christmas.

'I expect you've already made plans, but how would you feel if I came and stayed?'

He smiled his roguish smile, and I felt my heart melt. At last! Just as I had always known, deep down in my heart, things between him and Sofija were starting to disintegrate, and this was his way of starting to build a bridge.

I opened my mouth to reply when all my dreams came crashing back down to earth.

'Sofija's spending three weeks in Latvia (her dad had a heart attack) and I was thinking about flying out to see my brother Charlie in Dubai. But then I thought, what about the kids, and I don't like to think of you rattling about in this huge house all by yourself. So how about it?'

My mouth was dry. 'I won't be alone. Your mother's staying, and Mummy too.'

'Oh.' He frowned, ever so slightly. 'I don't want to be stuck in town over Christmas. Everyone's away. It'll be no fun. And a father's place is with his kids at Christmas. I can't miss them opening their stockings, Iss. Can you find a corner for me to lay my head?'

What could I say? So now I have the unholy trio of my philandering husband, my mother (who loathes him) and his mother as house guests. And a healthy dose of pregnancy hormones. Great! **#merrychristmas #familystrife**

Truly, I don't know sometimes how I do all I do. Along with keeping the household running, becoming a churchgoer (I may try it again next week. Perhaps), bringing up three children, nourishing and nurturing a fourth *in utero* and working full-time, I have also been project managing the remodelling of the south wing. Finally, after many months, the roof has been completed, the dry rot and infestation dealt with, and the walls are being papered and painted. It's all looking fabulous. Kevin, my builder, came to see me on Tuesday morning as I sat at the island checking my feed.

'We're on the home straight, Isabella. Just the carpets to sort out. I've got a fantastic local supplier – do you want me to set up a meeting?'

Well, of course I did. What Issy Smugge doesn't know about floor coverings isn't worth knowing! I was the first to spot that seagrass was over, to pioneer the use of engineered hardwood and master how to place Scandi-style rugs. I couldn't imagine that some local flooring person would have anything to tell me about carpets. How wrong I was.

Later in the week, a small van drew up on the drive and a smart-looking chap got out. I received him in the family room, offered him a coffee and waited to be bored to death. Whipping out his samples, he blew my mind with his encyclopaedic knowledge of floor coverings. I can't remember the last time I had that much fun in the family room!

We walked over to the south wing and he paced around the suites of rooms, eyeing up the proportions, making copious notes and talking all the while about things that Isabella M Smugge finds completely fascinating. Money was no object, obviously, so with my trademark eye for a good finish, I ordered what we needed and shook him warmly by the hand. I must follow him on Insta. #flooringluxury #loveagoodcarpet

With my remodelling project nearly complete, I turned my attention to courting the parents of the new boy in Finn's class, who, I find, is called Harry Baker. He is a scrawny, anxious-looking child who gazes at life through a large pair of glasses. I spotted him walking into the playground on Friday morning with his mother six paces behind him. She, too, is an anxious-looking spectacles wearer.

Finn has made it abundantly clear that I am, under no circumstances, to come anywhere near the Year Six line or to acknowledge his presence or speak to any of the parents until he is safely ensconced in his classroom. At a safe distance, I consulted Lovely Lou, Maddie, Kate and Lauren.

'Have any of you met the parents yet? Have they got other children? Do we know where they live?'

Just over a year away from London and I was starting to turn into a villager! I drew a blank. No one else had a child in Year Six, and while Maddie suspected that they had moved in to one of the new-builds by the bypass, she had no evidence for this.

'She looks worried, doesn't she?' Lovely Lou was peering short-sightedly across the playground. 'Those Year Six mums are a tough crowd. I don't think anyone's really spoken to her yet.'

I pondered. We could follow her home, which would answer question three, but was also borderline creepy behaviour. As the children streamed into school, we watched the woman turn around and start to walk slowly towards the gate, head down. I made up my mind. I had been welcomed with open arms the minute I set foot in the playground. It was time to share the love.

'Hello!' I beamed and did a rather ill-advised little wave with my hand. 'Are you a new mum? I'm Isabella. I've got a son in Year Six.'

The woman looked surprised, but a half-smile crept across her face. 'I am new. Very new. We just moved here a couple of weeks ago from Somerset. I haven't really got to know anyone yet.'

The girls introduced themselves and we walked slowly out of the gate, chatting all the way. I felt the question 'What would Claire do?' forming in my head and found myself asking the woman (Polly) back to my house for coffee. I hadn't really thought it through, and when we walked into the kitchen, to find Ali singing to herself and wiping the surfaces, I saw Polly's eyes flicker slightly, and for a second I saw myself through her eyes. I made her a coffee and lured her into the snug.

After an hour of determined chatting, I had learned that Polly had two sons, the eldest of whom was at high school, that her youngest, Harry, had been bullied at his last school and suffered from anxiety, and that her husband worked at the nuclear power plant. She herself worked part-time in a job share as the receptionist at another local primary school.

The old Issy Smugge would have revelled in the effect her beautiful house and many elegant accoutrements were having on her visitor. The new one felt a bit embarrassed and found herself talking more about her son than herself. One of the things I like most about Claire is the way she really listens. It's hard not talking about yourself when you are your brand and your own livelihood, but I managed to keep it zipped long enough to relax my guest, at least a little bit.

I was mindful that Finn would be horrified if he knew that I had enticed a fellow parent into the family home in order to craft a new friendship. On the way out, I struggled to find a tactful way of expressing my concerns about meddling in my son's social life. After I'd tried a few different ways of putting it, Polly laughed.

'We're both boy mums. I get it. This coffee never happened. It was really nice to meet you.'

She smiled, waved and walked off down the drive. I felt ridiculously pleased with myself as I headed off to the studio to sign the next batch of *Issy Smugge Says: Have Yourself a Trendy Little Christmas Limited Edition Festive Boxset.*

Christmas is usually a time of huge enjoyment for me. Mimi and I plan it out months in advance, book sales are up, I love all the glitter and sparkle and I'm overrun with excellent content. This year feels different. I'm struggling to get that festive feeling. This is partly because I am now five months pregnant with what appears to be a thrill-seeking mini acrobat (I couldn't tell you how many times I've been kicked in the ribs just as I drift off to sleep) and partly because the month of December appears to be the time when primary school teachers look at their calendars and decide to fill them up to the brim with events. Don't these people have homes to go to?

When Sofija and I ran the show together, I never had to worry about missing a play or a nativity or some kind of gruesome craft morning. We shared them out between us. Now, however, Issy Smugge is alone in a sea of forms and newsletters and requests for parental assistance, and she feels like a lone fishing boat cast out to sea with neither fish finder nor ship-to-shore radio.

I have been forced to create a large, laminated table of activities for this month which I have stuck to the fridge door, since otherwise I would most certainly miss something. We have a Christmas production, non-uniform day, Christmas Fair, Christmas Shopping Afternoon, Christmas Disco, Christmas Assembly and Carol Concert, Festive Make Morning (I dodged that last year) plus any number of other annoying little events which necessitate me laying down my important work and trotting up to the school.

To be scrupulously fair, I have shot myself in the foot, events wise. As the new secretary of the PTA, I hit the ground running, throwing myself into planning with gusto. My suggestions on how to increase the profit margin at the disco were met with rapture and, in a weak moment, I agreed to run the Christmas Shopping Afternoon. It's all taken vast chunks out of my working day and I find myself putting the children to bed and working until around midnight most nights. Thank heavens for my Miracle Lush Lash Serum and Wonderful Wide Eyed Luxury Eye Mask. My head is awhirl! **#christmasevents #addingvalue**

I've always looked on myself as a hands-on parent, encouraging my children to read, create, play outside and develop as well-rounded human beings without too much recourse to screens. Turns out it was really easy being that kind of mother when

Sofija was here. Facing up to a weekend alone with the children and a frankly terrifying to-do list, I found myself extending their screen privileges at an alarming rate.

On Friday, over tea, I made an attempt to have some quality conversation. I enquired how young Harry was getting on, to which Finn rolled his eyes and sighed heavily.

'He's OK. A bit nerdy, but OK. Mr Cresswell found out he likes football, so he's joined the team. Why?'

I reached out and stroked his arm. 'Just asking. I like to know what's going on in your life.'

He shook my hand off. 'Well, you don't need to know. It's fine, OK? And don't embarrass me and start chatting to Harry's mum or anything like that. It's lame.'

That was child number one engaged with. Honestly!

I turned to Chloë.

'Do you want me to hear your lines, darling? And we should talk about your costume.'

She swallowed a mouthful of Japanese cherry cheesecake (so deliciously light!) and shook her head. 'I've learned them all. It was easy. Maisie's mum is really good at sewing so she's doing most of the outfits. There's a letter in my book bag about it. We need to give Mrs Hill some money for the material.'

It was good to see my daughter so self-sufficient, but I felt a bit shut out. I smiled at my little Elsie.

'And how's your week, been, darling? What has Mrs Jenkins been teaching you?'

She beamed at me. Her smile is more gaps than teeth. Adorable.

'I love Mrs Jenkins, Mummy! She's so kind and nice. We're learning about castles. I've got to make one and bring it in next week. Charlie says he's going to make one out of cake and Amelia is doing hers out of Lego and Lucie said her dad is going to help her make hers out of wood and everyone else says they're going to get some big boxes and get their mums and dads to help them. I want to put jewels on mine and make a lovely queen who lives in the castle.'

She shovelled cheesecake into her mouth, continuing to smile at me. A castle? Yet another shot had been fired across Isabella M Smugge's crumbling bows.

I made an inarticulate sound, slid off my stool and rummaged through the book bag. Sure enough, crumpled and folded in half in Elsie's reading book, there was a letter from Mrs Jenkins giving us all plenty of notice (ha!) and reminding us that it was all about the children and please not to help too much. This meant that I had seven days to plan and construct a castle. Craft is not my thing. I yearned to have Sofija back, before recalling that she was out of my life forever and a good thing too.

I plastered a big smile on my face. 'How lovely, darling! Why don't we make a start this weekend? We've got lots of leftover paint and you can make a pretty queen and get her ready to put in the castle.'

Elsie leaned over and gave me a big hug, wiping her sticky mouth on the sleeve of my Scrummy Mummy maternity floral midi dress. Did I mention I am now the face of Scrummy Mummy? Beautifully made clothes, very on-trend and with immaculate provenance. **#mumtobe #beautifulbumps #styleambassador**

'Thank you, Mummy! I love making things with you.' She hopped off her stool and put her plate and spoon in the sink. 'Can I watch TV?'

I sighed. 'Go on, then.'

The girls ran into the family room and Finn sloped off upstairs, leaving me with all the washing-up, crumbs on the floor and a raging headache. If I devoted myself to all the children's activities and nothing else, that would be a full-time job. I don't know how people do it. I loaded the dishwasher, wiped the island, swept up the crumbs and opened my laptop to write up the minutes of our last PTA meeting and send out last-minute reminder emails to all the suppliers for the Christmas Shopping Afternoon. Then I wrote to all the local primary schools, asking them if we could advertise in their

93

newsletters. One job led to another and yet another and before I knew where I was, it was gone ten and Elsie was asleep on the sofa while her sister gazed at the television. I can see why parents use screens to get precious time for themselves. The way things are going, it seems that even Issy Smugge is going down that pernicious road. **#droppingmystandards #todolists**

By Sunday evening, having put the children to bed, done their packed lunches (boring old ham sandwiches, organic low salt vegetable crisps, a homemade flapjack and an apple for Finn), loaded the dishwasher, checked off my to-do list for the morning and posted a few inspirational bits of Christmas content, I was wiped out. Thank heavens Silvia is coming on Tuesday for a week. I've changed Johnnie's weekends with the children. We had agreed on two a month, but with Silvia's visit and Christmas, it's all over the place.

I was excited that my lovely mother-in-law would be christening my newly refurbished guest suite. On Monday, I dressed the bed, put fresh flowers and a scented candle on the dressing table and some posh toiletries in the en suite. I took lots of photos and wrote a quick piece about having family to stay. Harpreet and Mimi will be over the moon. Images of family togetherness really boost my brand. It's just as well she's coming as Mimi has booked me not one, not two, but three appearances, Lavinia has written an utterly poisonous piece in her hideous rag, I need emotional support and the week is full of school events.

Silvia appeared at lunch time on Tuesday, and never have I been so glad to see a bishop's widow. Anyone less like Mummy you couldn't hope to meet. She enveloped me in a warm hug, told me how wonderful I was looking and insisted I sat down and put my feet up while she made me some lunch. Silvia has some delightfully old-fashioned ideas about pregnant ladies. I've never let any of my babies slow me down, but my mother-in-law had other ideas.

'That's why I'm here, my darling. I had a wonderful time at Toby and Davina's (that baby is so sweet! An angel) and looked after them and now I'm here to look after you. Don't you move. I'll make a cup of tea and we can have a good catch-up.'

Really, I should have been working, but my eyes were still sore from the crying about the article and my ankles were a bit swollen. I allowed myself to be fussed over, covered with a cashmere throw and served a wholemeal tuna and rocket sandwich. Silvia had read Lavinia's offending piece over the shoulder of a fellow passenger on the train and was full of righteous indignation.

'What things to say! I never buy that terrible paper (all gossip and bad recipes) and I'll make sure none of my friends ever do either. You take no notice of her, my darling. Rise above it!'

I had been trying, but it's hard when you sit, alone and pregnant, in your studio with rampant heartburn, reading lies about yourself.

Isabella M Hugge: When Inspiration Turns to Desperation
Difficult times in the formerly picture-perfect world of sugar-sweet blogger and mumfluencer Isabella M Smugge. First her husband, dashing hedge fund manager Johnnie Smugge, ran off with her younger, prettier au pair. The red-faced influencer brazened it out with a stream of hypocritical content about family values. However, I can reveal that the author of *Issy Smugge Says: Turn the Lights Down Low* has been doing a lot more than that! As the festive season approaches, she has a little Christmas pudding of her own in the oven, ready to be served up in the springtime.

Sources close to the so-called inspirational blogger are concerned. 'Issy won't accept that she and Johnnie are over,' a family friend told me. 'He's never coming back, but she's convinced it's only a matter of time. I expect she got pregnant on purpose. It's just the kind of thing she would do.'

At this time of year, it's hard to get away from Smugge's outpourings. Her saccharine Christmas campaign ('Have yourself an Issy little Christmas') is everywhere. What next? A keep-fit DVD? Smuggerise Yourself Slim? This writer says, 'Stop jingling your bells and put a sock in it. We've all heard enough.'

Thank God for Silvia! I had been a little anxious about our first meeting after Johnnie's departure, but in between planning a hideous revenge on Lavinia and telling me all about Baby Matthew, there was no time to worry.

At 3.10, I heaved myself off the sofa and we walked down to school to pick up the children. Their faces lit up when they saw her, even Finn's. I was heartened to see him walking out of school with Harry Baker. Could a friendship be developing?

That evening was delightful. Silvia helped Elsie with the blasted castle, listened to Chloë's lines with rapt attention and sat looking interested while Finn talked at her about football. She put the children to bed for me ('Rest, darling! You look so tired') and cleaned and tidied the kitchen. I love her! #bestmilintheworld #pushoffharcourt

It's just as well I took Silvia's advice and had an early night. On Thursday, I had two appearances to promote my Christmas boxset and on Friday a meet and greet with some other mummy bloggers at a large out-of-town shopping centre. I tried not to feel guilty as I drove towards my first personal appearance in nearly eight years.

I had dressed with great care, putting together a very on-trend look with conceptual layered pieces. As I always tell my followers, there's no need to be a slave to fashion. Buying well, dressing to suit your shape and colouring and accessorising boldly will take you anywhere. That said, it can't hurt to have an entire dressing room of outfits from which to choose.

I felt a little nervous as I was shown to my seat. Things had moved on considerably since I burst on to the blogging scene and I didn't want to show myself up. I needn't have worried. From the moment the doors opened and the line of fans began to snake towards me, I was enveloped in a cloud of appreciation, admiration and, dare I say it, almost adoration. I signed books, answered questions and smiled for selfies until my cheeks hurt. I wonder if this is what the Queen feels like. After my three hours were up, I went to the loo, refreshed my perfume and make-up and drove to the next venue where I did it all again. On Friday, running largely on adrenaline, I granted my followers' wishes for selfies and autographs alongside a squad of fellow mummy bloggers and smiled until my perfectly made-up visage was throbbing. **#giving #feelingthelove**

Mimi had sent one of her underlings to help me. I had spotted her from afar, largely because of her frozen features. Bless her, she carried heavy boxes of books, stood by with hot drinks and was a tower of strength, even if she didn't crack a smile. Well, she clearly couldn't. At the end of the day, she counted up how many books we'd sold and told me the glad tidings with a poker face. I was delighted. Why haven't I done this before? I checked my socials and sure enough, **#imetissysmugge** was trending. I lost count of the shares, retweets and new comments. Magnificent! **#johnniewaswrong #bestgameintown**

By that evening I was worn out. Thank God for Silvia. She'd kept everything running like clockwork (but then I suppose she would!) and was waiting for me with a delicious shepherd's pie when I returned home. To my surprise, Finn was markedly more affectionate than usual, even telling me that he'd missed me. Perhaps absence does make the heart grow fonder. I was so wiped out that I had a long, lavender-infused bath and was in bed by nine. I need to rest up for the party at Boing! tomorrow.

I wouldn't want you to think that I've got ideas above my station, but Issy Smugge would rather be seen wearing neon colours two seasons after they went out than book a party at a large echoing warehouse full of screaming children on an industrial estate. I had brought all three children, plus Silvia, Jake and Harry. Finn had grudgingly agreed to join us on the understanding that I did not speak to him or approach him in any way. I was so happy that his friend count was going up that I would have done anything.

We parked up and walked into something calling itself 'Welcome and Reception'. A teenage person dressed in a lurid orange outfit with 'Boing!' emblazoned on the pockets stopped chewing gum and staring at her phone for long enough to ask us our intentions. I dropped Lauren's name and we were in.

My friend was sitting at a table with a helium balloon, a pile of presents and several plastic jugs full of a purple liquid. How much more enjoyable children's parties would be if only cocktails were served.

'It's mad, babes. I've had two no-shows so far and Lysander's feeling sick.' She glanced over to where Kim was talking earnestly to Hayley, who was crouching down beside her pallid son.

I introduced Silvia, who immediately offered to sit at the table and accept presents from incoming mums, while Lauren went off to speak to the party coordinator, who appeared to be in her early teens. Children were milling about everywhere, and the noise was deafening. Another orange-clad youngster joined us and announced it was time for the safety video. We rose from our seats and shuffled into a small, stuffy room which smelt strongly of feet, where we were treated to a short video telling us how incredibly dangerous trampolining was. Our duty done, we returned to the table and the children scattered to go and leap about on pieces of reinforced canvas suspended on bungee ropes.

Lauren and Kim sank into their seats and wiped their brows. 'Peace and quiet for an hour and a half!' Kim said, getting out her purse. 'Anyone fancy a coffee? First one's free, but I need chocolate.' Dear Silvia immediately got up and offered to help. I tried to identify my children among the frantically bouncing forms in the middle distance. I could see Elsie and Becky jumping hand in hand on a small trampoline while my son and his friends hurled themselves repeatedly at a wall, which fortunately appeared to be made of some kind of yielding material.

Lysander and his mother had inched a little closer to the trampolines, but there was no sign of any intention to actually bounce. I was thinking some rather uncharitable thoughts about Hayley when a familiar voice broke into my musings.

'Do you mind if we join you? Joel's in the ball pit and I need to be able to keep an eye on him.' It was Tom, pushing a sleeping Ben in his pram. We moved the chairs around to accommodate them and I introduced Silvia.

'Didn't we meet last Christmas? I'm sure I remember your face.' Tom was smiling charmingly, and Silvia was beaming. I left them chatting and turned to Lauren, Kim and Kate, who were talking avidly about the latest playground gossip. I sipped my hot chocolate and let my mind go blank. Once you got used to the screaming and the smell of hundreds of sweaty, bouncing short people, it wasn't too bad. My children were all entertaining themselves, I had a hot drink, and no one was asking me to do anything. I wondered if I should take a few shots. I could hear Mimi's voice in my head. 'So relatable, darling! Issy Smugge at a soft play centre, just like a normal person.' Maybe not.

Looking over, I could see that Lysander had been absorbed into the vast elasticity of the main play space and that Hayley was heading our way. Maybe it was because I was thinking of Claire, or maybe I really am becoming a better person. Whatever it was, I found myself smiling at her and inviting her to join us, ignoring Kate's deep sigh and Kim's rolling eyes. **#reachingout**

My week with Silva was bliss. Thank heavens she's coming back for Christmas. I don't know how I'd cope with Mummy *and* Johnnie otherwise. My friends wanted to know if it wasn't a bit awks, what with her being the mother of the man who cheated on me with my au pair, but on the first night she told me that she was horrified by his behaviour, absolutely did not condone it and would support me in any way I needed. I love her! **#luckygirl #emotionalsupport**

Lauren and I went up to the hospital to see Claire on Wednesday. Driving down the A12, we were both feeling a mixture of emotions. The poor girl had been through so much. First the placental abruption (which I didn't even know was a thing), then the emergency C-section to get Ben out, then the emergency hysterectomy, then the sepsis. All I wanted to do was throw my arms around her and tell her how happy I was she was still here. Lauren felt much the same. I was also very aware that I was walking in with a baby bump, glowing with health (apart from the swollen ankles, heartburn, pregnancy thrush and occasional skin breakout), while she was separated from her family and probably feeling pretty grim. I shared my concerns with Lauren as we parked up.

'Look, she's your friend. She'll be happy for you. You know what she's like, always putting other people first. Let's just spend some time with her, try to cheer her up if she needs it and be positive.'

We walked into the ward, having first thoroughly sanitised our hands with some nasty-looking blue gloop. We both spotted Claire at the same time, lying propped up on her pillows in a bed by the window. We forgot all the advice (take it easy, don't tire her out) and enveloped her in a hug, Lauren on one side of the bed, me on the other. I was surprised to find that my cheeks were wet with tears. I was always so good at managing my emotions before. Now, I found that I didn't care if anyone saw me crying.

Holding our friend's hands, we sank down into the chairs and beamed at her. She looked pale and tired, with circles under her eyes and tell-tale bruising in the crook of her arm and on the back of her hand, but at least she wasn't hooked up to lots of tubes and drips any more. We both started talking at once, sharing all the latest news about Hayley and her kitchen, me and Mr Rycroft, Chloë's starring role, my visit to church, the dramatic rescue of Max and everything else she'd missed. As Lauren recounted the tale of me mistaking my daughter's new teacher for a teenager, she laughed in the old way, her face lighting up just as it used to do.

'Oh, Isabella, how funny! Does he really look that young?'

'Honestly, about fourteen!' I assured her. 'How was I supposed to know?'

It had been funny at the time, but now, sitting in a ward full of ill people, looking out over the Ipswich skyline, it seemed the most hilarious thing in the world. All three of us rocked with helpless laughter, tears streaming down our faces. Lauren was trying to bring out the punchline between howls of mirth.

'And then he said…' She paused to wipe her eyes. '… I'll be twenty-three in January.'

That finished us off. It was about five minutes before we were able to speak without our voices shaking. I fell back in my chair, gasping for breath and feeling happier than I had in months. All the laughter had put some colour back in Claire's cheeks and she was grinning from ear to ear.

'Oh, girls, it's so good to see you! I can't tell you, honestly. I've missed you both so much. I can't wait to get out of here and be back at home.'

We assured her that there was a void in the playground that only she could fill and asked if she knew when she was being let out.

'They say before Christmas. I'm so much stronger now, off the drips and able to walk a bit. I feel so helpless lying here, and I miss the children and Tom so much.' She suddenly looked terribly sad. I yearned to be able to do something to help, but nothing came to mind. Just then, we heard the rattle of a trolley and something calling itself lunch was served.

I wondered how to bring up the subject of my own condition. I needn't have worried.

'So the other big news is that Isabella's expecting.' Lauren gestured towards my billowing stomach, encased in the well-cut lines of another Scrummy Mummy ensemble.

Claire dropped her fork with a clang. 'No way!'

'Yes way! Due in April. I only got it out of her in October. She's going on the NHS. Talk about relatable!'

'She only told you in October? Good heavens. So are she and Johnnie back together, then?'

At this point, I felt it was time to intervene. 'I am still here, you know. We are not. He knows and he's supporting me, naturally, but he still hasn't come to his senses. He's coming for Christmas, so I'll work on him then.'

Lunch forgotten, Claire was gazing at me in wonder. 'Not to pry, but if you're not back together, how did… I mean, were you… you know?'

'Got hammered, quick how's-your-father, left her in the morning to go back to London.' Lauren leapt in before I could think of a tactful way to break the news.

'No! That's shocking. How could he?' Claire was looking as angry as I'd ever seen her.

'I know. Talk about taking advantage.' Lauren appeared to agree.

I raised a hand. 'I appreciate you're cross on my behalf, but it really wasn't like that. We had a massive fight, I threw my best salt and pepper mills at him and they broke, and I smashed a wine glass over his head. Then Finn came down and saw, and after that, we started on the port and it just happened.'

As the words came out of my mouth, I seemed to hear them afresh. How many times had Johnnie mocked women who said exactly that?

'It just happened, Iss. Yeah, right!'

I'd had a choice, but then, so had my husband. I felt suddenly uncomfortable and unsure. Here I was defending the man who had cheated on me, left me, deprived me and my children of Sofija, and was now leaving me to bring up his children on my own while pregnant with a fourth.

I didn't have time to ponder further, as Claire was hurling questions at me. I filled her in, and we rejoiced at the thought of having another pair of children in the same class.

'I've told her she'll have to go to toddlers. She'll meet loads of people there.' Lauren appeared to have taken my social life in hand.

'Oh yes, great idea, Lauren. She will. Once I'm better I can go back to helping Mary run our group and you can bed her in at the one at the village hall. You know what it's like. Can be a bit scary.'

My friends seemed to have my future all sorted. I didn't know whether to be offended or pleased. I settled on the latter. It was quite soothing having other people deciding what I should do. Well, when those people were Lauren and Claire, anyway.

Lunch was cleared away and our friend let out a huge yawn. 'Sorry, girls, I think I'm going to have a nap. I get so tired out. It's silly, really, but even sitting and chatting takes it out of me. Will you come again?'

We assured Claire we'd be back every day if allowed and bade her a fond farewell. Walking out of the hospital, we were both silent, absorbed in our own thoughts. I don't know what Lauren was thinking, but my mind was a whirl of doubts and worries and anger. What was happening to me? I did what I always do and pushed it all down, where I couldn't see it any more.

Christmas was coming and with it three family members who had no reason to love each other. I was going to have my work cut out. #yuletidestress

January

Thank heavens that's over! Never, in all my life, have I experienced such a stressful Christmas and New Year. Mummy was the first to arrive at the Old Rectory, bristling with rage at the thought of sharing an abode with her philandering son-in-law. I had one night to convince her that telling him exactly what she thought of him in front of his mother wasn't the best idea. Heavily medicated by a succession of gin and tonics and cigarettes, she reluctantly agreed to behave herself.

Next to pull up on the drive was dear Silvia, who was charm itself. She and Mummy have always got on moderately well, and after a rather intense conversation over dinner, they reached an uneasy truce. I was exhausted after weeks of school activities, assemblies and events. The Christmas Shopping Afternoon was a triumph, but nearly killed me. The PTA coffers are healthier than they have been for some time, but Isabella M Smugge is not.

The children were beside themselves with excitement at seeing their father. I was pinning my hopes on his heart being softened by my charming Christmas decorations and the yuletide spirit. When he arrived, late on Christmas Eve, having missed the frenzy of dinner, the Christingle service at church, which Silvia insisted on us all attending, and a meltdown from Chloë (too much excitement brought on by her recent performance in the Year Three and Four production, plus unacceptably high sugar levels), I was more than ready to hand over the reins of parenting to him.

He came breezing in, as cool as an Early Pride cucumber, smiling, his arms full of presents. Having just got everyone calmed down, I was none too impressed when he started horsing around and getting the three of them all excited. From the look on Mummy's face, either she had accidentally ingested the lemon slice in her drink or she was plotting some kind of bodily harm. Silvia intervened, speaking quietly to him and stopping the horseplay. I wonder if she would consider selling her house and living with me forever and ever.

Sadly, that set the tone for the rest of Christmas. It was more of an endurance test than a time of peace and goodwill. Roll on New Year, was all I could say. **#stress #disappointment**

I've spent a lot of time thinking about Johnnie and why he behaved as he did over Christmas, and now I come to think about it, he must have been feeling threatened by the presence of not only my mother but also his own. If only we had been able to spend some quiet time together and have a really good chat, I might be sharing my king-sized, beech-framed bed with its hand-tied hourglass springs again. However, either Silvia or Mummy always seemed to be lurking around a dark corner, which put the kibosh on that.

It didn't help that Silvia was residing in Sofija's former bedroom suite and that Mummy was laying her head in the new en-suite double next door. Johnnie was relegated to the second floor, a part of the house we were intending to renovate this year. We've got three bedrooms and a bathroom up there, all in need of some TLC, but perfectly acceptable for a cheating husband.

After our Boxing Day dinner (roast lamb with cumin and rosemary yoghurt marinade, served with crushed minted potatoes and buttered spinach), Johnnie seemed particularly jolly. He had put away around three-quarters of a bottle of a particularly fine Gironde red and was slurring his words just the tiniest touch. Only a wife would notice. Mummy had ingested at least four gin and tonics and was hammering her way through a cheeky little Pinot Grigio while Silvia had had one glass of the Gironde and then switched to water.

I wouldn't want you to think that I've got a drink problem, but I am really missing having wine with dinner. Our wine merchant is marvellous, almost a family friend, and as he always says, 'Life's too short to drink bad wine.' I would have given almost anything to be allowed to wash my tender, flavoursome lamb down with a glass of Bordeaux, instead of watching my husband quaff it all.

I got up to go to the loo (again!), and when I emerged from the cloakroom, there was Johnnie, looking particularly handsome as he leaned against the frame of the kitchen door. His tie brought out the deep sapphire of his eyes and his aftershave was giving me painful flashbacks to better times.

'Iss, you excelled yourself. That was the best lamb I've ever tasted. Stroke of genius, pairing it with cumin and rosemary. Can I help you with the pud?'

He was smiling into my eyes and it took all my strength not to reach out, grab him and never let him go. I scuttled sideways, like a flushed and pregnant spider crab, to access the individual custard tarts with roasted pineapple which I was offering for dessert. I thrust a tub of organic free-range double cream (made by happy cows) at him.

'Put this in the blue jug. No, not that one. The one with the swirls on it.'

Having sourced the correct receptacle, he gazed into my eyes. 'The one we bought in the Douro. How could I forget? What a holiday that was!' He sighed and the spicy fragrance of his aftershave drifted over to me.

The moment was shattered by Mummy, stalking in with her cigarettes, en route to the boot room. She shot a look of pure loathing at Johnnie and marched past, scowling. My husband gave me a naughty wink and grinned. I could feel myself grinning back, and who knows what would have happened if Silvia had not joined us, offering to take the puds through.

Dinner finished and cleared away, there was an awkward moment. Johnnie and Mummy didn't want to be in the same room, I desperately wanted to spend time with my husband but could tell that Mummy didn't want me to, Silvia was trying to keep everyone happy, and I needed the toilet again. Sitting in my lovely cloakroom, I leaned my flushed visage against the cool, tiled walls and took some deep breaths. Every fibre in my body was yearning to take Johnnie's hand, run upstairs with him and restore our marriage.

As I sat gazing at my lightweight waffle-weave hand towels and inhaled the delicate fragrance of my wild mint and strawberry reed diffusers, my agent's voice suddenly popped into my head.

'Do I really have to remind you what he's broken?'

As the baby kicked me hard in the ribs and I felt the unwelcome stirrings of acid heartburn, I realised that it was going to be a sleepless night. For all the wrong reasons. **#whyme #sotired #issysmuggesaysivehadenough**

I wouldn't want to give you the impression that I'm spending every waking moment thinking about Johnnie. I'm really not. I've never been busier or more successful. Mimi is radiant with joy (so she tells me, at least. I wonder how long it takes for Botox to wear off), since my personal appearances are having an amazing effect on my reach. **#imetissysmugge** and **#smuggeselfie** are trending on Twitter and my book sales have rocketed. Things are normally quiet in January and February, but the excitement of meeting me in the flesh has encouraged many of my new followers to fill their bookshelves with Issy Smugge.

At our first weekly meeting of the new year, my agent was as animated as was physically possible.

'Sweetheart! A very happy New Year. Now, I hate to say I told you so, but (here she let out a harsh bark of laughter) I told you so! I'm sure Johnnie had his reasons for locking you away like a princess in a tower, but now you're free, I hope you can see which way the wind's blowing. You've lit up Twitter, Insta is going crazy and your book sales are beyond amazing.'

She leaned back in her chair and gazed at me through narrowed eyes as the smoke from her cigarette curled upwards. I wasn't at all sure about the way this was going. Free? If spending my evenings alone and tearful was being free, I didn't think I liked it very much.

'You're making it sound as if he controlled me, Mimi. Surely you're not saying that protecting me and looking out for me was wrong?'

I thought but didn't say that Mimi's marital track record hardly qualified her to criticise other people's marriages. She's never understood Johnnie and I and how we work.

My agent sighed and took a swig of something from a small silver flask. It could have been finest French brandy. Equally, it could have been cough syrup.

'I'm not his biggest fan. That's no secret. All I'm saying is that your career is already stellar and with a few more personal appearances, there's no knowing where you might go.'

I judged it best to make a non-committal reply and move on. We chatted figures, stats and strategy and I agreed to appear at three more events in January, four in February and six in March. ('Strike while the iron's hot, darling. Let's get in as many as we can before that little baby comes along and then we can concentrate on hundreds of newborn shots and links to your endorsements.') Mimi appeared to be salivating with excitement. Making a mental note never, ever to have anything injected into the facial region, I blew her a kiss and departed to get on with my busy day.

Thank heavens there are no PTA activities until Easter. I need a break. I made myself a mature Cheddar and tomato ciabatta, drank several cups of peppermint tea to combat my wretched heartburn and knuckled down to writing some serious content. My to-do list is vast.

After two hours of solid work, I awarded myself a short break. Idly scanning through the bestseller lists (call me shallow, but seeing my own name on there still gives me a secret thrill), I noticed two new names, both cleanfluencers. Clicking on the first one, I found that she was represented by Mimi Stanhope Creatives. Interesting. Her first book, *Neat Freak: My Life in Tidying*, was selling fast. Checking out the other one (Fabulously Fantastic Fiona, a woman who seems to live for vigorous exercise), a pattern began to emerge. She too was represented by my agent, who was clearly spreading her nets.

I went to the loo for the umpteenth time and took advantage of the weak winter sunshine by popping into the garden and taking some pictures. As I was framing a rather gorgeous shot of the leafless beech tree reaching up into the winter sky, my phone started ringing. Mummy. I sighed and let it go to answerphone. I just didn't have the strength.

My boy's birthday is coming up. Eleven years old! This last year has shot by. It seems only yesterday that I was being told not to embarrass him while Sofija calmed it all down. I miss her. I can't believe I've said it, but I do. I'm still angry with her, but I hadn't realised what a huge part of my life she was until she disappeared.

As I headed along the landing past Elsie's room the other day, I heard the girls whispering. I know it's wrong to eavesdrop, but sometimes I feel so shut out of my children's lives and I don't know how to be part of them again.

'What if Sofija has a baby like Mummy?' Elsie was talking. 'Daddy would never come back home because he would be looking after them.'

'She won't have a baby, silly. Remember she always used to tell us that we were her babies. Maybe Mummy and Daddy will get back together and then she can come back and live with us and everything will go back to normal. She could do all the work like she used to and then Mummy would be happy again.'

My daughter sounded wistful. I felt my eyes fill with stinging tears. Was that really how the children saw our situation? I went into my en suite, locked the door and had a good cry, interrupted only by the desperate urge to go the toilet. Perhaps eating quite so much Lebanese Fig Preserve last night was a mistake. Once the children were in bed, I absent-mindedly troughed through half a jar with a teaspoon before I realised what I was doing. The figs have had what you might call a freeing effect. #goodclearout

Once everything was restored to normal and I'd tackled the worst of the eye puffiness with my Cool as a Cucumber Eye Pads (a lifesaver!), I took a deep breath and resolved to be a better mother.

I don't know what's come over me. I used to get through so much work every day, but since Christmas, I've felt completely overwhelmed. My standards are definitely slipping. Even with Ali doing all the housework and most of the cooking, things aren't as perfect as they used to be when Sofija was here. The children seem to have got out of the habit of cleaning up after themselves. I had to have a serious talk with them the other day when I discovered that they've been leaving their beds unmade and scattering dirty clothes and toys all over their floors. I pointed out that Ali is not paid to pick up after them and that they would do well to return to the habits Sofija drilled into them. Finn scowled mutinously and Chloë chewed her fingernails while glowering at me. These days, I always feel like the bad guy.

This morning was frightful. I had a bad night's sleep, punctuated by constant trips to the loo to produce around a teaspoon of liquid. I dreamed that Mummy was moving house and had bought the cottage at the bottom of our garden, while Meredith made friends with Hayley and wrote a horrible article about me and put it in all the book bags. I woke up in a cold sweat, late, and we had the usual scramble to get everyone dressed, breakfasted and out of the door on time. We were late and had to gaze pleadingly through the double doors at Mr Cresswell, who took pity on us and allowed the children to scuttle in, rather than condemning us to the walk of shame through the office.

Walking back across the playground, I passed Liane Bloomfield.

'All right, Smug?' she greeted me.

I tried to smile in a gracious and natural fashion. While I was racking my brains for some kind of conversational gambit, she spoke again.

'What's the deal with that woman in the paper slagging you off? She's really on your case.'

She shifted her weight to her right hip and began rolling a cigarette. I sighed.

'She hates me. We were at the same school and she was vile to my little sister, so I sneaked into her dorm and cut her hair off.'

Said out loud on a cold and windy Suffolk playground, it made me sound like a psycho, but sometimes you need to tell it like it is. Liane frowned.

'What's a dorm?'

I explained.

'So, like a bedroom for posh people?'

'I suppose. Yes. Like a big room full of beds and washbasins.'

'Sounds more like prison to me. But you should know. And that's why she's writing all that stuff about you being huge and two-faced?'

I nodded. 'I don't really know what to do about it. If I respond, I'm fuelling the fire; if I stay quiet, I look weak, and she thinks she's won.'

'I can see that. She needs telling.' Liane got out her lighter and began walking slowly towards the gate. 'Have you got people on your side?'

I considered. 'Well, yes. My agent is, but she's paid to be pro-me. Obviously, my sister is, but what can she do? I've chosen to be in the public eye, so I've got to expect this sort of thing. That's what my husband says, anyway.'

Liane snorted. 'Does he, now? What you want is someone powerful on your side. You know, the sort of person who doesn't care what she says and could dish the dirt on her.'

I was pleasantly surprised but also confused by Ms Bloomfield's sudden concern for my welfare. Ever since the fight at Messy Church over her sausage rolls last April, we had circled warily around each other, and if I was honest, I was still a bit frightened of her. On the other side of the gate, she lit her cigarette and took a meditative puff.

'If you went to school with her, you must have something on her. You could threaten her and then she'd stop saying that stuff about you. Just a thought.'

I smiled, and this time it was a real one. 'Thanks, Liane! I'll have a think. My sister's moving back to the UK in a couple of months. I'll ask her if she knows anything. I would love to threaten Lavinia, but she'd use it against me.'

I found myself telling Liane about the fight with my old enemy. When I got to the bit about me knocking Lavinia down, she inhaled appreciatively.

'You're not nearly as wet as you look, Smug. That's what people like her need. A good kicking. Well, can't stand here chatting – things to do, places to be. See you!'

Turning on her heel, she trundled off with the pushchair in the direction of the village, leaving a thoughtful Issy Smugge facing up to the biting north wind and heading back to the warm embrace of her delightful abode. **#wellwell #frenemy**

One of the first things I do when Christmas is over is to update my labels list and repack my Christmas card box. It may surprise you to learn that an internationally renowned blogger of my calibre still writes her Christmas greetings by hand. Johnnie thinks I'm mad.

'Honestly, Iss, why don't you do e-cards like everyone else and save yourself the time?'

I don't know about you, but I still get a childish thrill of excitement when a letter or card comes through the door addressed to me. Nowadays, with online shopping, parcels are ten a penny, but I like the idea that they are still special. I handwrite all my cards, using my efficient label system, and I always will. Yes, it takes a lot of time, but it's all about adding value.

I packed the Christmas box and asked Finn to take it up to the top floor, ready to be stowed in the attic. I didn't want to climb up the ladder in my condition. Johnnie can do it when he's next at home.

My phone rang. Mummy. I'd been avoiding her calls. Sighing, I hit 'answer'.

'You *are* still alive, then, Isabella!'

I sat down at the island and braced myself for a tirade of sarcasm. I wasn't disappointed. Mummy hates not being able to get hold of people. Once she'd finished and asked after my health in a desultory fashion, she moved on to the main event.

'I've decided to downsize. I'm putting the house on the market. It's getting too big for me, even with help.'

My heart stopped for a second. Had my dream been some kind of awful prophecy? What if Mummy decided to move to Suffolk? How would I cope? Worse still, what if she asked to come and live with me? Appalling scenarios flashed through my mind before she let out a rattling cough and continued.

'I'm staying in Kent, obviously. All my friends and my social life are here. I've got my eye on a nice little two-bedroomed cottage on the other side of the village. I'll need to get rid of some of my things. I want you to come down for the weekend the next time that man has the children. You and Suzanne might want some of the furniture and there are some things I need to go through with you.'

The relief of finding out that Mummy had no intention of straying further north filled me with joy. I put a weekend in the diary at the end of the month and passed the phone over to the children. Their faces fell as I mouthed, 'Grandmother wants a word.' After each child had been addressed, I took the phone back for the concluding pleasantries.

'You looked very pulled down when I was up at Christmas. Make sure that husband of yours doesn't take advantage. The girls seem to be picking up a local accent. Terribly common. Bye!'

And she was gone. Sighing, I put my phone back in my pocket and started on the tea. **#womansworkneverdone #busymum**

What with the personal appearances, planning Finn's birthday, losing an entire weekend to Mummy and trying to create fresh, engaging content, my head is in a whirl.

I broached the delicate subject of birthday celebrations with my son just after Christmas. Maybe I am becoming a better mother, as I didn't try to impose my ideas on him but asked politely if he had any suggestions. We managed to have a conversation about the options without anyone slamming doors or exiting the room in a huff. It seems that he would like to go to Ipswich with Jake and Harry, mooch around a bit and then eat his own weight in burgers and chips. I suppressed the first question that sprang to mind ('How am I supposed to get any good images from that?') and the second ('Walk around Ipswich? Surely we can do better than that?') and contented myself with asking if he thought it was safe for three eleven-year-olds to wander around the county town. It's bad enough watching him disappear down the drive with Johnnie twice a month.

He sighed. 'Mum, don't be lame. It's fine. What do you think's going to happen to us?'

I agreed to contact Charlene, Jake's mum, and Polly, to see what they thought. We sat in silence for a minute then Finn reached out and patted me kindly on the arm. 'Thanks, Mum.' He smiled, slid off his stool and loped upstairs. I felt strangely proud of myself. Maybe I'm not doing such a terrible job after all.

January slid by in a whirl of doctor's appointments (I am starting to see why people go on so much about the NHS. They really are jolly good), personal appearances (exhausting, but so much fun!), parenting, work and general admin.

I've thought for a long time that what I really need is an executive PA to help me run my life. Looking back on it, in a way, that's what Sofija was to me. A lovely, smiling PA who made everything easy. It must be the pregnancy hormones, but I often find myself snivelling childishly these days. I was halfway through an uplifting piece on dinner party etiquette in the twenty-first century recently when I had a flashback to Sofija and me howling with laughter in the kitchen last June, surrounded by vomit-soaked sheets. Knowing what I know now, I realise she would have been in the throes of her affair with my husband and yet, just at that moment, I would have given anything to have her back and to be able to talk everything through.

Sometimes, lying awake at night or sitting in the en suite producing yet another teaspoon of liquid as the owl hoots outside my bedroom window I have imaginary conversations with my former au pair. I ask her when it started, why she did it, how it felt to deceive me, if she misses me as much as I miss her. And then I cry, pathetically, because I know that I will never have the opportunity to find out. That makes me think about Daddy and how much he loved me, and how different my life might have been if he hadn't taken that ill-fated holiday with Arabella, my godmother, the woman he left Mummy for. If only they hadn't run off together and then decided to go on holiday to Italy. Even now, some nights I still have that old, horrible nightmare where I'm plunging down a ravine in the car with Daddy and Arabella by my side. The weeping Issy Smugge, wracked with sobs, who lies sleepless on her Plump No Mores night after night bears no resemblance to the smiling, beautifully dressed and confident Isabella M Smugge, doyenne of lifestyle bloggers (that's what they called me in a recent magazine interview).

The dead of night is when I have my most depressing times. Every so often, some throwaway line or joke I made returns to me and I cringe. I never could remember where Sofija came from and I used to make little funny remarks and she'd laugh. But what was I really doing? I was telling her that she didn't matter to me. Not enough to bother looking up Lithuania and Latvia and working out the difference, anyway.

The realisation that I might have contributed to my au pair's decision to sleep with my husband reduced me to helpless tears, interrupted only by a sleepy, thumb-sucking Elsie walking in and clambering into bed with me. Being a mother means pretending everything is all right, I've learned, so I wiped my eyes, blew my nose and cuddled up with my little girl. I was asleep in seconds, worn out with emotion.

I have been trying very hard to be a better person. Part of that, I feel, is going to church more regularly and trying to understand the rituals of religious people. I haven't been to Claire's ladies' group very much. It's not the same without her there. I went to the traditional service after Christmas and rather enjoyed it. We sang hymns, read things off a screen which I didn't really understand but which sounded nice, prayed quietly with our eyes closed and heard a story from the Bible in normal language. No one put their hands up or shouted things. People were nice to me afterwards and I had a cup of tea. I felt strangely soothed by the whole experience, and of course, it must have added to my holy points. I don't know how long the contribution to fixing the roof will last. I expect God has some kind of balance sheet, and I need to show willing and put in the work.

Something has been bothering me and I don't know who to ask about it. How come someone like Claire, absolutely at the top of the religious tree, can have had such a bad time of it? Married to a vicar, running groups, praying all the time, going to church every single Sunday, and yet she almost died. If you're doing all the right stuff, how can things go so catastrophically wrong? I parked the question in the seething cauldron of my mind and resolved to ask my friend what God thought He was playing at, when she was well enough to consider such questions.

She didn't come out before Christmas after all. Another setback. How can this be? I talked to Lauren about it but she didn't understand it either. It's all very baffling. #difficultquestions #badthingstogoodpeople

Finn's birthday trip to Ipswich was a great success. Polly met me at the Old Rectory with Harry and Jake (Charlene was far too anxious to venture into Ipswich) and we drove to the town centre, deposited the boys at a burger bar with strict instructions to stay in touch via text and went for a lovely wander.

There was some delightful architecture and a plethora of little coffee shops. I found myself enjoying the experience, snapping away, adding to my bank of images and getting to know Polly a little better. We had to keep stopping so I could go to the loo (so annoying!). For a little while, I forgot that I was Isabella M Smugge, renowned and beloved blogger and influencer, and reverted to Bella Neville, searching for exactly the right angle and perspective. People don't realise that you can't just point and click. Really good photos take some planning and I flatter myself that I know exactly how to do that. Sitting down and enjoying a hot chocolate and a piece of lemon drizzle, I looked back through my gallery and felt a pleasant glow of achievement.

My followers would never forgive me if I missed one of my children's birthdays, so I posted some fairly anodyne content, with lots of pictures of a young, cute Finn and mixed it up with some shots of the town. It's so important to keep engaging with your followers. My busy little brain is always looking for the next opportunity and, mindful of Harpreet's suggestion about building up a good stock of evergreen content (social media guru-speak for images that aren't time-specific), I photographed the heck out of every medieval church, blue plaque, narrow alley, Georgian mansion and municipal edifice I could find. All the while chatting non-stop to Polly and maintaining a smiling face. Sometimes I don't know how I do it.

The boys met us at the appointed time and place, beaming. I felt that I had done a truly good thing. Polly and Harry headed off and, driving Jake and Finn home, listening to their happy chatter, I pondered the way forward. Maybe it was time for Issy Smugge to look at her life plan and rewrite it a bit. Would the world stop turning if I didn't flood my feed with pictures of all three children, perfectly posed? Probably not. I felt so jolly that I gave in to the boys' pleadings to stop at some kind of drive-through establishment and lavish hot chocolate and sugary treats upon them. I had a sneaky chocolate brownie myself (for the baby). #funmum #lovemyboy

A WhatsApp from Suze. Hooray!

'Hi Bella, great news! We've set a moving date. End of February. House all going through, sorted out Lily's school. How are you all? xx'

I stopped going through some rather lovely black and white shots of a perfect medieval church I'd found in Ipswich and focused on my sister.

'That's the best news I've had all week! Come up and stay as soon as you can. Dying to see you all. Have you heard from Mummy? She's moving, apparently. Wants to go through her stuff and give us some of it. Keep me posted, lots of love xx'

Hard on the heels of this wonderful news, Tom sent out a group message with the glad tidings that Claire is coming home in a fortnight. Chatting with the girls in the playground that afternoon, we agreed that we wanted to welcome her home with a lovely surprise. What it was to be was a more vexed question. Maddie and Lou were all for putting a hamper together, Lauren and Kate wanted to do housework vouchers, so she didn't have to worry about doing anything around the vicarage for a while, whereas I was dreaming big and thinking about doing a makeover on the front room.

In my mind's eye, I could see the transformation. These days, I don't even notice the worn carpet, the badly sprung sofa and the tired paintwork at the vicarage. That said, the dual-aspect, south-facing living room would really benefit from the inspired touch of what *Gorgeous Home* magazine once called 'Britain's Most Relatable Mum Designer'. Claire loves yellow and bright, sunshiny colours. I was seeing broken-plan living (so now), pared back Scandi style, clever storage, warm earth tones and splashes of yellow. With four children in the house and all the clutter that brings, plus the need to use the space for meetings and social occasions, my designer's mind yearned to rip out the whole sorry lot and start all over again.

I let the girls finish twittering about local produce and ironing vouchers and posited my idea. There was a silence. Taking the bull by the horns, I invited everyone back to mine for coffee and a chat. These days, even without Sofija, I don't think twice about opening up the Old Rectory for social occasions. I could see they weren't sure about my brilliant idea, but when Issy Smugge has the bit between her perfectly white and even teeth, there's no stopping her!

Coffee made, we plonked ourselves down on the modular sofas in the family room. I am getting quite good at making flapjacks and had a plate stowed away in the pantry. Offering them around was a stroke of genius. Before anyone could get a word in edgeways, their teeth were glued together with a delicious mixture of cherries, golden syrup and oats. That gave me the chance to start talking, which I did, persuasively and at some length.

As you know, I do regular makeovers on my blog. They are some of my most popular features and I've been on quite a few TV programmes as the resident interiors' expert. My heart beats just a little faster every time we schedule in a room transformation. The work at the Old Rectory has kept me going for well over a year, but now, in the depths of winter, what could be more fun than a gorgeous, sunshiny sitting room refresh?

I wouldn't want you to think that I'm using my friend as a way to get myself more likes and shares. That's not it at all. I remember going to a talk once about something or other (I forget what. Social action, probably), and the woman on the stage telling a story about someone she once interviewed. Faced with a huge, global emergency, this person asked herself, 'What can one person do to change it?' The answer she came up with was, 'Use what is in your hand.' I always liked that.

And what is in Issy Smugge's perfectly manicured hand? Why, talent, drive and an address book simply stuffed with fantastic contacts. We could have the whole room transformed in just over a week, for pence.

The girls had regained the power of speech. The general feeling seemed to be that Tom might not like it. I couldn't imagine why not. If a renowned lifestyle specialist (daughter of the founder of award-winning interior design firm Carobella, let's not forget) offered *me* a completely free makeover, I'd jump at the chance.

'But babes, put yourself in his shoes.' Lauren was leaning forward and looking serious. 'We all know you want to do it because you're kind-hearted and generous. Tom's a vicar, though, and he's used to living like that. People don't expect vicarages to look like they come out of a glossy magazine. The church decorated the whole place before Tom and Claire moved in. They might not like it either.'

Everyone else seemed to feel the same. They didn't seem to understand that feeling so unsure and unsteady in my personal life, I was yearning to make my mark somewhere. I searched through my memory banks for phrases from the chapel at St Dymphna's.

'"It is more blessed to give than to receive."[2] That's out of the Bible, isn't it? And that's what I'm doing. It's not for me, honestly. I just love the idea of Claire's face lighting up when she walks in.' To my horror, I began to cry, helplessly. 'I've missed her so much and I want to do a lovely, kind thing for her. I'm not being selfish or thinking of my reach. I'm really not.'

I dissolved into wracking sobs and dropped my face into my hands. There were supportive murmurs from the girls, and I felt arms go round my shoulders. After a few minutes, my nose running and my eye make-up ruined, I felt like a complete idiot. What had happened to that old, poised Issy Smugge who never gave painful emotions house room? She'd gone, and it didn't look as if she was ever coming back.

Lauren supplied me with a crumpled tissue. I dabbed ineffectually at my eyes and blew my nose in a rather louder and more fluid fashion than I had intended. My voice wobbling, I tried to explain how I was feeling.

'We totally get it, Issy.' Kate was smiling sympathetically. 'We've all seen how hard you've been working to keep

---

[2] Acts 20:35, KJV.

everything going. And none of us think that this is about you benefiting from a makeover. It's a lovely thought. Lauren, you know Tom best. Why don't you chat to him and see what he says?' She patted my arm and proffered the flapjacks. Sighing, I took one. **#babyneedssugar #onemorewonthurt #hungrymummy**

The last weekend of January was looming. I agreed to drive the children to City Airport and meet Johnnie there, then brave the Friday evening traffic through the Blackwall Tunnel towards Kent. I can't say I was looking forward to spending a weekend in Mummy's lair. It's hardly a relaxing experience. I can probably just about manage two nights, but I'll leave straight after breakfast on Sunday and amble back to town in a leisurely fashion. I wonder what Mummy wants to give me. Unconditional love and support would be nice, but it's a bit late for that. **#sadness #stress #motherlove**

February

If Mummy didn't live in it, the Coach House would be a charming and welcoming abode. She was lurking at the door when I turned on to the drive. I pride myself on my city driving, but a year in the country has blunted the edge of the killer instinct one needs when venturing through the Blackwall Tunnel and down the A2.

All I really wanted was a cup of peppermint tea and a sit down. Mummy insisted on showing me what she'd had done to the drawing room before I was allowed to eat my supper and wend my way to bed. Surprisingly, I slept like a log, lulled into my slumbers by the surprisingly soothing hooting of an owl outside. I awoke to the sound of rain lashing against the windows and the wind howling through the lime trees.

Dressed and made up, I presented myself to Mummy, who I found making tea in the kitchen. I accepted two slices of granary bread with butter and grapefruit marmalade (pregnancy has changed my tastebuds – I find I can't get enough sharp and sour flavours) and sat down in the breakfast room with her to consume it. We made desultory conversation about the children, the weather and the political situation, before washing up together. Mummy doesn't believe in dishwashers. I can't imagine why.

We made our way to the drawing room. Mummy's eye for interiors is excellent (one of the few good things she bestowed upon me), but her style is firmly rooted in the past. Would you believe she still has damask wallpaper and fluted lampshades everywhere? I have always eschewed clutter, but Mummy is a big fan of silver-framed photographs, standard lamps and unfashionable prints. No doubt it will all come back into style one day, but Isabella M Smugge certainly won't be having it in her house when it does, thank you very much!

Settled in a wingback chair, I sipped my tea and awaited her remarks on downsizing. She started prattling about photo albums, furniture, heirlooms and silver and my mind wandered, as I gazed out of the drawing room window behind her head, watching the rain drift across the garden in great sheets and the wind batter the trees. Turning my attention back to my parent, I noticed that her hands with their crimson nails had a slight tremor as they rested on the arms of her chair. She still wears her wedding and engagement rings on her left hand and her mother's cabochon cut emerald ring on her right. The light from the table lamp was falling on her face, illuminating the march of time. The lines around her mouth and eyes seemed deeper, more pronounced, her eyes hooded, and the well-defined planes of her face blurred.

My reverie was interrupted by her sharp voice.

'Isabella! Are you listening to me? What do you want me to do with them?'

I had to admit that I had no idea what she was talking about. She tutted loudly.

'The photographs! I've got a cupboard full of albums and I can't take them all with me. They go back to my grandparents' time. Very valuable, some of them. I'm sure there's one of your great-grandfather with the King at Sandringham, at a shoot. Why don't you take them all back with you when you leave, and you and Suzanne can decide who has what?'

I agreed that this was a good idea. Mummy coughed, a deep rattling cough, and dabbed at her lips with an embroidered handkerchief. 'I can't get rid of them. But I won't have the room in the new house.' She glanced at me, then looked out of the window. 'One day you'll be doing this with your children. Clearing out all your treasures and hoping that they won't be hurled into a skip when you die. And it'll be sooner than you think.'

I didn't really know what to say. Spending any amount of time with my mother can tip me into mindless depression, but this was a particularly uncomfortable conversation. Not for the first time, I swore that I would never be like her.

The albums allocated, we moved on to furniture. There were several pieces that I was happy to accommodate at the Old Rectory. Suze would have to make her own decisions when she moved back. Mummy arose.

'I've put aside some things I thought you girls might like. They're in the back bedroom.'

We made our way upstairs, both of us leaning slightly more heavily on the banisters than we once would have done. Age and pregnancy seemed to be slowing us both down. As we ascended the staircase, I began writing the property details in my head.

'Set in an enviable village location with excellent road and rail links, this charming seventeenth-century house offers delightful, mature gardens, several spacious reception rooms, four bedrooms and three bathrooms. The present owner...' Here I broke off as we reached the door of the back bedroom. It was full of boxes, heaped up with books, pictures, ornaments and bric-a-brac.

'I'll leave you to it. I've got some things to clear out in my bedroom.' The present owner marched briskly away across the landing and I was left crouching by a pile of memories, wondering what I would find. **#blastfromthepast #nostalgia**

I'm thirty-nine years old, insanely successful, a mother myself, and yet rummaging through Mummy's boxes catapulted me back to my childhood. A large, silver-framed studio portrait of my mother looking young and happy took me back to our old house in Kent. The picture used to stand on the piano in the lounge, lovingly polished and dusted by our help. It was strange seeing Mummy without those deep lines of disappointment carved into her face, looking pretty and carefree. I analysed the photo, taking in the single ring on her left hand, the string of pearls around her neck, the long eyelashes and the sparkling eyes. It must have been her engagement photo.

Further excavation turned up a companion photo of Daddy, looking handsome and happy. Underneath were baby pictures of Suze and me, all chubby fingers and downy hair. I had to look twice. Elsie really does look exactly like my sister.

By the time I'd finished, I had seven boxes of photos, books, ornaments and sentimental treasures to take back to the Old Rectory. Thank goodness I'd brought the estate car. I found Mummy in the pantry, searching for components for lunch. I was suddenly seized with the urge to get out of the house. It had stopped raining and the familiar scent of Mummy's abode (cigarette smoke, perfume, lavender furniture polish) was bringing back memories I didn't relish.

'Let's go out to lunch,' I suggested. 'The weather's cleared up and we've been working hard all morning. We deserve a treat.'

We put on our shoes and coats and sallied forth into the village. It's your standard Kent commuter belt community, full of chichi boutiques, converted oast houses, tea rooms and half-timbered houses. I allowed Mummy to steer me towards an establishment with steamed-up windows which was already half-full of genteel diners, many of whom seemed to know her.

I wedged myself behind a wobbly table on what appeared to be a former pew, painted a rather nice shade of on-trend sage green. Mummy was so busy waving at acquaintances that she ignored the menu completely. Aware that I had been massively overdoing the carbs of late, I decided on a fresh ginger infusion and a bowl of celeriac, bacon and barley soup followed by a warm chicory and halloumi salad.

Mummy ignored the menu and clicked her fingers at the harassed-looking waiter who was busy making up bills, serving lunches and answering the phone. There seemed to be a chronic staff shortage if the wild, staring eyes of the poor lad were anything to go by. Caught in the tractor beam of Mummy's glare, he scuttled over and stood hopefully by our table, pen and pad poised.

'My usual. And a large glass of dry white. And don't forget to warm the focaccia. I warned you last time.'

I cringed inwardly. Nanny brought us up to have perfect manners, emphasising that little ladies never forgot their pleases and thank yous and should always be absolutely charming to those who waited upon them. I had long suspected that she was acting on her own initiative, and so it seemed.

We made perfunctory conversation while I sipped my infusion (so cleansing) and she made inroads into the wine. It was barely twelve o'clock, far too early to be drinking, in my humble opinion.

The terrified-looking waiter appeared at our table and laid Mummy's lunch reverently before her. She hovered her hand over it, sniffed it and gave him a curt nod. Honestly. While I ate my soup, she held court, talking loudly about local matters and her plans for the new cottage between bites of her Parma ham, buffalo mozzarella and beefsteak tomato. Every so often, another well-preserved lady would bellow, 'Caroline!' across the café and we would have to stop eating while I was introduced. By the end of lunch, I felt about five years old.

'This is my eldest. Moved out to Suffolk. Three children and, of course, we now have a fourth on the way. She writes for a living. All over social media. I don't pretend to understand it, but she seems to do rather well. No, Suzanne is still in Hong Kong. Oh yes, *her* husband is delightful. They're moving back at the end of the month.'

I wondered if anyone would notice if I went to the loo and clambered out of the window.

After what seemed like half a lifetime, Mummy gesticulated to the unfortunate waiter and called for the bill. While she was in the loo refreshing her lipstick, I quietly paid it, leaving a huge tip. The poor boy had earned it. **#cringe #soembarrassing**

When we returned to the Coach House, all I wanted to do was go to bed and sleep until it was time to leave. Sadly, the large glass of white and the brisk walk through the damp streets seemed to have livened Mummy up no end. We repaired to the drawing room where, it seemed, she wished to address me again.

'Now, don't interrupt me. I have often wondered if I should have given you this before, but there's no point repining. Don't read it here. I want you to wait until you get home.'

She opened the drawer of her Georgian escritoire and drew out a white envelope. My name was written on it in spidery black letters. I was completely at a loss.

'There's one for your sister too. When I dismissed Nanny, she made the most frightful fuss. She was convinced that her absence would traumatise you and Suzanne. I assured her that I was perfectly capable of looking after my own children and refused to listen to any more nonsense. She insisted on writing to you both and I promised that I would deliver her letters to you when I felt the time was right. Perhaps I should have given them to you before, but to be honest, when your father left, I forgot all about them and they got lost in the move.'

She lit a cigarette and looked down at her hands. I tried not to cough and prayed that the toxin-laden smoke would drift in the opposite direction.

'I am aware that we haven't had the easiest of relationships, Isabella. I did what I thought was best for you. Your father wanted you to go to school with Arabella's girls, but I knew you would benefit from getting away from home and learning to stand on your own two feet. Your sister was a different matter, but we agreed it would be unkind to separate you. When she joined you at St Dymphna's, I made a concerted effort to improve my marriage. Your father and I had drifted apart, and of course I know now that Arabella was carrying on with him behind my back. However, when I found I was pregnant, I truly believed that we might be able to make it work.'

'Pregnant?' I spat out my tea and mopped at my skirt with the doily from Mummy's nest of tables. 'Why haven't you ever mentioned this?'

'Your father and I had a brief rapprochement on a weekend in the Peak District. You and your sister were back at school when I found that I was expecting. Your father was delighted. I now know he broke it off with Arabella and things got better between us. I went for a scan and we found out we were having a little boy. We were so happy.'

She broke off and stubbed out her cigarette in the heavy glass ashtray at her elbow.

'I started getting the night nursery ready. I was so excited that I just couldn't wait. Your father said we should wait until I was further along, but I ignored him. I went out shopping to get curtain fabric and paint. I spent ages choosing the most adorable sky-blue material with little white ducks on it. I've still got it hidden away upstairs.'

To my amazement, a tear rolled down her cheek, then another, then another. I have never seen my mother cry. I didn't know she could.

'I got home and showed your father. He told me off for going out and exerting myself, but he was just concerned for my health. We had a lovely evening, sitting together on the sofa as we used to when we first got married. We went to bed and I woke up in the middle of the night with the most terrible pains. I knew it was all over. We drove to the hospital, but there was nothing they could do. I think I went a little bit out of my mind. I couldn't stop crying and blaming myself. I didn't leave the house for weeks. Your father didn't know what to do to help me and we drifted apart again, but this time we couldn't find a way back.'

I sat in silence. I genuinely did not know what to say. Mummy's shoulders were heaving, and sobs that seemed to be dragged painfully from the very depths of her being were taking her over. I repeated my usual mantra when difficult situations arose. 'What would Claire do?' She would probably comfort the person and listen to whatever they had to say. Reluctantly, I heaved my pregnant self out of the chair and patted Mummy awkwardly on the shoulder. It seemed to make no difference. The words and the sobs kept coming.

'I suppose nowadays people would say I was depressed. Stuff and nonsense, of course.' Here she broke off and blew her nose. 'Whatever you want to call it, I was heartbroken. I couldn't seem to get over it.'

She dropped her head into her hands and continued crying, tears falling onto the skirt of her wrap dress. My mother never showed emotion, not like this, anyway. I knelt awkwardly by her chair and put my arm around her shoulder. We sat like that for so long that my arm started to go dead, and I got pins and needles in my feet. After I don't know how long, she let out a long, shuddering sigh and blew her nose loudly. Kneeling uncomfortably on the floor, I let out an involuntary yelp as the baby gave me a sharp kick under the ribs.

'Can I get you a glass of water, Mummy?' I enquired, not sure what to do.

'You can get me a large gin and tonic, Isabella.' Mummy had taken out her powder compact and was examining her face in the mirror. 'Easy on the tonic.'

I trotted obediently into the pantry and made Mummy a weakish G&T.

'I'm sorry you had to see me in that ridiculous state.' Mummy was frowning and knocking back her drink at top speed. 'Naturally, one doesn't talk about such things, and I had no intention of allowing my emotions to take me over like that.'

'But Mummy, this is really important. I can't believe you've kept it to yourself all these years. I'm so sad for you. I've never lost a baby, but I imagine it must be terrible.'

She nodded. 'It is. Yes.' She continued to drink her gin and gaze out of the window. I felt that we had reached an important point in our relationship but wasn't sure how to continue. Mummy and I don't have cosy chats, but her revelation of heartbreak and loss had touched me. To think that Suze and I could have had a little brother and that she and Daddy might have patched things up. How different my life would have been.

I let my mind drift back to the terrible homecoming when we found that Nanny had gone and our ponies had been sold. Now that I knew that my mother was suffering from depression and grief, it made more sense. The memory still stung, but perhaps I could start to work through my own feelings and build a better relationship with her.

My musings were interrupted by Mummy rising from her chair and announcing that supper wouldn't make itself. #revelations #sadface

Sometimes I think that my life would make a jolly good TV series. I envisage a six-part drama, on BBC One, naturally, perhaps in the teatime slot on a Sunday. I'm not quite sure who would play me. Someone gorgeous like Vanessa Kirby would do it. Joanna Lumley would make a good Mummy. I can see the scene in her drawing room morphing into one of those soft-focus flashbacks and her honesty leading to a better mother–daughter relationship.

Mummy clearly doesn't watch the right kind of television. At supper, she was her old, brittle, critical self. I tried to start up an open conversation a couple of times but was shut down.

After we'd finished eating and washed up, we sat in her lounge, watching television in silence. By ten I was in bed. So much for breaking down barriers.

I woke up to the sound of china clinking on a tray and the delightful fragrance of hot, buttered toast. I opened my eyes to find Mummy pouring me a cup of tea. Sleepily, I struggled upright in bed.

'What's all this in aid of?'

'Can't a mother bring her daughter breakfast in bed?' Mummy handed me a plate of buttered toast with a little pile of marmalade on the side. 'I remember being very tired when I was expecting you girls. No one ever thought to bring *me* toast and tea and give me a lie-in.'

I was rather taken aback. 'Thank you, Mummy. What a treat. Are you joining me?'

It seemed she was. We sat munching our toast and sipping our tea. It was rather nice. Mummy was the first to break the silence.

'How are things going with your husband? Christmas was rather strained.'

I couldn't disagree. I told her that the flat had sold, and that Johnnie was buying a three-bedroomed apartment nearby so that the children could stay over at the weekends. 'We've got Davina and Toby's christening in half term. Obviously, he's coming. I'm hoping that having his family around him might help me to persuade him to come home.'

Mummy threw me a sideways glance. 'You really do still want him back after what he did to you, don't you, Isabella? You're far more forgiving than I ever was, I must say.'

'Of course I want him back! He's my husband and the father of my children. I married for life. I can't imagine being divorced and having to start all over again, like…'

I broke off, aware that I had said too much. Mummy finished my sentence for me.

'Like me? I'm a widow, not a divorcee. There's a big difference.'

She stood up and took my cup and plate. 'I'll see you downstairs.'

Driving home through the rain, having picked the children up, I was dying to open the envelope, but something told me to wait until I was back home. The girls fell asleep in the car and I drove up the A12 in silence, the rain lashing against the windscreen. Glancing in the mirror, I could see Finn gazing out of the window, apparently lost in thought. I didn't have the energy to start a conversation, and by the time we reached Chelmsford, he was fast asleep. **#longdrive #sadthoughts #mysteryletter**

February is a very depressing month. The only bright spot is Valentine's Day and this year I hadn't even got that. Standing on the freezing cold playground the next morning, I still felt distracted and sad. My reverie was interrupted by Lauren.

'Have you heard the news? Claire's home!'

I cheered up immediately. I hoped that she would be enjoying the celebratory hamper put together by all of us. Tom had thanked me for my lovely idea, but explained that a makeover might offend the church, who had paid to decorate the vicarage, and his parents, who offered to overhaul the entire place every time they came to visit. I put Mummy out of my head and listened to Lauren, Maddie and Lou as we walked out of the playground.

'Shall we go over for coffee? I'll text her. Tom said his parents arrived on Friday. He didn't look too happy about it.'

There was nothing I wanted to do more than run straight to the vicarage and see my friend, but I had my weekly Zoom with Mimi booked. 'I'll message her and see how she's fixed for tomorrow.'

We said our goodbyes and I trudged back up the lane to my cosy house for a full day of work.

The letter is lying on my bedside table, waiting for me, like a snake curled up in the grass. I'll read it tonight before I go to bed.

I can hardly write for crying. I can't believe that Mummy kept such an important document to herself for all these years. I spent so long wondering where Nanny was and why she never wrote to me, and now I know why. My feelings of sympathy for Mummy have been washed away in a torrent of tears.

One of the most painful memories of my childhood is losing Nanny. She was such a warm, loving, stable influence on Suze and me, and when we returned from school to find her gone, without even a note, it broke my heart. I blamed myself. Perhaps I hadn't written home enough. Perhaps I'd been naughty. Whatever it was, it had sent my Nanny away to work for another family and sing her lullabies to other children. I cried myself to sleep for months once she'd gone. Asking Mummy about it only made it worse.

'Stop asking impertinent questions, Isabella! You're far too old for a nanny. You need to learn to stand on your own two feet.'

I read my letter again and again until I could remember every word.

My dear Isabella.

I'm writing this as when you get home from school I will have gone. Your mother has decided that it is time for me to leave, as we always knew I would one day. I haven't been able to say goodbye to you in person, so this letter is doing it for me.

I want you to remember your manners, keep up with your drawing and be a good girl for your mother. I know you will look after your little sister. I will miss you both very much indeed.

I am going to work for a family in Scotland. They live in a castle, a real one with turrets and a moat. I will think of you often and will blow you a kiss every night before I go to bed.

Your own loving Nanny xx

Nanny had seemed ancient to us as little girls, but thinking back, she was probably only in her forties. I had often dreamed of finding her and having a loving reunion, but then I would tell myself not to be so silly and to crush that dream underfoot.

As soon as I could bear to speak to her, I planned to ask Mummy where she'd gone. I couldn't wait for Suze to read her letter, so I WhatsApped and told her the news. She was just as horrified as me. #secrets #cruelmother

Isabella M Smugge is nothing if not resilient. In spite of the emotional storm which had reduced me to a sobbing mess on Monday night, by Tuesday morning I was up with the lark, fully moisturised and enveloped in a rather lovely pair of Scrummy Mummy tailored black trousers and a boat-neck stripey jumper. I accessorised with a pair of silver and crystal power hoop earrings and slicked on some pale pink lip gloss. I might be pregnant, I might be sad, but as I say in my bestselling go-to manual, *Issy Smugge Says: Let's Dress for Success*:

> Wear your clothes, don't let them wear you. A few well-cut pieces and the right accessories will take you anywhere and make sure you turn a few heads along the way.

The minute the children were in school, Lauren and I headed for the vicarage. I was hoping that Tom's parents wouldn't be there, but those hopes were dashed when the front door was opened by a woman who clearly bought all her clothes from a catalogue.

'Hello! You must be Claire's friends. Do come in. Thomas is on the telephone and Claire is having a little rest upstairs. I'm Patricia, Thomas' mother. We've come to stay and give them a bit of help. Not here, obviously, they're packed together like sardines as it is. We're camping out at the hotel in the next village.'

Her voice was loud and her eye penetrating. She made Mummy sound like Eliza Doolittle, pre-makeover.

'Can I offer you coffee? We brought it from home. Properly roasted, not like that awful cheap stuff Claire will insist on buying. Now, who are you? Thomas has told me about Claire's school friends, but I do get rather confused with all the names.'

Lauren was the first to speak. 'We've met before, Mrs Fitzwilliam. I'm Lauren. I go to Claire's ladies group.'

'Oh. Yes. So you do. Milk? Sugar?'

I declined the coffee and asked for a tea. We plumped ourselves down on the sagging sofa and I prepared for the interrogation.

'Now, I haven't seen you before, my dear. Are you new to the village?'

I explained who I was. Tom's mother pursed her lips and fixed me with a beady gaze.

'Smugge. Smugge – where have I heard that name before?'

It was unlikely that Mrs Fitzwilliam followed me on Instagram.

'I expect you're thinking of my late father-in-law, Bishop Smugge.'

Her cold, grey eyes lit up. 'Of course! Good heavens, he was your father-in-law? Well, well. My husband and I thought he did such good work. And what is it that you do?'

I explained that I wrote for a living. Mrs Fitzwilliam did not seem very interested. The questions continued.

'And who are your people? Where did you go to school?'

I felt a nudge in the ribs from Lauren and tried desperately hard not to laugh. I'd come to see my friend and here I was trapped in her sitting room being interrogated by a twenty-first-century Lady Catherine de Bourgh.

I admitted that I was a Neville ('One of the Kent Nevilles?') and that I had been educated at St Dymphna's.

'Are you Caroline Neville's girl? We had our house done up by Carobella back in the mid-eighties. That was when we were living in Brockenhurst.'

Mrs Fitzwilliam seemed to have an encyclopaedic knowledge of posh English families and their scions.

'I was so sorry when I read that your mother had sold the business. She was the only woman I ever met who truly understood pelmets. Henry! Come here. This friend of Thomas' is Caroline Neville's daughter.'

Tom's father, who appeared to have been thoroughly coated in quick-drying varnish, came trotting through in response to his wife's command. We went through introductions again and the two of them started quizzing me about my father's background. Very rude, I thought, particularly as they were showing absolutely no interest in Lauren and her family tree.

Once we had galloped briskly through Daddy's genealogy and discovered that Henry had worked with him briefly and that Patricia had gone to school with Mummy's cousin, I felt it was time to assert myself.

'Such a pleasure chatting to you, but we would love to go and see Claire now. Do you mind?'

Apparently they did. 'Such a lovely girl. Not *quite* who we had in mind for Thomas, but they seem very happy, considering. We've had clergymen in the family before, of course, but they pursued proper careers. Thomas seems quite content to fritter away his talents in a little rural backwater like this. We told him, didn't we Henry, we told him, you could be archdeacon if you work at it, but he doesn't seem interested. And now all these children! Four! I ask you.'

She lowered her voice and leaned forward. 'I don't say it in front of Thomas, but we are glad that the children aren't too dark. He got so cross with me when Hannah was born, and I mentioned it. Those lovely dark eyes and curly hair, but no sign of her mother's – well, lineage. If you know what I mean. And the baby with that beautiful olive skin. More Mediterranean than anything else. Although as Henry said to me the other day, they've got one in the Royal Family, so it's obviously acceptable now.'

The room seemed suddenly stuffy and too small to contain us all. Mrs Fitzwilliam was leaning forward, boring into me with those fishy eyes while her husband towered over us, hands clasped behind his tweed-clad back. These days, leaping to my feet is a challenge, but I did my best, with Lauren's help.

'You'll excuse us if we go and see Claire now.' I used my chilliest tone, the one guaranteed to strip the shine off a mixed reactive glaze dinner plate at 100 paces. 'She must be wondering where on earth we've got to.'

I spun on my heel and marched upstairs with Lauren behind me. On the landing we turned to face each other.

'What was *that*? How *dare* she?' I was spluttering with rage. 'I knew they weren't very nice, but I didn't realise they were racists into the bargain.'

Lauren opened her mouth to reply, but as she did so, we heard Claire's voice calling to us.

'Are you two coming in or spending the rest of the day on my landing?'

In we went, to find our friend lying on her bed with baby Ben asleep in his Moses basket next to her. She took one look at my face and burst out laughing.

'What on earth have you been doing down there, Isabella? You're as red as a beetroot.'

'She met your in-laws,' Lauren was quick to explain. 'They were on top form. No interest in my family tree, but it was twenty questions with this one.' She put on an imitation of Patricia Fitzwilliam's voice. 'Which school did you go to? Ohhhh! Yah! My mama was there, head girl, of course.'

Claire grinned. 'Did they offer you their special coffee? And discover that they were at school with your parents? They're a bit obsessed with family and stock and breeding. I don't really make the grade. Mixed race, fostered *and* a former addict. It couldn't be worse, really.'

It was bliss to be chatting with our friend again, none of us able to talk fast enough and cover enough ground. Claire looked so much better, her face filled out and that old sparkle in her eye. It seems that she takes refuge upstairs for a nap every day, to escape from her in-laws.

After an hour of non-stop chatting, we descended to the ground floor where the Fitzwilliams were lurking in the hall.

'Must you be off?' She pronounced it 'orf'. 'So lovely to meet you! Do remember us to your mother.'

I mumbled pleasantries and fled. Lauren and I vented our feelings about Tom's parents all the way back home, and I'm not ashamed to tell you we used quite a few naughty words. Honestly!

As February wore on, my stomach became ever larger and my heartburn ever worse. The only thing that assuaged it was milk, and that led to issues down below. I tried adding organic pitted prunes to my porridge every morning, which solved the problem but gave me another, rather antisocial, one. If men had babies, everyone would be an only child.

Midweek, snow was forecast on the evening news. The children were wildly excited. We never saw snow in London, and thanks to Johnnie and Sofija's perfidy, we haven't had a skiing holiday since last Easter.

Snow is the successful influencer's best friend. It transforms even the most humdrum of landscapes into a gleaming winter wonderland, and if you put frolicking children into the frame, you're guaranteed any number of likes and shares. On Friday evening, yells of excitement from the girls alerted me to the fact that snowflakes were falling thickly from the sky. It was a Mummy weekend, thank heavens, an absolute gift for me.

I was awoken early the next morning by the sound of heavy breathing in my ear. For a minute, I thought Johnnie was back, but rubbing the sleep from my eyes, I realised it was my daughter.

'Mummy, there's loads of snow out there. Can we go out and build a snowman, please, please, please?'

I gazed blearily at my phone.

'Chloë Smugge, it's half past seven in the morning! Go and make yourself some breakfast. I'll be down shortly.'

Opportunities like this don't come along every day, I can tell you. Looking out of my bedroom window, I saw that the garden was wrapped in a sparkling mantle of snow. I dressed hurriedly, for practicality rather than fashion, and walked briskly downstairs. There was no sign of Finn, but my daughters were eating granola and already dressed for outside. I shook my head.

'Come on, girls, you know the drill. I've laid out your special snow clothes in the family room. Hats and scarves on, please; don't forget the gloves. I'll be as quick as I can and then you can change back.'

I checked them both for stray breakfast fragments and brushed their hair. With the correct, Insta-friendly outfits on, they looked as though they had just stepped out of a high-end childrenswear catalogue. We marched out into the snow and I started taking shots. Thank heavens they know what they're doing and don't look the wrong way or mess around. They did a lot when they were younger, but Sofija always knew just what to say to help me get the right images.

By the time they had built a snowman and had a couple of snowball fights (difficult to capture – I had to keep asking them to stop and start again), they were starting to shiver and look rather fed up. 'Can we have hot chocolate now, Mummy? We're cold.'

I bargained with them, as we must often do when dealing with children. 'Mummy needs a few snow angel shots and a bit more standing by that big tree looking into the distance, then you can have whipped cream *and* mini marshmallows in your chocolate.' That did the trick, and by nine o'clock I had a whole library of gorgeous, wholesome family snow shots. I was as good as my word, whipping up two calorie-laden hot chocolates and letting them relax in front of the television. I still had plenty of work to do. It was eleven by the time I finished, having captured a whole heap of amazing images.

As I came in through the boot room, shivering and stamping my feet, I was met by all three children, rosy-cheeked and excitable. 'We're going out to play for real now, Mummy. Can you help us build a proper snowman, please? And can we ask Hannah and Becky if they want to come and play in our garden? Please, Mummy, please?'

I was exhausted and cold, and all I wanted to do was sit down with a cup of tea and relax. However, they had held up their part of the bargain and it was only fair that I reciprocated. It was an aching and exhausted Isabella M Smugge who texted her friends and asked if they would like to deposit their children in my garden, and a tired and dyspeptic mumfluencer who whipped up a large batch of roasted sweet potato with rosemary and pecorino when it was time for lunch.

When I first moved up here, I would have thought nothing of feeding ten children. But then I wouldn't have been doing the cooking. Lauren's three didn't seem terribly keen on sweet potato, and Finn and Jake turned their noses up at my warm winter salad. Sighing, I fished some emergency pizzas out of the chest freezer in the utility room and bought myself some supermum points.

My altruism was rewarded by Lauren offering to take the girls back to her place for the rest of the day and Polly texting to ask if Jake and Finn would like to go and play at hers. Result! I left all the dirty dishes, abandoned the wet clothes by the washing machine, lay down on the sofa with a hot chocolate and binge-watched a boxset. You'll appreciate the depth of my exhaustion when I tell you that I didn't even post a snow image until the evening. **#everyonewishestheywereme #workitlikeme #followme**

Before I knew where I was, half term was upon us. The big news was the trip down to Buckinghamshire for Baby Matthew's christening. Davina and Toby seemed terribly keen to see as much of us as possible and had invited us for the entire week. Johnnie, they told me, was joining us on the Friday and, of course, Silvia would be there all week too. Xenia and Rafe were coming on Saturday morning, just for the christening and after-party. Their house was going to be awash with Smugges.

I can't pretend that I wasn't nervous about seeing Johnnie. Surrounded by his family, all of whom appeared to be resolutely pro-me, I worried that he would feel threatened. I hoped that spending time with me and the children might soften his heart and make him realise what he was missing. As godparents, we would be standing toe to toe at the font, and with his own incipient child very much in evidence under the well-cut folds of my gorgeous linen-blend trench coat, how much longer could it be before he begged for forgiveness and came home?

My snow pictures had made Mimi a very happy agent. 'Beautiful, darling, beautiful! No one does unstudied naturalness like you. How long do you think you'll need off when this new one comes along? A couple of days? We can fill in with guest bloggers and evergreen content while you're *hors de combat*.' She laughed, a deep gravelly laugh.

I snorted. 'I can tell you've never had children, Mimi. At least a week. I'll drop some spontaneous baby shots, but I don't know how all this natural birth business is going to go. They tell me it hurts.'

I worked extra hard all week to get everything scheduled, and by Sunday lunchtime we were packed up and ready to go. I had laid in a stock of healthy travel snacks, books and puzzles. The old Issy Smugge didn't approve of children being on devices for more than one hour a day. So bad for their developing minds. By the time we reached Colchester, however, the fighting and whining from the back had drilled so deeply into my aching head that I caved in and dug their tablets out of my suitcase just to keep them quiet.

All was calm until we hit the M25, when it all broke out again. I offered travel snacks, which kept them happy for about five miles. Attempts to play fun car games were rebuffed with cries of, 'That's boring! When are we going to be there? I want the toilet. I'm hungry. I'm thirsty.'

I managed to last until South Mimms where I confess that I parked up and allowed them to feast on a most unhealthy meal composed of hamburgers, chips and a drink allegedly containing fruit. Blissfully replete, my children sank back in their luridly coloured plastic chairs. Chloë let out a small burp.

'That was so lovely, Mummy. Why don't we have takeaways more often? Maisie's mum lets her have one every Friday if she's been good.'

My standards are slipping at an alarming rate. Still, my children seem happy and that's what it's all about, they tell me. We strapped ourselves back in and I drove towards the affluent green expanse of the Chilterns, more than ready to enjoy the delights of my brother and sister-in-law's hospitality. **#ineedarest #tiredandemotional #lovethosechilterns**

March

It's a funny thing, but I'd never looked upon Davina and Toby's house as a home. On the few occasions we'd stayed, it felt that it was more of a convenient place to lay their heads before they got back to mucking out horses (her) and doing insurance (him). There was no real personality there, I always felt. Arriving on Sunday evening, however, I noticed a difference straight away. Our host and hostess were standing eagerly awaiting us as we swept up the badly kept gravelled drive, and someone had tied a bunch of blue and silver helium balloons to the stone pillars holding the porch up.

I'm not the biggest fan of Victorian architecture. For me, it's got to be Georgian or Edwardian – far cleaner lines. The Beeches (for such is the name of Toby and Davina's abode) is everything that is worst about late nineteenth-century design, in my opinion. Red brick, unnecessary porch, and lower ceilings than one would like.

We were ushered into the hall (ill-advised paint, chipped original quarry tiles) and embraced warmly by Davina. 'Oh, it is so lovely to see you! We've been looking forward to it so much. I can't believe how much you three have grown! I can't wait to introduce you to Baby Matthew. I know you're going to love him. Isabella! How are you? My goodness, you are looking well. I expect you'd like a nice cup of tea and a sit down.'

She said all this almost without taking a breath. Toby was his usual reserved self, kissing me on both cheeks, taking my suitcase and encouraging me to come and take a seat in front of the fire in the lounge.

Last time I was at The Beeches, this room was rather bleak, cluttered up with horse brasses, photos of Davina's hunters and what appeared to be an elderly horse blanket draped over the back of the sofa. Now, with a roaring fire in the grate and pictures of Baby Matthew everywhere, a more human influence appeared to be in play. My keen eye noted a baby bouncer, a play gym, several teddy bears and various other pieces of infantile paraphernalia littering the space. The young man himself was lying on his back on the said gym, gurgling incoherently and batting at a dangling winged creature of some kind, suspended above his fluffy little head.

His mother scooped him up and presented him to the assembled Smugges like a prize marrow at an agricultural show. I found myself holding my nephew in my arms, breathing in that indefinable baby smell and being clutched by a fat little fist. Baby Matthew was almost completely spherical, with round rosy cheeks, bright blue eyes, blond fluff on his head and a distinct problem with intestinal gas. The noises coming from his well-padded rear end reduced the children to helpless giggles.

Davina beamed fondly. 'He likes you! I knew he would. He only does that when he's feeling really relaxed. Now, can I leave you with him while I go and make the tea? Toby, darling, can you take everyone's cases up to their rooms?'

She bustled off, leaving the newest member of the family to get to know his aunt and cousins. He seemed to be excessively relaxed as the popping and rumbling from his posterior built up to a full-on production. The children were intrigued. It had been a while since we'd had a baby in the house and their inner workings, loud and smelly, seemed to fascinate them.

We lay him back down on his play gym and watched him as he chuckled and burbled to himself. Elsie was delighted when he grabbed her finger and held on to it hard, and Chloë gently stroked his fluffy little head. Finn, I could see, was not quite sure what to do, but the frightful aroma wafting from the legs of his cousin's dungarees was certainly a talking point.

Davina burst back into the room with a large tea tray in her hands. 'I've got scones and butter and jam. No need to worry about spoiling your appetites. We're just doing potluck tonight.'

She plonked the tray down unceremoniously on an underpolished walnut table and joined us by the son and heir.

'Isn't he beautiful? Look at his tiny hands!' She gazed adoringly at the little pudding, who was dribbling copiously and blowing bubbles. 'Have you done something in your pants? Have you? Have you done something for Mummy?' She leaned over and kissed his tummy, unleashing fat chuckles and yet more malodorous wafting. I vaguely remembered not minding the smell of the contents of my own babies' nappies, but not being a fan of other people's.

To my relief, Baby Matthew was carried away to be cleansed and Toby took over hosting duties. Duly supplied with a cup of tea and a scone, I settled back on the sofa and engaged in small talk. I'm not really into babies but managed to keep the conversation going with compliments about Baby Matthew's good looks and charm. I'd never seen my brother-in-law so animated. Davina, it seemed, was taking to motherhood like a Muscovy duck to water and was spending more time in the nursery than in the stables. Toby had gone down to three days a week in the office and was working from home to help her out. Not that it seemed she needed much assistance. #earthmother

The rest of the evening was strangely enjoyable. Davina and Toby don't have the first idea about interior design, proper window dressing or style trends, but their house is oddly comfortable just the same. We enjoyed an informal tea of ham, cheese, crusty bread and butter, various salads and a huge treacle tart with clotted cream to finish. The children ate like horses (appropriately enough) and seemed quite relaxed when, halfway through our repast, Davina adjusted her clothing and began feeding her son. Trying to ignore the loud slurping, I asked when the rest of the family was arriving.

'Ma's going to be here around teatime tomorrow. Johnnie will be joining us late on Friday.'

I saw Toby's eyes flicker sideways to Davina just for a second when my husband's name was mentioned. I have decided to be calm and adult about the whole thing. Why shouldn't I spend a family weekend with my husband and extended family? No one will see Isabella M Smugge losing her rag or being anything except well bred and polite.

'Then Rafe and Xenia will be here on Saturday afternoon. We're putting them in the annexe with Johnnie. You've got the big spare room with the en suite, Isabella, and the children are next door. We're at the other end of the house, so hopefully we won't disturb you in the night. Although Matthew is down to one feed a night, aren't you, you clever little man?'

Since Baby Matthew was engaged in taking his evening meal, he did not reply, but from the way his parents carried on, you'd think he had won a scholarship to one of the major universities.

Tea finished and cleared away (I volunteered the children to load the dishwasher and clean up, in spite of our hostess' protestations), we repaired to the big comfy TV room. Toby disappeared to put Baby Matthew to bed and I sank back into the badly upholstered sofa with a sigh.

'What do you all fancy doing tomorrow?' Davina was beaming at the children. 'We've got some lovely parks, there's the pool where we take Baby Matthew for his swimming lessons, or we could go for a walk. I don't want you three to be bored.'

I assured my sister-in-law that the children would fall in with whatever plans we decided to make, but she seemed keen to consult them rather than me. The girls were yawning and looking heavy-eyed, so I left Davina and Finn chatting and put them to bed. I wandered into my room (unfashionable paint colour, bed not properly dressed) and unpacked. It was only just gone 8.30, but I felt absolutely exhausted. I decided to have a little lie down on the bed, and the next thing I knew, it was pitch black and my neck was uncomfortably cricked. Sighing, I consulted my phone and found it was two in the morning. I undressed, climbed into bed and was out like a light. **#sotired #issysmuggesaysgetyoureighthours**

I'm fed up with being pregnant. I haven't seen my feet for months and my fingers and ankles are swollen. I've been driving myself hard at home to get through all the work and personal appearances, but here in Stoke Poges, the very air seems to suck all the life out of me. I don't mean that in a rude way. I believe that normal people quite often take naps and go to bed early with a good book, but Issy Smugge doesn't have time to waste.

Life at The Beeches appears to revolve almost entirely around Baby Matthew. Such is Davina's maternal devotion that she has given over care of her horses to a trusted chum. I never thought I'd see the day. After breakfast, we were washing up together in the kitchen while the children played with the baby. Crows and chuckles indicated that he was very much enjoying getting to know his cousins. He seems particularly fascinated by Finn, following him around the room with his eyes and grizzling when he is out of sight.

I dried a plate and stretched out my aching back, massaging the tired muscles. 'I'm sure I wasn't this worn out with the other three. Honestly, I feel about 150 most days.'

Davina glanced admiringly at me. 'I think you look amazing. I don't know how you do it. I've completely given up on my appearance since Matthew came along. I made an effort because you were coming, but normally I look like a terrible old fright!'

She laughed comfortably and rinsed a juice glass. She wasn't wrong. Even pre-Matthew, Davina didn't follow a proper skincare regime, and I'm as sure as I can be that she's never had her colours done. A thought popped into my head.

'What are you wearing for the christening, Davina?'

'Oh, my navy suit will do, and that hat I wore for Rafe and Xenia's wedding. It won't be a dressy affair.'

My suspicions were confirmed. Over a cup of tea in the lounge, I persuaded her to come out shopping with me. After putting up the expected resistance, Davina caved, agreeing that a girly day would be rather fun. I wanted to get her into the hairdresser to have her hair properly done (she had once told me that she cuts her own fringe – I ask you), and I wondered if I might even be able to persuade her to have a proper manicure. #girlyshop #goodhair #stylemeup

I was surprised by how much I enjoyed my week, especially once Silvia arrived. Naturally, I was taking advantage of my new surroundings to build up a bank of good content. Who doesn't love images of happy, laughing children? Our walks through woodland, our visit to the soft play park for Baby Matthew's benefit, our fun swim with the wave machine and giant inflatables and our sojourn to the local play park; all were grist to my blogging mill.

On Thursday, Davina and I headed off to town with Baby Matthew securely strapped into his car seat. He still relies entirely on his mother for nutrition. Like many first-time mothers I've come across, Davina is reluctant to move on to solid food. Personally, I couldn't wait until my children were more self-reliant, but my sister-in-law seems to be clinging to the most draining and irksome stage of motherhood. I suppose it's because it took her so long to conceive. I don't know.

At the hairdressers, I approached the senior stylist, Michele, with a full brief. I'd already spent twenty minutes on the phone with her explaining that a proper makeover was required. Davina's hair resembles a shaggy mane and has never had a proper cut or colour in its life. The stylist's eyes widened as she took in the enormity of the situation, but soon Davina was installed in a chair with a latte and a stack of magazines, and the transformation began. My hair was in tip-top condition, naturally, so I took my nephew out for a recce round the shops.

Davina had issued with me a list of instructions as long as my arm, which seemed to boil down to nutrition, cleanliness and entertainment. I pride myself on being a good aunt. Every time Baby Matthew hurled Mr Monkey out of his pushchair, I picked him up again. Every twenty minutes or so, we had a pit stop so that he could chew on a rusk. Fortunately, nothing too catastrophic seemed to be going on in his nether regions, leaving me to check out what the clothing emporiums of Stoke Poges had to offer.

At the appointed hour, Baby Matthew slumbering peacefully in his pushchair, I returned to the hairdressers to find that there had been a transformation. Gone was my sister-in-law's mousy brown mane and in its place a glossy long bob, chestnut highlights and a choppy fringe. Davina looked ten years younger. I was very nearly speechless.

Having given Michele a large tip and the promise of a five-star review the minute I got home, I whisked my sister-in-law off to the shops. Davina is one of the most modest people I know and seemed unable to accept the compliments I loaded upon her.

'It is lovely, Isabella, but I don't know how I'll keep it up. Michele gave me this special shampoo and conditioner. I normally use the cheapest stuff I can find, two for one.'

That explained her dull, out of condition locks. Tutting to myself, I whisked her off to find the right outfit for her son's christening. **#makeoverqueen #prettywoman**

Davina's hair and nails properly done and a delightful outfit hanging up in her wardrobe, I felt that I had done my duty as a good sister-in-law. Sitting in the lounge in front of the fire, I sipped on a mango and strawberry herbal tea (so invigorating). Davina seemed to be preparing herself to say something. The children were upstairs, and Toby and Silvia were attending to Baby Matthew's bedtime routine.

'Thank you so much for taking all that time to buy me the outfit and get my hair done, Isabella. You're so jolly kind when you're such a busy person yourself.'

I waved away her gratitude. Really, it was the very least I could do.

'Toby always says to spend as much as I like on what I need, but I've never really needed anything. Now I've got my little Matthew, I couldn't wish for any more.' Here she looked down at her lap and blushed. 'I am glad we bought that outfit because it'll save us having to get another one for the next christening.'

Poor Davina has no idea about seasonal style. I began to explain that an ensemble which works in February is absolutely no good in July, but she interrupted me.

'I don't mean for your baby. I mean for mine.'

She was smiling shyly and resting her hand on her stomach, which was still protruding considerably. I always snapped back into shape after each one of my babies, but that's C-sections, private care and a rigorous exercise routine for you. I gazed at her, wondering if the chemicals at the hairdressers had somehow seeped into her brain.

'What do you mean, yours?'

'Well, this is a little bit embarrassing, but I'm expecting again.'

I gasped, rather rudely, but who could blame me?

'Again? But you've only just had this one! How on earth…'

Davina giggled. 'Well, at Christmas, Toby took us away for a little break and we stayed in a lovely hotel. I suppose we got a little bit carried away. I thought you couldn't get pregnant when you were breastfeeding, but it seems that you can.'

Well! I ask you! Irish Twins, I think they call it. I did some rapid calculations in my head and worked out that Davina would be giving birth to baby number two in September, nearly two months before Baby Matthew's first birthday. I spluttered out my congratulations and listened to her enthusing about how wonderful motherhood was and how much she loved it. Takes all sorts, I suppose.

In bed, gazing at the walls and mentally repainting them in something gorgeous and on trend, I looked back on the week. Much to my surprise, I'd truly enjoyed spending time with Davina and Toby and getting to know them better. Johnnie has always had a downer on his brother, and I suppose I inherited his view when I joined the family. Next to Johnnie's sparkle and wit, Toby never shone, and they always seemed to bring out the worst in each other. Johnnie hero worships Charlie, and Rafe is the perennial little brother.

Tomorrow my husband would be arriving, and surely this would be the beginning of our reconciliation. With only a few weeks left before the baby came along, I was sure Johnnie would be calling it a day with Sofija and coming back to the woman he adores.

The night was spent in a series of unsettling dreams featuring Mummy, Johnnie and Bertie Pryke-Darby, Arabella's husband, of all people. I woke feeling tired, grumpy and apprehensive. Peering out of the window, I saw that heavy raindrops were falling from a leaden sky and that the paddock beyond the garden had turned into a quagmire.

After breakfast, I found myself in the kitchen with my brother-in-law. As we loaded the dishwasher, he cleared his throat and I realised he wished to make an announcement.

'There's something I want to say to you, Isabella. We asked you and Johnnie to be godparents before we knew about his behaviour, and had we known, of course, we would have restricted the invitation to yourself. Davina and I are 100 per cent behind you. We both think he's behaved appallingly. I can only hope that he sees sense this weekend and comes back home.'

Toby does sometimes speak as though he were addressing a board meeting, but his heart is in the right place. I felt rather touched.

'Honestly, it's fine, Toby. But I do very much appreciate your support. It means a lot.'

Dishwasher loaded and speech delivered, we ambled into the lounge to talk about the plans for the day. Since the rain showed no sign of ever stopping, we agreed to go swimming and have lunch afterwards. I had packed a Scrummy Mummy bathing costume with cleverly hidden stretchy panels and shoulder detail, so I was ready for anything. Davina stated her intention to take to the waters and paddle Baby Matthew around in his little flotation suit. What with me and my enormous bump and her with her baby weight and smaller bump, we'd be lucky if any of the water stayed in the pool. **#displacement #makingwaves**

An air of stress and tension hung over The Beeches as we loaded the washing machine with wet towels and swimming costumes and put Baby Matthew down for his afternoon nap. I went upstairs to do my hair and make-up. I wanted to look my best for Johnnie. Shimmying back down the stairs, delicately fragranced with his favourite perfume, I admired myself in the hall mirror.

'You look lovely, my darling.' It was Silvia, who had been watching me from the kitchen door. 'If my son doesn't see the light and beg you for forgiveness, he doesn't have the sense he was born with.'

I laughed, lightly. 'I'm sure he'll get his silly little fling out of his system soon and come back home.'

Silvia nodded. 'I'm sure he will. Now, what do you think about this wonderful news about Davina and Toby? Another grandchild! I'm so excited.'

Although I'd never thought about it, Johnnie and Toby were perilously close to being Irish Twins themselves. Only thirteen months separate them. Silvia and the Bishop obviously decided to have a bit of a break, as Rafe is five years younger than Toby.

I planned my children carefully, with just the right amount of time between each.

The sound of clattering pots and pans drifted from the kitchen. Davina has a lady who helps in the house and who can, on occasion, produce a meal. Tonight, she was giving us roast beef with all the trimmings, something that could go one way or the other. I heard the crunch of wheels on the gravel outside and my heart started beating in double time. My instinct was to throw open the front door and run to him, but this wasn't my house. Taking deep breaths, I walked down the hall to find my hostess and inform her that her latest guest had arrived. #beatingheart #soexcited

Sitting down at the big table in the dining room, I gazed at my husband. His blue eyes were tired but still sparkling, and his dark hair needed a cut, which made him even more attractive. The children were delighted to see him, and he'd made a big fuss of Baby Matthew and brought him a huge teddy bear. I was just a little narked as I'd already texted to tell him I'd purchased a silver engraved christening mug and a Children's Bible for him on behalf of both of us as godparents.

I'd set the table, using some rather nice crystal glasses that I'd found packed away at the back of the sideboard. I'd also lit the fire, put candles on the table and dug out a pretty, embroidered runner. We all sat down while Davina's help came puffing through with a selection of tureens and a huge joint of roast beef. Toby had opened a bottle of very good red wine which I was eyeing up longingly. My husband, I noticed, had put away an entire glass before the beef was even carved.

In similar circumstances, I would have produced an elegant starter, then the main course, followed by cheese, dessert and coffee. I've always known that Davina doesn't value food and presentation as I do, but this particular meal was one that I would want to forget.

The beef was tough, the gravy was too salty and had lumps in it, the roast potatoes were singed, the carrots were undercooked and the cabbage was watery. None of this would have mattered, however, had the conversation been light and sparkling. It was anything but.

We'd all fallen into the habit of having lovely, informal meals punctuated with jokes and chatter. Davina and Toby are so good with my children, and in turn, they seem to really love their aunt and uncle. Johnnie (quite unconsciously, I'm sure), seemed to be casting a shadow over proceedings. Sprawled casually in his chair, he sawed away at his meat, a quizzical smile playing around his lips, drinking red wine as though it were going out of fashion.

In an attempt to break the ice, Davina told him the news about baby number two.

'Toby, you old dog! Well, well, I never knew you had it in you.' He threw back his head and laughed loudly. 'Many congratulations to you both. You're really going for it.'

Davina's cheeks turned red, and I saw Toby's lips compress. Silvia hastily changed the subject to the weather and that carried us through to dessert. Sticky date pudding with a caramel sauce was plonked down in front of us. What Davina's help lacked in meat cookery prowess, she more than made up for with her desserts. I let out an involuntary murmur of delight as I plunged my spoon into the fragrant mass and poured double cream over the top. Over the table, I could see Johnnie frowning. He wagged his finger playfully at me.

'Steady on, Iss. Don't overdo it. You're going to look like a sticky date pudding at this rate.'

Toby banged his spoon down on the table, making me jump.

'I say, Johnnie, leave Isabella alone. I think she looks absolutely marvellous.'

Davina, her mouth full of pudding, nodded vigorously and as soon as speech was possible, added her compliments on my appearance to her husband's. I must confess, I was a little hurt by Johnnie sniping about my weight. It wasn't the first time, either, now I came to think about it. I could feel my cheeks burning as I pushed my dessert around the plate.

The silence grew, hanging over us like a pendulous rain-filled cloud as I racked my brains for the right thing to say. My voice came out rather shriller than I'd intended as I complimented Davina on her hair.

'It's so you. And you were right to go for that paler colour on your nails. It's going to look fabulous with your outfit. What time are your parents arriving tomorrow?'

Davina's family and her new look kept the ladies going for several minutes, Silvia adding in her compliments on her glossy locks. I was just starting to think that my adept social manner had steered us out of the choppy waters of awkwardness when Johnnie spoke.

'You look very smart, Davina, I must say. I hardly recognised you. That's my dear wife's trademark, of course. Taking people who don't want to be made over and transforming them for her own ends. Don't be surprised if you find yourself on Instagram. How many likes and shares do you think Davina will bring in, Iss?'

Something cracked in me. I wanted nothing more than to rise to my feet, walk around the table and bean Johnnie with the decanter. However, Isabella M Smugge had good manners dinned into her from the egg and it would be morally wrong of me to attack a fellow guest under the roof of the host. I fixed my husband with an icy stare and spoke in a calm, level voice.

'Davina and Toby have been absolutely wonderful to us this week. They've welcomed me and the children with open arms and been incredibly kind and supportive. Davina and I went out for a girly afternoon. That's all. No pictures will appear on my socials. I wouldn't do that.'

I certainly didn't want the children hearing any more of this toxic dinner party conversation. Also it was getting late. I smiled radiantly at them, sitting in a forlorn little row on the other side of the table.

'Come on, you three, time for bed! Do you want me to take you up?'

Even such an innocent subject as the children's bedtime seemed up for debate. Johnnie scowled.

'Don't be such a killjoy, Iss. It's not that late. I see little enough of them as it is.'

'And whose fault is that?' Toby's face was red, and he was shaking with rage. 'Three smashing children, a wife like Isabella and you behave like an idiot and break her heart. You should be ashamed of yourself.'

Silvia jumped in. 'Now, now, Toby, this isn't the time or the place. *Pas devant.*' Her eyes flicked across to the children, who were gazing at their uncle with shock written across their faces. 'Come on, my darlings, let's go up. Say goodnight to everyone.'
#awks #cringeworthy #idiothusband

I cast about desperately for a safe topic of conversation and decided on clothes. Davina and I talked determinedly for ten minutes about the outfits we were sporting on Sunday and then moved on to the church service, what time the rest of the family were arriving and what the weather was likely to do. That's part of the training they give you at boarding school. Avoid the unpleasant at all costs and if all else fails, talk about the weather.

As everyone sipped their coffee and nibbled on petit fours (shop-bought, but jolly nice), the conversation took another unfortunate turn.

'There's a super little pre-school just up the road from here, Isabella.' Davina was talking, little glints of candlelight reflecting off her new chestnut lowlights. 'I can't imagine Baby Matthew ever being old enough to go, but Toby and I are thinking about two days a week in due course, just to get him used to it.'

Johnnie cut in. My heart sank as I saw that he had started on the port.

'Get him into a good private school as soon as you can. That's my advice. I listened to Iss and now my son is off to some state sinkhole.'

His eyes were dark and angry, and his brow furrowed. I swallowed hard and felt my cheeks flame.

'That's really unfair of you, Johnnie. We've discussed this already. Finn's going to be with his friends and living at home, which is what he wants. Listening to your children and doing what is best for them is the hallmark of good parenting, wouldn't you agree?'

Johnnie poured himself another glass of port and looked at me for a long moment before he spoke.

'You know my views, Iss, and you trampled on them to get your own way. You're taking away all the advantages that Finn would have had if he'd gone to my old school. I give it six months at that place you're sending him to before you're running back to me, begging me to get him a place. I noticed he's already picking up a local accent from that commonplace little school you insisted on sending him to.'

There was a horrible, brooding sense of impending doom in the dining room. My heart was banging hard in my chest. I opened my mouth to speak, but was beaten to it by my brother-in-law.

'So what if he is? He's a super chap. I've spent all week getting to know your children and they're a credit to Isabella. We won't be sending Matthew to our old school. We want to find somewhere that's right for him. One size doesn't fit all, but you should know that.'

There was naked hostility in Johnnie's eyes as he leaned across the table and addressed his brother.

'And what's that supposed to mean, Mr Boring? Do I detect a touch of jealousy? Here you are, buried in commuter-land with your dull job and no prospects and breeding like rabbits. You always did like to try to copy everything I did.'

Toby rose slowly to his feet. 'Shall we remember our manners? There are ladies present. Will you excuse us?'

Straight-backed and dignified, he exited the dining room with Johnnie following him, port glass in hand. Davina and I were left sitting staring at each other over the ruins of the family dinner. Johnnie had always made little jokes about his brother, but now the naked antagonism between them was shocking.

The door opened and Silvia walked in.

'I read them all a story and they went out like lights. Why don't we…' She stopped and looked at the empty chairs. 'What happened to the boys?'

We explained.

Silvia tutted loudly. 'For goodness' sake! I will go and find them and sort this silly situation out once and for all.'

She turned on her heel and marched in the direction of the library.

Davina was looking upset. 'Oh, Isabella, this is awful. What do you think they're saying? I wish we knew, but I don't suppose we can listen outside the door.'

This was fighting talk. I could think of no better plan than to creep down the hall and eavesdrop. Toby's honourable nature would probably preclude full disclosure and I wasn't keen to quiz my husband about the conversation. I stood up and stretched my aching back.

'Come on, Davina. Let's go and find out what this is all about.' #spillthebeans #brotherlylove

I've loved Johnnie for such a long time. I never thought I would be without him, and now it's been eight months of solo parenting and living, I'm almost getting used to it. Sitting at dinner tonight, I saw him through different eyes. Still devilishly handsome, but rude and boorish too, and drinking too much. I felt ashamed of him, and that's something I never thought I'd say. We tiptoed down the hall and positioned ourselves outside the library, where we could hear angry voices.

The Victorian builder who constructed The Beeches didn't stint on materials. I will say that for him. The internal doors are made of oak and are extremely thick, sadly. Even with our ears pressed against the panel, we could hear only a low murmuring. Suddenly, however, there was an eruption, and we heard Silvia's voice, loud and furious.

'Jonathan *Smugge*! Apologise to your brother at once. I will not have such language.'

Davina gazed at me, her eyes bulging.

Silvia continued talking in a loud, angry voice, but we had no idea what she was saying, nor to whom, as she lapsed into German. That's the trouble with having a bi-lingual family. They wander between languages, which is absolutely no good at all in a situation like this.

'Davina! How's your German?'

Davina looked abashed. 'I can say what my name is and talk about the weather, and ask where the hospital is, but that's about it. Sorry. I do feel like a chump. I wish we knew what she was saying.'

Just then, Toby's voice cut in, fortunately speaking English at high volume.

'... your attitude, so disrespectful. What have I ever done to you?'

'You *know* what! You *know* what you did!' My husband was raging. I could feel the emotion even through the door. 'Everything was fine until you came along, taking Ma away from me and being so needy. Then I had to put up with you tagging along after me at school.' He put on a childish voice. 'Jonathan, where's my tuck box? Jonathan, will you help me with my prep? Jonathan, I really miss Mummy and I want to go home. You were so wet! I couldn't wait to ditch you.'

'I am so terribly sorry! How inconsiderate of me.' Toby was clearly raging too. 'You were a rubbish older brother. Charlie helped me far more than you ever did.'

'Oh yes, of course, Charlie, the perfect brother. Well, I had him first! It was great with just the two of us until you came along.'

'I can't believe you're still angry I was born. It wasn't my choice, believe me. You've clearly got some serious issues and I suggest you deal with them before you get much older.'

There was a muffled bang and the sound of grunting. I heard a chair being knocked over. Could they have resorted to fisticuffs?

'Stop this at once! Jonathan! Tobias! Put that chair down. What would your father have said to see you two fighting like this?' Silvia lapsed into German, so we never did find out what the Bishop would have thought.

Toby was speaking again, sounding slightly out of breath. 'You can't blame me for disapproving of your appalling behaviour towards your wife. Taking her away from everything she knows in London, carrying on with the au pair behind her back, stringing her along – I'm ashamed of you!'

'I'm sorry you don't approve of me, Toby. At least I've got some interest in my life, not like you, buried down here with your dull wife and your boring job.'

There were more banging noises and a yelp as – I assumed – something hard connected with someone's person. For two pins, I would have burst into the library and assaulted my husband with one of Davina's horrible candlesticks, but my sister-in-law was sobbing quietly and looking distressed. It was time to take action. I marched her back to the lounge and sat her in front of the fire. Looking out of the window, I noted to my dismay that it was still pouring with rain. I had considered walking outside and peering in through the library window, but I didn't fancy catching my death of cold or being spotted by the feuding Smugges.

All I could do was sit down next to Davina and apologise for Johnnie.

'You're not dull. You're absolutely lovely. Take no notice of him. He's drunk.'

To my surprise, I found I meant it. My week at The Beeches had opened my eyes to a few home truths. The sound of a door being flung open and banged shut floated down the hallway. Before we could heave ourselves off the low-slung sofa (pregnancy is so terribly limiting), we heard the front door open, then crash shut. The sound of high heels came tapping down the quarry tiles and Silvia appeared in the doorway. Her face was flushed and her eyes glittering.

'Your husband has stormed off to the annexe, Isabella. Toby is just calming down. I'm afraid that quite a lot of repressed feelings came to the surface. So typical of the English. I suggest that we all go to bed and start again tomorrow.'

She helped us both off the sofa and with an affectionate kiss, sent us off to bed. I had a disturbed night, rising repeatedly to go to the loo and being joined by Elsie in the small hours. I prayed that she wouldn't lose control of her faculties, and when I awoke to the watery winter sun peeping through the window, she was gone, and the bed was dry. **#smallmercies #cosleeping**

I was up, showered and dressed by 7.30. I tiptoed downstairs to make myself a peppermint tea, the entire house still wrapped in slumbers. The sky was clear and little fairy cobwebs of dew were spread all over the garden. I headed outside to take some early morning shots. The light was wonderful, and I didn't want to miss the opportunity.

There are some pretty walks down by the paddocks, and I took full advantage of this unlooked-for free time to wander about taking shots of trees, wildlife and open countryside. I posted a story on Instagram and tweeted a couple of pictures, then headed back to the house.

I walked past the annexe, glancing in the window as I passed. To my surprise, I saw my husband doing press-ups in the lounge. On impulse, I rapped on the glass and had a brief moment of satisfaction as he jumped out of his skin. I decided to take the opportunity to chat, as we weren't going to get any alone time over the weekend.

Wiping his face with a towel, Johnnie greeted me.

'I'm all sweaty, Iss. Don't get too close. Coffee?'

I declined and took a seat on the futon in the lounge. Surely, Toby and Davina must be the last people in England to own such an outdated piece of furniture. But I digress.

I came straight to the point.

'What got into you last night?'

Johnnie frowned. 'I've had enough of my sanctimonious brother judging me and looking down on me. I've wanted to hit him for years and last night we had a bit of a punch-up before Ma broke it up. If I hadn't said I'd be the chosen one's godfather, I'd be straight on the road and back home.'

I was shocked. Has my husband always been this rude and entitled? Surely not.

'I've really got to know Toby and Davina this week. They've been sweeties. And the children love them. I want to spend more time with them, not less. It would be so good for the children to spend time with the baby and build up a good relationship.'

'You do you, Iss. I've had enough of boring old Toby and his opinions.'

I took a deep breath. 'You were so rude last night, Johnnie. I've never seen you like that before. Why are you so jealous of Toby?'

He frowned. 'Jealous? What are you talking about? I wouldn't live his humdrum life for anything! Stuck in this horrible house with Horse Features and a whining baby? That's no fun. I've got everything I ever wanted in life.'

'Davina is a lovely woman, and the baby is gorgeous. How can you be so mean? And what do you mean, everything you ever wanted? You ran off with my friend, the woman I trusted, a huge part of my life. You told me *I* was the one you wanted.

Remember that first night, in my flat? You said you would never ever love anyone but me.'

'But you broke the promise, Iss. You broke the promise you made to me.'

I was stumped. 'What are you talking about? What promise? I've always been completely faithful to you. I've never even looked at another man.'

Johnnie was staring at me. 'You must remember. We were in bed, and I asked you if you were prepared always to put me first. You promised me I would always be number one for you, before anyone else. Anyone.'

It was coming back to me. 'But I have always put you first. We moved into the flat *you* liked, I didn't take that job at the gallery in Edinburgh because you wanted me to be in London with you, I fell out with my sister because of you – how could you possibly think I've broken that promise? What more could I have done?'

'Oh, Iss. I should never have agreed to move away from town. That's where it all went wrong for me. I wasn't your main focus any more.'

I couldn't believe my ears. 'But you were the one who suggested it! You always got your own way.'

He shook his head. 'That's not how I remember it. I supported your career just as much as you supported mine.'

'But what about the personal appearances? I stopped doing them because you wanted me to. And I had C-sections because you insisted on them. I've built my entire life around you, Johnnie Smugge. Don't you realise that?'

He was smiling and shaking his head. 'I was just trying to protect you from yourself, Iss. You needed direction. Left to yourself, you'd have been rushing around from pillar to post wearing yourself out and making yourself a target for weirdos.'

I heaved myself to my feet. 'You always put yourself first – stuff your stupid promise. You carry on living your pathetic little life in London with Sofija and see how long it is before she works out just who you really are.'

'She knows who I am. The handsomest, most charming man she's ever met. She adores me. And that's a very attractive quality in a woman.'

Well. Maybe it was the pregnancy hormones or maybe it was time I cut him down to size. I grabbed his phone from the coffee table and threw it at the wall. Then I slapped his face and walked out. Darn, it felt good. **#notaviolentwoman #promisenopromise #isabellatellsitlikeitis**

The rest of the weekend was fine. Rafe and Xenia were fine. Davina's parents and sister were fine. The christening was fine. It was all totally fine. We left mid-afternoon on the Sunday and for the first time, I didn't kiss Johnnie goodbye. I couldn't bring myself even to speak to him. I need a long, long time all by myself to figure out where I'm going and how I'm getting there. Not that such an opportunity will present itself any time soon.

On the way home, I didn't even bother packing the children's tablets in the suitcase. I let them play on them the entire time, and when they asked for food, I pulled into a motorway service station and let them have whatever they fancied. Go me.

At school on Monday morning, the girls asked for details of my week away. I omitted all the stuff about Johnnie and showed them pictures of Baby Matthew, and Davina's makeover. Hayley, it seemed, had given birth at the very beginning of half term, two weeks late. The child was a girl, to be called Cressida. No other details were forthcoming as Hayley was cocooning and letting her husband do the school run.

It was good to be back home. I had a productive day, meeting with Mimi on Zoom, writing loads of content and teeing up some more guest bloggers.

From the outside, it must look as though I am invincible. I never miss a deadline, I win awards, I influence. If there's a trend, I surf it. Alone in my beautiful house, however (Ali had the day off), I sat in my writing studio wondering where I'd gone wrong with my life.

Tuesday morning brought a salvo of abuse from Lavinia, who had been very quiet of late.

That's Swell: What Next for Isabella M Hugge?

Self-promoting trend hunter Isabella M Smugge has built herself a very successful life by jumping on every passing fad and weaponising it for her own ends. Ms Smugge has toyed with veganism, meditation, wellness and anything else she thinks might harvest her a few more followers.

The shameless mumfluencer lost her hedge fund manager husband to her au pair and found herself accidentally pregnant, yet still continues to pump out saccharine content about her perfect life. But there's more to Ms Hugge (now enormously pregnant) than meets the eye.

A source close to the bragging blogger says, 'First she took three primary school places, when everyone knows she can easily afford to send her children to private school. Now, she's having this baby on the NHS. The village surgery is already overstretched. Lots of locals are seething. They can't understand why someone so rich and entitled is draining our hospital heroes. She's wangled her way on to the PTA, buying friendships by handing out money left right and centre. She even goes to church, although I'm sure she doesn't believe in God. It's sickening.'

The ever-swelling mumpreneur is obviously building bridges with her husband's family. Last week, she was posting nauseating shots of her 'wonderful family time' in the depths of Buckinghamshire.

Smugge needs all the friends she can get, as very soon she'll be a single mum of four. This writer says, 'Give it a rest, Ms Hugge.'

I must be changing and becoming a stronger person. Not that long ago, I'd have cried myself to sleep and brooded over Lavinia's unkind words for weeks. Now, I simply shrugged them off and wondered who the 'source close' to me might be. I am starting to have my suspicions. Vainqueur Designs kitchens don't come cheap. #theplotthickens #bloodmoney

I am determined to enjoy my last few personal appearances before I have the baby. Once upon a time, I relied on Sofija for everything. These days, I have a much more reciprocal arrangement with friends. Every other Tuesday, Finn goes to football with Harry and has tea at Polly's, and I return the favour the following week. The girls always have friends to play with, and on this particular Tuesday, with a meet and greet plus a book signing in Essex, I've had to call in quite a few favours. I won't be back until at least ten, so Finn's staying over at Jake's, Chloë at Maisie's and Elsie at Lauren's.

In the car driving south on the A12, I relished the unaccustomed headspace. My life is so much busier these days, what with clinics and blood tests and weigh-ins for the baby, PTA work and so on. I'm glad I listened to Mimi and agreed to all these personal appearances. The numbers are making her very happy (we may be looking at a third reprint of the *Issy Smugge Says* series next year), plus she's been approached by some serious journalists for interviews in the glossies and broadsheets. Isabella M Smugge does not belong in the grimy pages of Lavinia's rag. She should be gracing Scandi designer coffee tables up and down the land.

Upon arrival, I was greeted by a member of Mimi's team, her features mobile again as the Botox had finally worn off. Such a relief. In addition to the book signing and meet and greet, Mimi had booked me an interview with Emma Ford, who writes the 'Net Results' column and has been a fan of Issy Smugge ever since she discovered that Lavinia hates me. Emma's a great writer. Her paper is the diametric opposite of Lavinia's: measured, intellectual, inspirational. I was genuinely excited about meeting her.

Mimi had also arranged for me to chat with a woman called Katie Moran who is the cultural editor at *Cursive*, a very high-end magazine which is so desperately intelligent that hardly anybody reads it. It's a shame I can't drink coffee at the moment as my brain is not quite as sharp as I would like. Still, Isabella M Smugge can pull it out of the bag when she has to. #feelingthefearnaddoingitanyway #climbingtheladder #inyourfaceharcourt

Gliding back up the A12 with Radio 4 burbling comfortingly away in the background, I reflected on the past few hours with great satisfaction. Emma is delightful and clearly has history with Lavinia.

'She's a piece of work, isn't she? Loves nothing more than upsetting people with her stupid column. I got really drunk once and had a fight with her in the ladies' at an awards' ceremony. When you're ready, we could write a really incisive think piece on what makes gossip columnists such sad people. Dig into her background a bit.'

Five years ago, I would have leapt in and done the interview at once. These days, a wiser and more-experienced woman, I smiled in a non-committal fashion and agreed to think about it. Our interview went well. I think I've made a friend. Well, as close to a friend as one can be with a journalist.

Katie Moran was exactly as I expected her to be, dressed head to foot in Alicia de Montfort. Not many English designers sport a nobiliary particle, or even know what one is. Alicia was the year below me at St Dymphna's. She's done jolly well for herself.

Nothing as common as a digital recorder for Ms Moran. She took a fat notebook from her handbag and produced a fountain pen with which she made tiny, neat notes. She's sending a photographer to the Old Rectory next week. The production values are so high on *Cursive* that the piece won't see the light of day until June, but that's fine. I feel that I have taken an important career step. **#issysmuggesaysaspire #glossies #poshmag**

I've just realised that Chloë hardly bit her nails at Davina and Toby's and Elsie didn't wet the bed once.

It was Johnnie's birthday today. Came home from the school run and wasted fifteen minutes of precious work time crying and torturing myself by looking at photos of us when everything was perfect.

Most days, I'm just a normal mum in the playground. A mum who writes for a living and is having her picture splashed across the nationals. I've found it much easier to be relatable since Johnnie left and I have had to do most of the childcare myself. Hayley has returned to the playground, pushing young Cressida in a mid-range pram while Lysander trots along beside her in a pallid fashion.

This morning, I lured the girls back to mine for coffee. I must confess that I had an agenda.

I had hardly fired up the machine when there was a knock at the front door. To my amazement, a woman was standing there holding the most enormous bouquet of flowers. I hefted it in and plonked it down on the island.

'Look at that, babes! Have you got enough vases?' Lauren was open-mouthed and all the girls were gazing at the fragrant blooms with amazement. I opened the little card.

Darling Iss. I was a complete bore. Am I forgiven? Johnnie xxxx'

My heart was racing. What a beautiful gesture. Johnnie doesn't do apologies, as a rule, so this one meant a great deal to me. I was about to seize my phone and text him when Lauren leaned over and read the card.

'Am I forgiven? Errrr, no! Typical bloke, thinking he can mend everything with a few flowers.'

I was rather taken aback. 'What do you mean? He's obviously sorry and I think this is the first step towards reconciliation.'

Lauren sighed and, looking at the other girls' faces, I saw that they were unsmiling.

'Babes, no offence, and don't be cross, but this is such a ploy. All he's done is get his wallet out and splash the cash. Has he changed anything? Is he going to? I doubt it. He's got the best of both worlds, Sofija in his bed and you still thinking the sun shines out of his rear end. And he hasn't actually said sorry. If you text him, I think it'll be a mistake.'

'Agreed.' Kate was frowning. 'From what you told us, he behaved really badly at your sister-in-law's, and like Lauren says, these flowers don't really mean anything. If he was truly sorry, he'd start trying to mend things with you. Please don't text him. We've all seen you get so much stronger since he's been gone.'

It was a minute or so before I could speak. My head was whirling. Nothing made sense in my world any more. I consoled myself with the thought that my friends had only known me for eighteen months or so and didn't really know Johnnie at all. I felt a bit sick, so excused myself and went off to the cloakroom for some quiet time.

As I returned, I heard a snippet of conversation.

'What would you expect? Bless her, she can't seem to see it.'

Everyone stopped talking as I waddled back into the kitchen and heaved myself back onto my stool.

Lauren was looking worried. 'Please don't be cross, babes. We all care about you and we don't want to see you getting hurt any more. You're going to be having that baby soon and you need all your strength.'

How could I ever be cross with Lauren? She doesn't know anything about my relationship with Johnnie, but I know she has my best interests at heart.

I waited till the girls had gone and texted Johnnie. **#reconcilation #lovelyflowers #stilllovehim**

My suspicions are confirmed. I'm as sure as I can be that hirsute Hayley has been blabbing to Lavinia. Who else could know so much about my everyday life? It seems that her husband works at the council, in the planning department, which explains my old enemy's jibes about the so-called desecration of the Old Rectory's garden in her stupid column last year. She'd accused us of building our gorgeous, heated indoor pool room on an ancient camomile lawn and I'd put it down to Ted the gardener talking indiscreetly at the pub. If Hayley's husband had seen our planning application, maybe he had been the one to tell her and she'd passed it on to Lavinia. I don't know what to do about it. The girls counselled caution.

'Look, you can't accuse her. It'll only make things worse. Rise above it if you can.'

Easier said than done. I wanted to know why she'd done it. Maddie ascribed it to jealousy.

'She's resigned a couple of times before and we always asked her to come back. She was a good secretary, but she made such a fuss about everything. It was hard work, but getting people to join the PTA is difficult enough, let alone filling the posts. When she stood down at the fête, I don't think she meant it. Then you came along and volunteered to take the role. I bet that's what upset her.'

'How was I to know?' I was flummoxed. 'Game playing, that's what it is! Honestly.'

I was so cross that I went into the pantry and brought out the granola bars I'd made with Elsie the night before. I had meant to save them for the children's after-school nibble, but sometimes sinking your teeth into the sweet, yielding deliciousness of a little snack is the only thing that cheers you up. I must overhaul my diet once the baby comes. Davina told me I looked well when I was at her house, and we all know what that means.

In other news, Suze and the family are back! They're coming to stay the last weekend of March. I am beside myself with excitement. My due date is 5th April, but I have no idea what that means in natural birth terms. What I do know is that it's put a real crimp in our Easter celebrations. Issy Smugge's Easter Egg Hunt is justly famed, so we must hope and pray that the baby doesn't emerge too soon.

I always had a date in the diary for giving birth before, but now I have to wait until he or she is ready to emerge. The girls have given me chapter and verse on what to expect. A bewildering range of experiences all round, ranging from pooing a bowling ball to producing a melon. My heaviest child was Chloë at 7lb 3oz which sounds quite a lot of person to encourage out of one's lady bits. I am trying not to think about it.

April

I had the best weekend with Suze, Jeremy and Lily. It was absolutely perfect, and that isn't a phrase I've been bandying about much of late. The children were over the moon to see their cousin and, after a few awkward moments, they rushed upstairs to bond.

On Saturday evening, the girls repaired to Elsie's room where they have built a camp. They are insisting on sleeping in the same bedroom and have dragged duvets and sleeping bags in to make some kind of pink, girly cocoon. It's rather sweet, actually. Lily is delightful. Beautiful manners and an infectious giggle.

I sank onto the sofa in the family room with an involuntary grunt and put my swollen feet up on to the ottoman. Jeremy and Finn were playing chess at the table, leaving Suze and me to have a chat. Once we'd covered all the usual ground (school, new house, how they're getting on in Chalfont), we moved on to the family.

'We're off to Kent next weekend to see Mummy before the house sells. I've been on the phone with her a lot since we got back. Did you notice anything strange when you were with her?'

'No stranger than usual.'

'Hmm.' Suze was looking thoughtful. 'She's been repeating herself a lot and she called Jeremy Johnnie. I wonder if there's an underlying health issue. She drinks far too much and the smoking can't help.'

I just did not have the headspace for Mummy concerns, but mentally logged Suze's comments. I wondered if she was having some kind of emotional blip because of the move. Who knows?

Suze put her hand on mine. 'How are you doing, Bella? Really and truly?' She glanced across at Finn and dropped her voice. 'It must have been hard seeing Johnnie at Toby and Davina's.'

I thought about it for a bit. How was I, really and truly? Confused. Sad. Worried. Apprehensive. Certainly, all of those things, but also, strangely, strong, optimistic and proud of myself for getting through the last few months.

I gave Suze a précis and told her about the flowers.

'So of course I texted him to say he was forgiven. I honestly think he's going to come back. He said he's taking a week off work when I go into labour and wants to come and spend it with us here at the house, helping out with the children and bonding with the baby.'

'That's big of him.' Suze didn't look impressed. 'And what do you think Sofija will make of that?'

I truly didn't know. An image of her face, sad and downcast, flashed into my mind and I swallowed hard. It was all such a tangled mess.

'Everyone seems to think I should forget him and move on, but how can I, Suze? He's my husband, the father of my children. I still love him so much and I'm prepared to forgive him and mend our relationship.'

'You're a good person, Bella. I just hope he appreciates how fortunate he is. Shall we stop talking about him now, before I smash something?' Suze's cheeks were flushed. I can't blame her. Her own history with Johnnie must still rankle. I felt a bit awkward and tried to smooth things over with the offer of wine.

'No thanks, Bella. I'm cutting down. Anyway! I have got some exciting news for you.'

It seems that Suze has been doing some research and has found Nanny! Johnnie forgotten, I hung on her every word. Once Mummy dismissed her, Nanny got a job working for the Marquess of Bathgate at Chriochan Castle in the Scottish Borders and is still there. Suze had looked them up and found that when Nanny left us, the twelfth Marquess of Bathgate had

175

five children, three boys and two girls, ranging from twelve years of age to two. Nanny must have had her work cut out.

Scrolling through pictures of the castle with its fairy-tale turrets, I tried to imagine our beloved Nanny in such wild and beautiful surroundings. It was quite a leap from suburban Kent.

'I seem to remember Mummy telling me that she had an offer of marriage from the Marquess before she met Daddy. She turned him down because her parents were mad keen for her to say yes. That might explain some of her anger towards Nanny and why she didn't pass these letters on sooner.'

Suze is so kind. I was still raging about the whole Mummy and Nanny situation.

We worked our way through the complex genealogy of the Bathgates.

'So, Edward Douglas Moncrieff Bathgate, twelfth Marquess of Bathgate (born 5 June 1949, died 9 February 2019) was an Anglo-Scottish aristocrat and entrepreneur. He was the elder son of Douglas Sholto Moncrieff Bathgate, eleventh Marquess of Bathgate and his wife, the Honourable Catherine Drummond. They had five children, Lady Flora Rose Catherine Bathgate, Lady Iona Violet Caroline Bathgate, Viscount Douglas Edward Moncrieff Bathgate (the present Marquess of Bathgate), Lord David Alistair Callum Bathgate and Lord Archie Ewan Sholto Bathgate. (Did you notice Lady Iona's middle name? That's interesting.)'

'Wow. She had her hands full.' I was rather taken aback by the roll call of aristocratic names. Reading through the five children's bios, we learned that Lady Flora was married with four children, Lady Iona was an artist, the present Marquess was married to an Honourable someone or other and had four children, Lord David was a businessman and Lord Archie worked in New York.

'And to think that could have been Mummy's life. The chatelaine of a castle, running an estate and being a Lady.' Suze was looking thoughtful. 'Apparently the Marquess inherited quite a lot of debt and turned it all around with events and good land management. The family live in the castle, but they let a lot of it out for weddings and conferences.'

'Mummy would have relished that. Imagine her marching around with a cigarette holder, bossing the staff around.'

'Do you think she and Daddy ever really loved each other, Bella? I often think about that and wonder if things could have been different.'

I recounted the story of our lost little brother with tears in my eyes. I was surprised by the wave of emotion that broke over me as I remembered Mummy crying helplessly in her cluttered drawing room. For a minute, I seemed to move outside myself and look down on my charming family room, two sisters weeping together on the sofa. **#sosad #whatmighthavebeen**

Over breakfast on Sunday, we chatted about being reunited with Nanny again. The very idea filled me with joy. I wasn't quite sure how we were going to make the introduction. How does one invite oneself to the home of a Marquess? Suze assured me she was on the case and I allowed my mind to drift to idealised scenes of the two of us being reunited with Nanny. The church bells were ringing and I realised that if I was going to make it to church on time, I'd need to get going. Suze had agreed to come with me while the children stayed at home with Jeremy.

I'm starting to get the hang of church and being around religious people. Tom was speaking this morning and it was really rather lovely. He was talking about doubt and how hard it can be when life is difficult and we don't know which direction to take. It felt as though the whole thing had been planned out just for me and was enormously comforting.

After we'd had the talk and some prayers, Keith, the retired vicar, bounced up from his chair and addressed us. It seems that the couple from Kenya are coming over for a fortnight in July and will need somewhere to stay. Their house is let out and they don't have a place to lay their heads.

Now, I don't know if you've ever had an experience like this. It could have been indigestion. It could have been my imagination. As Keith was speaking, I felt a tiny little nudge at the base of my ribs. It wasn't the young occupant of Isabella M Smugge's insides, as he or she is more of a kicker than a nudger.

'Should I offer them my en suite room at the Old Rectory?' I thought to myself. There was the nudge again. Odd. I'd never met these people, but I admired their selflessness in leaving a comfortable life in Suffolk behind them to go and look after babies in Kenya. By July, I would be back into my stride. Keith had made it clear that they would be out a great deal, visiting supporters and giving talks. I do love offering hospitality and I hadn't done anything particularly altruistic of late.

As I was sipping my tea, Keith himself appeared.

'Hello, my dear. How are you today?'

We chatted for a little while. I wondered if I should say anything about the nudge, but before I could, Keith spoke.

'As I was looking across the church, I felt God give me a little nudge to come over and chat to you.'

I started. A nudge? What a strange coincidence.

'How odd. I was just sitting here thinking that I could offer Jess and Andy accommodation at my house. Since my staffing arrangements changed, I've got a lovely big bedroom with an en suite bathroom just sitting empty, except for when my family come to stay. There's plenty of room for us all and my housekeeper could help out with the cooking if I'm too busy. Of course, they've never met me and there's probably someone else at church who wants to offer them a home.'

Keith was beaming. 'How wonderful. No one else has offered yet and I have mentioned it a couple of times from the front. I am aware that you've got your hands full, but if you really feel this is something you could offer, I know you would be an answer to prayer.'

I was feeling ridiculously pleased that a retired vicar thought that I, Isabella M Smugge, might be an answer to prayer. This was the second time in eighteen months. We agreed that Keith would email Jess and Andy to see what they thought.

Suze, Lauren and I walked out of church, full of tea, biscuits and good cheer. Jeremy was cooking the lunch, so all I had to do was relax on the sofa and chat to the children. Bliss! **#nudge**

Only twelve months ago, I was at the top of my game, happily married and looking forward to a holiday in Verbier. As a family, we always enjoyed at least two holidays a year, and good ones too. I don't mean the type where you stay in the UK and make the most of the scenery. Not that there's anything wrong with that. I wouldn't want you to think I'm being snobbish.

Before the children came along, Johnnie and I used to have the most marvellous holidays. We worked round the clock and we felt that we deserved to give ourselves wonderful experiences. One of our first holidays together was at a rustic Eastern Mallorcan getaway, all rugged scenery and azure seas. We've stayed everywhere, in villas, stylish boutique retreats, overwater bungalows and ski lodges. We had a particularly wonderful week in Zakynthos in April one Easter, and nine months later, our boy was born.

Once we'd started our family, we missed those buzzy towns with their hip bars and DJ sets by the pool, but then we had different things to look forward to. I wouldn't change a thing about that, but the fact remains that it's nearly a year since we had any kind of holiday. I'm not counting the week with Toby and Davina. I may have to have a chat to Silvia and see if she's up to accompanying us for a couple of weeks of sun in the summer holidays.

I am rather hoping that the baby will be late. I'm packing in as much work as I possibly can before its arrival. I've got lots of guest bloggers booked in, plenty of evergreen content and enough buzz around my personal appearances to tide me over, but still, I want to deliver the first draft of *Issy Smugge Says: Let's Do a Spring Refresh* before I give birth.

If you've followed me for any length of time, you'll know that I am passionate about interiors. So many people live with the same old dull look year in, year out, and there's really no need. I always say you can elevate the everyday with careful curation. Bedrooms can often be rather dowdy spaces, but it's the easiest thing in the world to update them with new linen and the right dressing. I always start with pure white Egyptian cotton sheets and duvet cover, add a waffle throw and layer the bedding in complementary shades with contrasting textures. You can add in cushions and match your curtains if you're feeling extravagant. Elegant bedside lamps and some scented candles and you're good to go.

I've never been a slave to my socials, but I flatter myself that I am always Insta ready. I've curated my own collection of cups, saucers, jugs and silverware. Mismatched vintage never goes out of style. Once you've got the basics, you can switch up and refresh as you go.

I spent several days writing non-stop, and by Wednesday, I had finished. I think it's one of my best books. My readers simply adore makeovers, and everyone likes to look to an expert for tips on a refresh.

Three days till my due date. Easter is ruined, of course. I've organised an Easter Egg Hunt but will barely be able to waddle round the lawn.

Dear Silvia is coming to look after me. She's cleared her diary and will be with me for as long as I need her. I haven't told her about Johnnie coming to stay yet.

Two days till my due date.

A phone call from Keith. Jess and Andy are so grateful for my kind offer and would love to come and stay. Excellent.

One day till my due date.

A call from Mummy. Do I want her to keep all my old school reports from St Dymphna's? Yes, of course I do! One day, those reports will be selling on eBay. She seemed perfectly normal to me. Her usual spiky self.

Baby due today.

Nothing. Not a twinge. I hate waiting.

Still nothing. Find myself ambling into the baby's nursery at least twice a day and rearranging all the books and clothes and toys. Ankles hideously swollen. Hate all my Scrummy Mummy clothes. Have had legs waxed and pedicure done so that I am completely ready. Kate says she always had her toenails done just before she had her children so she had something to look at while she was pushing. Revolting!

Not sleeping well. Up on the hour every hour to go to the loo. Honestly.

Feeling guilty that poor Silvia is hanging around the house with no baby yet. She says not to worry and that it's a delight to spend time with us all.

I am going to be pregnant forever and ever. When will this baby appear? When? I almost find that I don't care about the pain as I just want it to come out. Consulted the girls on the playground who told me hilarious stories about their own birth experiences. Maddie offered to take me for a drive along a notoriously bumpy lane which is often used to encourage village babies to come out. Declined.

Not a twinge. Find myself standing in the nursery in front of the full-length mirror addressing my bump.

'Now, look here. This is your mother. Everything's ready. I've got all the nappies, lotions, clothes, pram, cot – you name it. Just come out. I've got things to do, you know.'

Nothing.

Spoke to Silvia about Johnnie's offer tonight. She says it's up to me and that a woman needs her husband at a time like this. Asked her to be my birth partner. She cried. I cried. Texted Johnnie and told him to come up as soon as the baby is born. He can sleep in one of the frowsty little rooms on the second floor.

Email from the publisher. They love my first draft. Am posting lots of artful shots of the nursery, spring flowers, buds, foliage, etc. Outside in the garden, everything is bursting with new life. Much like myself.

Come *on*, baby!

Standing in the playground, I feel grumpy and almost violent. If one more person – *one more!* – says, 'Oh, are you still here?' or 'Hasn't that baby come out yet?' I think I'll scream. The girls were on hand to give me helpful tips. Lovely Lou suggested pineapples, which apparently contain some kind of enzyme rumoured to start labour off. Long walks, a hot curry, raspberry leaf tea and hearty marital relations were all suggested, although I don't know how they think I'm going to manage the latter. That's what got me into this fix in the first place.

I found myself crying in a pathetic, half-hearted way on the way out of the playground.

'That's actually a good sign, babes.' Lauren gave my arm an affectionate squeeze. 'I cried and shouted at Scott for a couple of hours before Ruby came. I could have killed him, honestly. I was consumed with rage. Then my waters broke. It could be tonight!'

Maddie renewed her offer to take me on a ride down the lane. Chicken dhansak and a pineapple upside-down cake for tea tonight.

I have got raging heartburn and appalling wind. I had to send Silvia on the school run as I didn't trust myself to stray too far from the en suite. I see now that the taarka dhal was a mistake.

Contented myself with a glass of pineapple juice at breakfast. I took the children to school and was scrutinised by the girls for signs of impending labour.

'Have you been doing loads of housework? Obsessing about anything? I went out and bought 200 clothes pegs the day before I went into labour.'

I was feeling tired and cross, but apart from that, had no symptoms. A familiar voice assaulted my delicate ear.

'Oi! Smug! Are you still here?'

I turned round to see Liane Bloomfield walking towards me.

'Of *course* I'm still here! What sort of stupid question is that? What do you think *this* is?'

I gestured at my bump, and as I did so, felt the most peculiar sensation. I haven't lost control of my faculties since Minty Pryke-Darby's fourth birthday party, an unfortunate occurrence involving too much orange juice and the toilet being occupied by another four-year-old. My Scrummy Mummy black combats were soaked and I could feel hot liquid pouring down my legs. My stomach cramped and with joy , I realised that young Master or Miss Smugge was finally effecting their egress.

I burst into tears and hugged Liane Bloomfield.

'Thank you! The baby must have heard you. How long have I got before I have to go to hospital?'

Ow. Ow, ow, ow, ow! This is terrible. How do ordinary people manage? Ouch!

Oh, the indignity! When will all this water stop coming out? My beautiful smoke-blue Egyptian cotton towels will never be the same again. Silvia has put a wash on. Am bent over the sink in my en suite with more towels soaking up the waterfalls of fluid.

Texted Johnnie. He didn't reply. Texted again. Nothing. Used lots of swear words and left him an angry voicemail. This is all his fault. Ouch!

Silvia has rung the hospital five times. They say not to come in until the contractions are closer together. Am relying heavily on the mums' WhatsApp group. Helpful and supportive messages pouring in from the girls, plus funny memes to take my mind off the pain. The girls are going home with Lauren tonight and Finn's staying with Jake. In between contractions, ordered flowers to be sent with sincere card of thanks. The fact that I can still multitask at a time like this gives me hope that the pain may end one day and my life return to normal.

Tell Silvia it's time. I don't care what the hospital says. I must be almost fully dilated by now.

The NHS are marvellous, and all the nurses and doctors are heroes. However, being greeted by somebody in a badly cut navy-blue ensemble who snaps on a pair of surgical gloves and rummages around in one's cervix is not the welcome I was expecting. At Mr Aggarwal's fine establishment, I would have been relaxing in my suite and being prepped for my surgery by now. No pain would have been involved and certainly no such indignities visited upon my person.

Four centimetres. How can this be? I'm in agony and I'm sure I can feel the head. The midwife says I've got a long way to go and offers me pain relief. I say yes to whatever's on the menu.

A mask is attached to my face and I'm breathing in and out heavily. Everything suddenly seems hilarious. I laugh and laugh and laugh and Silvia and the midwife (Jayne) look at each other and smile. It still hurts, but I don't care.

WhatsApp the girls. *'4 centimetres. Really hurts but am having gas and air. Are the children all right?'*

Back come many supportive replies. *'Keep pushing.' 'You can do it.' 'Go girl!' 'Kids playing happily, told them baby on way. They send love.'*

I love gas and air. I love the NHS. What lovely, kind people, giving of themselves, all the while being interfered with by the government. When this is all over, I will do a campaign on my socials to make sure they get paid more.

The gas and air have run out. I shout at lovely Jayne to get me more, immediately! The pain is unbearable. How did the

Victorians manage? I wish I was having a Caesarean. I am now at seven centimetres. Every moment lasts for an hour. Ouch.

Silvia is now in charge of my phone. Johnnie has rung and is on his way up. Do I want him to come straight to the hospital?

'Nooooo!' I shout between gritted teeth. Silvia sends a tactful text.

Waves of crushing pain. Thank heavens for the gas and air. It's been hours. When is this baby going to come out? Start crying and say I've changed my mind and can I please have a Caesarean after all. Lovely, kind Jayne strokes my arm and tells me I'm doing brilliantly. It certainly doesn't feel like it.

Eight centimetres.

I am standing up, leaning on the bed with Silvia on one side of me and Jayne on the other. The room is spinning and there's a roaring in my ears. I grip the mask so hard that I wrench the gas pipe out and Jayne has to re-affix it.

'Nearly there, Isabella. Nearly there. You're doing amazingly. When I tell you to push, push.'

Genuinely, I cannot do this. It's too hard. Start sobbing and saying I can't push, yet feel my body obeying Jayne's commands. I can't do this for much longer.

Silvia is holding my hand and reading out messages from the WhatsApp group. She's been keeping them updated. Claire has sent me a private one.

"Trust in the LORD with all your heart and lean not on your own understanding."[3] You can do this, Isabella. We are all here praying for you and cheering you on xx'

---

[3] Proverbs 3:5, NIV.

The words give me just enough strength to do an almighty push, and with a rush of fluid and a tearing pain, the baby is born. I collapse forward on to the bed, resting my head in my hands as I listen to my child crying. Silvia is hugging me and telling me how brave I am. She's not wrong.

I am lying in my bed with the baby in a little glass cot by my side. I ache all over. Down below is a region I don't even want to think about. Jayne let me hang on to the gas and air and stitched me up. Going for a wee is agony.

The baby is lying on his back with his head to one side, gazing at me. I don't know what to say to him. I try a faint smile and gently stroke his cheek. His tiny fingers clench around mine and I feel a jolt of primal love and devotion, in spite of the pain and exhaustion. Johnnie has been in, clutching a balloon and with a big smile. No name yet, but I'll be choosing it, thank you very much! Silvia has gone home to get some sleep. Thank heavens that texting and updating my socials don't use the muscles that are currently hurting so much.

I've managed to take some black and white shots of the baby's little feet and his face. I've done this sort of thing often enough to know what people like. Already, I'm lighting up Twitter, and my stories are being reshared constantly. As I was being stitched up, I texted Mimi to tell her the glad tidings. She's already swung into action, God bless her.

I never knew it was possible to be so crushingly exhausted.

I'm home and every day is like forty-eight hours. The baby is up all night and all he wants to do is feed. He has reduced me to a blubbering wreck with sore and tender extremities. Silvia is a tower of strength. Life is a strange, sleepless roller coaster. I look appalling but do not care.

All the things I loved about having my other babies are a chore with this one. Without Sofija to keep the household running like clockwork and deal with all the paperwork, I am constantly trying to keep up. Silvia has instructed me to stay in bed and I am too weak to disobey. Johnnie is residing on the second floor and is doing the school runs. When he comes in to see me, I don't even bother brushing my hair. Let him see his wife in the full horror of post-childbirth, wreaked upon me by his drunken carelessness.

He is delighted it's another boy. I think fathering a male child makes him feel good about himself. Which is weird. Mimi is delighted with the perfectly symmetry of the newly expanded Smugge family. 'Two boys and two girls, darling! You are clever.'

WhatsApps from the girls.

Johnnie being very charming and chatting to everyone. Hayley cornered him this morning and was asking loads of questions. Soz babes, couldn't get over there fast enough xx do you want anything from the shop?'

'Trying hard to be polite to your husband but struggling a bit. He's really working the playground. Even tried chatting to Liane, but she gave him short shrift. How are you doing? Do you need anything? Love, Kate xx'

'Still praying for you, Isabella. Please rest and get your strength back. Let me know when you're ready for a visit xx'

'Blooming Hayley! She was lurking by the gate waiting for Johnnie to walk in at pick-up. Lou and I are going to come in five minutes early every day to cut her off. We're on the case. Take care, Issy. Maddie xx'

I have decided to call the baby Milo. Johnnie made a little face when I told him. It's impossible for me to express just how little I care.

I awoke this morning with rock-hard bosoms, greasy hair, sore lady bits and a feeling that my life as I knew it is over. I've been cocooned in my bedroom with the baby for four days now and I'm ready to start receiving visitors. I sent a WhatsApp to the mums' group. *'Please, please come and see me today if you're free. Dying to catch up. I really miss you all. Look like a state but give me some notice and I'll have a shower xx'*

The baby started squawking and, with a sigh, I heaved him out of his basket and attached him to my bounteous chest. I lay back on my pillows and closed my aching eyes. I must have nodded off because when I awoke with a jerk, he was fast asleep in the crook of my arm and I was in a state of rather embarrassing undress. A steaming cup of tea and a plate of toast and marmalade sat on the bedside table. I only hope that Silvia didn't have her glasses on when she came in.

Amazing what you can do with one hand. I demolished the toast and gulped the tea down before checking my phone for notifications. The doorbell kept ringing, but it's been like that since the minute the baby was born. Flowers, chocolates, gifts from people I endorse, cards – my room looks like Kew Gardens. Silvia has had to go down to the village to buy more vases.

I heard footsteps on the stairs. Before I had a chance to smooth my hair down, in walked Claire and Lauren.

'Why didn't you tell me you were coming? Look at the state of me!' Being seen with greasy bed hair, stains down my top-of-the-range maternity nursing pyjamas and no make-up on was hideously embarrassing.

'Don't be so silly! We don't care what you look like. I wasn't exactly a supermodel when you came to see me in hospital.'

Claire sat down on the bed and gave me a kiss. The baby, sensing that new fans were in the room, stirred, passed wind and opened his inky-blue eyes.

'Look at him! He's so tiny! Can I hold him, Isabella?' Lauren was beaming all over her face.

'Please do!'

I took the opportunity to get out of bed and go and smarten myself up. Who knew there would be so many emissions when one gave birth naturally. Isabella M Smugge never thought she would see the day she was sporting a large pair of disposable pants. Really, it was the only way. I certainly wasn't mentioning *that* on the 'gram!

Glancing in the mirror, I realised to my horror that while the baby had drained my left-hand side almost completely, the right was horrifically enlarged. I looked as though I had wandered out for a mochaccino halfway through a breast augmentation procedure.

I settled myself back on the pillows for a good catch-up with my friends. The baby seemed perfectly happy in Lauren's arms, which was a relief. I've never endorsed the notion of baby wearing but for the last four days, it's been like having a tiny, flatulent stalker.

'So tell us everything! How was it? How long were you in labour? How much did it hurt? Is it weird having Johnnie back?'

I ran through the main takeaways. Hellish, hours and hours and hours, loads and yes.

'He's spending time with us, bonding with the baby, but it doesn't feel like I thought it would. I'm glad he's here, and it's great for the children, but I can't relax because I don't know if he's going back to Sofija after his leave is over. Would you believe he's told her I went into labour really late, because otherwise the dates don't add up? What am I, an elephant?'

Claire nodded. 'That's awkward. Do you think he'd be up for a really honest chat?'

I smiled in a non-committal fashion. I didn't particularly fancy an honest chat.

We moved on to playground matters and I shared my suspicions about Hayley. The evidence was fairly damning. She had been attaching herself to Johnnie every morning and afternoon until pincer action from Maddie and Lou cut off her access. I was bracing myself for a piece from Lavinia which would confirm that Hayley was indeed the village snitch.

'Have you decided on a name yet?' Lauren was still gazing adoringly at the baby, even though my trained nostrils had detected a yeasty aroma drifting from his rear end.

'Milo Lawrence. My father-in-law's name was Lawrence and I like Milo. It goes well with Smugge too.'

'Milo Smugge! What a lovely name. Isn't that a lovely name, you precious little man?' Lauren started kissing the baby's head and cuddling him, things I am struggling to make myself do on a daily basis.

'The best part is, Johnnie doesn't like it. He didn't have a say this time.'

Lauren begged to be allowed to change the baby's nappy and I directed her to the en suite. Such a relief. When he emerged, he began rooting at her shoulder and making the noises which I have come to realise mean that he is ready for refreshment.

Sighing, I propped myself up and unhooked my gigantic *Je T'Aime Maman* nursing bra. I signed a deal with them six months ago and have hoovered up any number of pregnant followers. Which I suppose is good. Their underwear is rather lovely. If one must wear a hammock on the upper part of one's body, it may as well be constructed by French ladies who understand embroidery.

The baby burped loudly and started pawing at my bra while grunting quietly to himself. For a minute, it was like having Johnnie back. A miniature version with appalling wind. **#twentyfourhourservice #jetaimemaman #demandfeeding**

On my fifth day, I had a long, luxurious, hot shower, trying to ignore the milk leaking from my ludicrously enlarged bosoms, got dressed and made my way downstairs. Silvia is being absolutely marvellous, keeping everything ticking over and making sure the children are all right. They have been so sweet with the baby and so lovely to me. I wonder why it is I can feel emotions and love for them, but very little for the baby. It's not that I'm not glad he's here. It's just that he's such a drain on my resources. Without Sofija, everything feels wrong.

A WhatsApp from Suze.

'*Good news, Bella. I've made contact with the Marquess. Absolutely charming, says Nanny was always talking about us and we're welcome to come up any time. How about October half term? I'm going to write to her and send some photos. How are you doing? How's little Milo? Lots of love xxxx*'

In other news, the baby is either feeding, asleep on me or pooing. It's like having a tiny bald vampire as a flatmate. Every time I pass him over to his father, he screams at the top of his voice and goes red in the face. He's clearly an excellent judge of character.

The rest of April stretches ahead of me, a hideous desert of feeding, changing and sleep deprivation. It's my fortieth in June. We were going to do so much to celebrate and now it's all ruined.

I'm tired of writing. Who cares about my stupid life? #blahblahblah #babiesofinstragram #fedup

May

Spring is here and I feel a tiny bit better. The baby has knuckled down to learning about good sleep habits and I am starting to feel more like my old self.

As all my followers know, the seemingly effortless nature of my content conceals a vast amount of work. Behind the scenes, I'm doing interviews, guesting on podcasts, meeting with those I endorse, scouting for trends and inspiring others. Balancing all that with family life takes some doing, I can tell you.

I have had to speak to Mimi and ask her to fill in the gaps with more guest bloggers. With my constant stream of baby pictures, interior shots and pre-publicity for the new book, I am just about keeping up. I need someone to take the baby away for most of each day and see to him so that I can get on with my work, but this seems impossible. I am wrestling with nap times, precious chunks of the day that allow me to work. The baby has not really got his head around this concept.

Now that I have my trim ankles back, can see my toenails (gorgeously painted in lilac, so on trend) and am not getting up four times a night to wee, it's time to seize the reins and sort out Lavinia Harcourt once and for all. We had a nasty little drip feed of toxic comments all through April, culminating in a particularly acid attack a week after the baby was born. It was enough to turn my milk sour! **#enemy #cheapshots #justyouwait**

Bootee Call: Is This the End for the UK's Most Annoying Mumfluencer?

Just when you thought self-satisfied mummy blogger Isabella M Smugge couldn't set your teeth on edge any more, she weaponised her latest child, pretentiously named Milo Lawrence Smugge (8lb 8oz) in the shameless fashion we have come to expect. 'So happy to announce that my husband, Johnnie, and I have welcomed Milo Lawrence to our family, a little brother for Finn, Chloë and Elsie. Couldn't be happier or more in love with him. **#preciousmoments #babybaby #welcomemilo**' The two-faced scribbler then proceeded to flood her unfortunate followers' feeds with endless moody black and white shots of the hapless tot's feet, hands and head.

What I can exclusively reveal is that Ms Smugge's sugary outpourings are all complete bunkum. Sources close to the reluctant new mother tell me, 'She didn't plan the baby and all she's done is complain right through the pregnancy. She blackmailed her poor husband into coming up and spending time with her, using the new baby as an excuse. He was supposed to be taking a much-needed break at his chalet in Switzerland, but instead had to toe the line and do what *she* told him. He's told her it's over again and again, but she won't listen. I feel very sorry for him. He's invested so much into the marriage and put up with her cravings for online affirmation. To be honest, no one can understand why he stayed for so long.'

And that's not all. The mendacious mumfluencer has been showing off her endless free products on the playground, rubbing in her wealth and status to the many parents who struggle to make ends meet. I've been told that she paraded the baby in a top-of-the-range bespoke pram by pretentious French company, *Mon Petit Trésor*, and has dressed the unfortunate infant head to foot in ridiculously expensive designer clothing. 'It was bad enough that she went on the NHS when everyone knows she's loaded,' confided a school mother. 'She was too posh to push with her other children, but she's always trying to appear relatable to her followers, so that's why she took an NHS bed which a terminally ill person could have used and made a point of being seen at the doctors' surgery in the village. Honestly, it makes me sick.'

Pretentious? Selfish? Hypocritical? Isabella M Smugge is all these things and so much more. I say, 'Accept your marriage is over and stop shoving images of your so-called perfect family down everyone's throat.'

Well! If that school mother isn't Hayley, I'm a Dutch person. The old Issy Smugge would have cried and ranted. The new one gritted her teeth and plotted revenge. **#thatsenough #scribblerindeed #talktothehand**

The joy! I can drink coffee again. I tried out a decaf instant round at Claire's and to my delight, it tasted normal. There is a God! Surely quaffing decaf won't affect the baby's shaky grasp on normal sleep patterns. Claire says not, so I am ordering a shedload for my beloved coffee machine. Oh, how I've missed it!

I switched to a local coffee supplier just after we moved up here. He came round in person and gave me some tasters. The one that stood out for me was his single-origin Swiss Water decaf. Absolutely delicious and 100 per cent organic. He claims it has sweet notes of peanut, milk chocolate, cookie dough and burnt sugar, and he's not wrong. I cannot tell you how much I enjoyed my breakfast latte this morning. I shared on my socials, a shaft of very convenient sunlight falling across the cup. So many likes and shares! I'm trending!

My more honest content, via Open Brackets, is quite difficult to write. If I were being truly transparent, it would run something like this:

> Baby filled nappy and it squirted out of his vest on to my lovely rug. Cried. He cried. Changed nappy, got poo under my nails, cried again. Turned my back for a minute and found he'd done another one, liquid this time. Just want it all to stop. Why is everyone else doing all this right and I'm not? Am useless, incompetent mother with faecal matter under my nails. **#notbonding #feelingblue #overwhelmed**

I suppose I would accompany it with a couple of shots of the poo on the rug and my haggard face. But of course I'm not going to do that. Who wants to read about someone else's epic fails, especially someone like me who is a shining beacon of inspiration to the nation? At least I can drink coffee now. Made myself a decaf cappuccino and grimly attached the baby yet again. I think he may have a drink problem.

Received a text from Nicki Hartington, my lovely friend from London. She's in Suffolk for a short break and wonders if we could meet for lunch. I can hardly wait!

I took all four children to church this morning. It wasn't a resounding success, but I was in a vile mood, had had a sleepless night and am tired of pandering to everyone else's needs. I found myself placing the baby into the award-winning depths of his *Mon Petit Trésor* perambulator and bellowing at the other three to stop whining and look lively. I am never going to become as good and holy a person as Claire if I don't go to church more often!

We arrived and I had no sooner settled myself than the organ started playing. Most unfortunately, it was a tune I recognised from Daddy's funeral (an occasion I have pushed to the very back of my mind) and it reduced me to helpless sobbing. Keith's wife, Hope, appeared and sat down next to me. While everyone else belted out a rousing chorus, she hugged me and said nothing, allowing me to snuffle pathetically all over her shoulder.

I had planned to depart at high speed the minute the service ended, but it seems that the draw of a newborn is irresistible to many. Ladies came to fuss over him, lift him out of his pram and carry him about, talking abject nonsense to him. He seemed to love it. Being stuck in the house with boring old me can't be much fun. The girls scampered off to play with Becky and Hannah while Finn ate his way through a plateful of chocolate digestives and sulked.

'Are you OK, Isabella?' Claire appeared, looking concerned.

I explained that I had had a bad night and was a miserable failure and began crying again. She suggested that I went over to something calling itself the Lady Chapel to have prayer ministry. I didn't see how it could make things any worse. When we arrived at the said chapel, equidistant between the font and some chairs that had seen better days, I saw that Wendy the jam maker was sitting there with a sympathetic smile.

'Do you want to tell us what's troubling you, my dear?' Wendy has such a kind face. I blew my nose loudly and gave them the overview. They asked for permission to put their hands on my shoulders and started addressing the good Lord in a familiar manner. They talk to Him as though He's a friend, someone who knows them inside out. I can't imagine ever getting to that point myself.

After five minutes or so, they both sighed and said, 'Mmm,' which seemed to signal the end of the conversation. I opened my eyes and we had a debrief. Wendy felt that God wanted to remind me that I am lovely in His eyes and don't have to strive.

I didn't point out that He clearly does not understand the world of blogging.

Claire started telling me a story about her past. 'I hadn't been a Christian long and I was really struggling with forgiving myself and believing that Tom truly loved me. I felt unworthy and dirty and kept looking back at my past and all the things I'd done wrong. One Sunday morning, I burst into tears. One of the older ladies took me to one side and prayed for me. She gave me a verse which I'd never heard before. It's from Joel.

> I'll make up for the years of the locust,
> the great locust devastation –
> Locusts savage, locusts deadly,
> fierce locusts, locusts of doom,
> That great locust invasion
> I sent your way.
> You'll eat your fill of good food.
> You'll be full of praises to your GOD,
> The God who has set you back on your heels in wonder.'[4]

I was touched that she wanted to share, but didn't really understand what it had to do with me or, indeed, what locusts had to do with anything. Seeing my furrowed brow, Wendy explained further.

'I think that what Claire's saying is that God often speaks directly to us when we pray. That encourages us to keep going, and to know that we're not alone. Claire and I have often talked about how she used to feel that her past was full of disappointment and missed opportunities. When we first got to know each other, you were still very unhappy about that, weren't you?'

Claire nodded. 'I really was. I hated myself and I couldn't believe that anyone thought I was worth bothering with. I used to compare my family life to Tom's and I always came off worst.

---

[4] Joel 2:25-26, *The Message* translation.

I did feel that my past had been stolen from me and I'd never get it back again.'

I had to interrupt. 'Sorry, you were comparing yourself with Tom's parents? Those two are toxic! I don't think I've ever met anyone so racist or narrow-minded, and I'm upper middle and went to private school!'

Claire and Wendy glanced at each other. Wendy grinned. 'They certainly are – challenging. But the point is, those words from the Bible were just for Claire, to reassure her that she would be compensated for all she'd lost.'

I still didn't really get it, but Claire obviously believed that God had sent her a direct message. It wasn't for me to question it. A thought occurred to me. 'Is that why you decided to call Joel, Joel?'

She confirmed that it was. Unaccountably, I felt better, as though a weight had been lifted from me. I walked back into the main church to find the baby being cooed over by hordes of middle-aged women. His face was beatific. 'Look, Mother,' he seemed to be saying. 'This is what I need. Mass adoration and lots of stimulation.' **#prayerministry**

The rest of Sunday was rather lovely. I popped the baby into his pram and wheeled him outside to take his afternoon nap in the shade of the wisteria tree. Replete with milk, he nodded off straight away while I challenged the children to a game of tennis. I found myself laughing in an almost carefree fashion, and it was only when we'd finished that I realised I hadn't taken a single picture. Oh well.

Just before tea, a text came in from Lauren.

'Hey babes, did you think about going to toddlers? You should give it a whirl xx'

I hadn't, but while I could ill-afford an entire morning away from work, perhaps it was what the baby needed. Loud noises, stimulation, people who might pick him up and carry him around and infant socialisation. I booked myself in for the following week.

One of the reasons I partnered with Scrummy Mummy is its acute eye for trends. As you'll know, tea dresses are very in, teamed with colourful spring flats. Issy Smugge is justly famed for her way with colour and if I can just lose another few pounds, I shall be able to sport a gorgeous new pair of hot pink jeans with a dark-green top. Thank heavens for the current trend for spring day dresses. Nothing says 'toddler group-ready' like a yellow and cream day dress with an olive-green cardigan to pull the look together.

On the appointed day, I sashayed out of the playground and followed a ragged crocodile of parents towards the village hall, apparently built in the Dark Ages (by which I mean the 1970s).

Several harassed-looking women were setting out tiny tables and chairs, there was a baby corner with lots of soft toys and blankets and a plethora of overexcited toddlers whizzing about on various plastic vehicles. The baby's eyes were glazing over. I gave his pram a little rock and he fell asleep, a miracle with the racket going on.

Various women, some of whom I vaguely recognised, started to wander over and say hello. As the noise intensified, the door creaked open and Liane Bloomfield appeared with her daughter on her hip. Seeing me, she grinned and headed my way.

'Smug! We're honoured. How jolly kind of you to join us.'

She appeared to be mocking me, but was smiling. I decided to respond in kind.

'I was going to go home and eat some caviar, but I decided to pop in here and wave and smile a bit instead.'

Amazingly, this appeared to tickle my frenemy. 'Caviar, what, what!' She adopted a ridiculous upper-class accent. 'Frightfully sorry we haven't got any champers. Can one interest you in an orange squash?'

I was terribly thirsty from all the feeding, and the weak squash in a tired-looking plastic cup tasted like nectar. Liane plonked her daughter on the floor and sank into the chair beside me.

I'm a veteran of baby groups, and the one I used to patronise back home, *Les Petits Fours*, was full of beautifully dressed yummy mummies like myself and no one expected you to actually look after your own child. Helpers in smart, drab, green tabards did all the work while we sipped excellent coffee and networked. In the village hall, this did not seem to be the case. A blonde woman wearing colours that went out three seasons ago ambled over to join us.

'Hi, Liane. Who's your friend?'

'This is Isabella Smug. Lives in the big posh house next to the church. Writes stuff and puts it on Instagram.'

The woman gazed at me. 'Oh. Hang on. Is she the one whose husband ran off? The one Hayley Robinson hates?'

'That's the one. Smug, this is Ashley. Ashley, Smug.'

'It's Isabella, actually. And it's pronounced Smugge as in Bruges. Or rouge. Or indeed, luge. But do please call me Isabella.'

I smiled charmingly as the woman stared back at me. Thinking on my feet, I came up with a conversational gambit which would surely kick things off.

'Which years are your children in? I've got Finn in Year Six, Chloë in Year Three and Elsie in Year One. And this is Milo.' I indicated the baby, still out for the count.

'So why does Hayley Robinson hate her?' The woman continued to address Liane.

'Some PTA drama. You know what she's like. Wants to be queen bee.'

'I heard she'd come into money. Lottery?'

'No one knows for sure. I've got my suspicions.'

I wondered if I had become invisible. I considered leaping to my feet and shouting, 'Hello! Hello!' in Ashley's face, but decided against it. I didn't want to stand out on my first visit.

'Going to get a coffee. See you.'

And that was that. Liane Bloomfield turned to me, rolling a cigarette with one hand and scratching her ear with the other.

'Ashley's not a fan of change, or new things. Takes her a while to accept them. Don't take it personally, Smug. By the time your baby's in Year Six, she'll be talking to you. She's got a girl in Year Four and that kid over there hitting the other kid on the head with the toy hammer. Going outside for a fag.'

And she was gone, leaving Issy Smugge wondering what on earth she had got herself into.

Ever since Johnnie's paternity leave came to an end, he's been seeing the children up here. He tells me that he is having the new flat completely redecorated and it wouldn't be appropriate to have them there. I can't see why he doesn't do what he did before and book a hotel, but he says he likes being in their natural habitat. First I've heard of it. I asked him how Sofija had taken the news about the baby and he changed the subject. I detect trouble in paradise.

Lunch with Nicki Hartington. I served organic roasted red pepper hummus, a torta pasqualina, strips of organic wholemeal pitta bread, soy-infused quails' eggs with celery salt, a dressed salad of wilted green leaves and a delicious apple slaw. I parked the baby in the kitchen while I was making lunch.

Ali had put a whites wash on and as I peeled the quails' eggs under the cold-water tap (so fiddly, but worth it!), I noticed that my son was gazing at the revolving drum with utter fascination. I steeled myself for the demanding squawks that I had learned meant that he required refreshment and/or entertainment, and which had been having such a detrimental effect on my daily life, but the next time I looked up, he had fallen fast asleep.

I ran upstairs to find Ali making the girls' beds. I warned her that the baby was crashed out in front of the washing machine and to please, please not disturb him. We had a brief chat and she told me that her older boy used to nap in front of the washing machine while listening to heavy metal music.

'I used to get a solid two hours out of him every afternoon, Mrs Smugge. And now he's a drummer in the school metal band and listens to it round the clock. I can't help but think the two are connected.'

Metal is not really my genre, but Ali suggested that even heavy rock might do the trick. It seems it's something to do with white noise and regular rhythm. I'm more a Goldfrapp kind of girl, but needs must.

I had the back door and the kitchen window open and placed my top-of-the-range baby alarm on the worktop next to the pram. By some miracle, the baby slept for two and a half hours. An all-time personal best! **#thankheavens #lovelylunch #metalhead**

Since the beginning of our marital difficulties, Nicki and her husband, Max, have taken my side and refuse all Johnnie's invitations to dinner. Meredith, on the other hand, is sucking up to Johnnie and has the two of them over for supper at least once a month.

Lunch consumed, we relaxed on my garden loungers and contemplated the cerulean sky. Ted was fiddling about with a hoe near the greenhouse and the faint sound of whistling drifted up on the warm spring breeze.

Nicki runs a gallery in London and her husband, Max, is a venture capitalist. On the surface, they are two very comfortably off people who live in a beautiful house with their four children. However, things haven't always been perfect for them. Nicki had just had her second child when her first husband died in a traffic accident. Somehow, with the help and support of both families, she got through, and several years later, she met Max. They've got two children together and are one of the happiest families I know.

'How are things, Isabella? Can I say I think you're doing amazingly? It's no joke managing alone with a newborn.'

I sighed. 'I'm putting a brave face on it, but if I'm honest, it's really hard. I feel so horrible saying it, but I can't seem to bond with the baby. I didn't plan to have him and the fact that Johnnie's off with Sofija living a separate life I know nothing about really hurts. I cry a lot and I feel utterly exhausted.'

Nicki smiled sympathetically. 'Don't blame yourself. It takes time to form a relationship with your children.'

I pondered this and sipped my coffee (such rich notes of burnt sugar and cookie dough! The coffee man was right). 'How did Johnnie seem to you when you last saw him? Are he and Sofija happy, do you think?'

Nicki looked straight at me. 'He seemed exactly the same as he always is. I'm not that interested in his happiness, to be honest. The person I care about is you. I have to speak frankly, Isabella. You look so much better and healthier now that you're apart than you ever did when you were together. I don't want to offend you, but that's how I see it.'

I was dumbstruck. I've spent years maintaining my weight, staying healthy and investing in what I thought was the perfect marriage. To hear that my friend saw things differently was a shock.

'I look in the mirror now and I see a tubby, tired-looking woman with awful hair. I used to be in control of everything, and now I'm not.'

To my horror, my voice wobbled and my eyes filled with tears. The contents of my lace-trimmed *Je T'Aime Maman* brasserie tingled and throbbed uncomfortably and my stomach rumbled loudly.

'You are not tubby! You used to be far too thin. Johnnie controlled you. I am sorry, Isabella. I hadn't meant to say it so bluntly, but Max and I have been worried about you for a long time.'

'That's just not true!' My voice cracked. 'Johnnie always wanted me to be the best I could possibly be. Since he's been gone, I've been eating far too many carbs and this is the result.' I patted my legs, far less lithe than ever they used to be, encased in a pair of wide-leg trousers a size larger than I'd like. They felt disgustingly huge.

'You used to sneak little sideways glances at him when you said something, almost as if you were looking for approval. Max struggled with some of the things he used to say to you – dressed up as jokes, but really quite offensive. He was horrified when he heard that Johnnie had left you for Sofija. He was so fond of her. So was I, if it comes to that.'

Sofija and the Hartingtons' au pair, Mari Luz, were great friends, and when we moved to Suffolk, Sofija often stayed with Nicki on her days off. My heart was banging in my chest and my mouth was dry.

'Did *you* suspect anything? For me, it came out of a clear blue sky. Sofija always told me she was staying with you, when in reality she must have been off with Johnnie.'

Nicki sighed. 'Max and I knew something was up but we couldn't work out what. Sofija nearly always stayed with us when she came up to London but she was often out. She had her own key, so she could come and go as she pleased. We were so surprised when we heard what had happened. She's a lovely person and she was so devoted to you.'

There were tears in my eyes. 'That's what I thought too. We had such a wonderful relationship. I relied on her in so many ways. But since this all happened, I've been going back over things in my mind and wondering if I treated her right. I took her for granted and perhaps I wasn't as sensitive as I might have been.'

Nicki reached over and gave my hand a squeeze. 'It's heartbreaking. We both feel for you so much.'

I blew my nose and took a sip of my cucumber water. It was painful to hear what my friends thought of my husband, but they weren't the first to express opinions that surprised me. I had some hard thinking to do. Nicki looked serious.

'If you don't mind me asking, do you know how she feels about Milo? She must have realised that he was conceived after you and Johnnie split up.'

'I genuinely don't know what she thinks. We haven't spoken since I confronted them at the flat.'

There was a squawk from the baby monitor and an ominous surge in my *Je T'Aime Maman*. I heaved myself out of the chair and trotted to the kitchen to liberate the baby, who had slept soundly and was now ready to feed and socialise. **#hearttoheart #afternoonnap #lunchwithafriend**

Once I had sated the baby's insatiable appetite, I put him in the pram and Nicki and I went for a walk. Our lane runs uphill, past the farm and out into beautiful open countryside. I've discovered a circular walk (I used to do a run round it when I could still do such things) which leads back to the centre of the village. Nicki hasn't seen the children for an age and was keen to meet them in the playground.

'I've got something I want to run past you, Isabella. I'm planning an exhibition later in the year and I'd love you to be part of it. Your photographs are so good and I know that's always been your first love. I chatted to Jen and she's totally up for it.'

Jenny Bell is Nicki's partner at the gallery. She's a huge noise in the art world. Her last exhibition was simply stunning.

I found my face breaking into a wide smile. 'Really? I would absolutely love that. I need a new project, something creative, and that would be perfect.'

We walked and talked and by the time we got to the playground, Isabella M Smugge was happier than she has been in a very long time. #truefriend #pasturesnew

My little Elsie is turning seven and I have planned the perfect party! I found a local farm which hires out alpacas for two-hour slots. Elsie and her friends will be spending time with the animals, doing an obstacle course and having their faces painted. Issy Smugge sure knows how to throw a party! I've invited the whole class and everyone's coming!

I had a phone call from Mummy asking if she can come and stay for a few days. 'I haven't met my grandson yet, Isabella. How is little Finn?'

'Finn? Not so little now. He's shooting up.'

'No, the baby! What's his name? And I would like to be at whatever you're planning for Elsie too.'

Well! Could Mummy be softening in her old age? Her memory certainly wasn't getting any better. I booked her in for a four-day stay and braced myself for criticism and snidey remarks. #familyties

The party was an utter triumph! Only Isabella M Smugge could take a herd of South American cameline mammals, mix them with a squad of excitable children in a back garden in Suffolk and make it the party of the year.

Elsie was wildly excited to have real-life alpacas walking around on the lawn and the obstacle races were a huge hit. I did mocktails, face painting, some crafts and of course laid out a wonderful spread. I felt almost like my old self and we were blessed with a beautiful, sunny afternoon. I had invited Johnnie, but found myself hoping he wouldn't come.

He didn't.

To my utter amazement, my mother behaved almost like a normal human being. Rather than attending for half an hour and then melting away to smoke furiously by the hostas, she helped me to carry out the party food, spoke to my friends and even entertained the baby, who seemed to have taken a violent fancy to her. I gave him a gigantic feed twenty minutes before my guests were expected and hoped that the unwonted social interaction would keep him going for the duration of the party. He was passed around from person to person and seemed to be enjoying himself hugely.

My organic cocktail sausages marinated in soy sauce, honey and sesame seeds are one of my signature dishes for children's parties. I'd ordered in five kilos of them and was on my third tray. Lauren was helping me put them on my giant crackle glaze platter and spear them with cocktail sticks.

'What's going on with your mum, babes? She smiled at me and asked me how I was.'

'Honestly, I don't know. I've never seen her being so nice before.' I shook some extra sesame seeds over the fragrant sausages and grabbed some bags of organic popcorn. 'She seems to like the baby too. I found her walking about with him in her arms this morning after breakfast, talking to him! She's hardly said anything horrible since she got here.'

'Wow!' Lauren poured the popcorn into a large glass bowl. 'Wonders will never cease.'

We walked outside to find Mummy deep in conversation with Tom and Claire, the baby in her arms gazing up at her face. Have I perhaps stumbled into an alternative universe? Or is sleep deprivation making me hallucinate? Perhaps Mummy's exotic scent of Chanel blended with filter tips is catnip to babies. Who knows? #surprising #intergenerationalbonding

The next morning over breakfast, Mummy was almost back to her usual self. She tutted when Chloë started chewing her nails

and told Finn off for putting too much butter on his toast. The baby was lying in his bouncy chair, gazing at the washing machine, perhaps in the hope that it would soon start up. I made his dreams come true by loading it up with the contents of Finn's laundry basket (the smell! I'm sure his feet never used to reek like that) and pressing start.

Mummy sighed. 'I'm going to have to harden my heart to this little one, Isabella.'

I was rather taken aback. 'What on earth do you mean, Mummy?'

'It's fatal to start loving them too much. It only leads to heartbreak.' She fumbled in her handbag and pulled out her cigarettes. 'I expect you've got work to do. I can take Milo for a little walk, if you like.'

I was speechless. It was Sunday, and I tend not to do too much on the day of alleged rest, but I was happy to see that my mother was finally bonding with one of her grandchildren.

'Thank you, Mummy. That's really kind of you.' I touched her arm and looked into her eyes. 'It's hard being the only adult in the house.'

I waited for an acid remark, but she contented herself with nodding and saying she was sure it was. The baby safely ensconced in his pram, she marched off on a tour of the grounds.

Mummy's visit was almost pleasant. I would go so far as to say I enjoyed her company. Most of the time. The baby, incontinent, flatulent and unpredictable, appears to have made the most unlikely ally he is ever going to in my uptight, chain-smoking, emotionally constipated mother. I managed to get quite a lot of work done by dint of feeding and changing the baby then handing him over to Mummy and galloping down to my garden studio before being summoned back for the next feed. I can see what Suze means, though. She mixed up the children's names several times, kept calling the baby Finn and forgot she'd told me about Bertie Pryke-Darby's latest operation, twice. I suppose she's not as young as she was, and her liver must be pickled with gin.

When she left, I was genuinely sorry to see her go. Our farewell embrace was several degrees warmer than usual and she insisted on giving the children £20 each. Could it be the beginnings of dementia? I must google the symptoms.

I am trying to count my blessings. Yes, I am bringing up four children by myself while my husband gallivants with my former au pair, but the baby is now having two regular naps a day. Thank you, baby-care wash cycle and Status Quo. Who would have thought it? Yes, Lavinia Harcourt has got her putrid claws into me and I am fairly sure that Hayley is the village snitch, but Emma Ford's latest 'Net Results' column is a love letter to Isabella M Smugge and all her works. Yes, I am struggling to get all my work done in a severely restricted timeframe, but my new book is out in a month and I have an exhibition to get ready for. On the whole, things aren't as bad as they might be. **#thebestisyettocome #stayingpositive #watchithayleyrobinson**

June

I have caved. A combination of broken sleep, constant needling from Lavinia, vast amounts of work and the baby's remarkable ability to mess up my days has led me to reach out to a local agency. They sent over a charming person called Sue Parkin who looks after the baby three days a week.

On good nights, I get away with one feed. On bad nights (and there are more of those than not), it can be up to four. Three mornings a week, I am jerked from my slumbers by the wails of the baby, feed him, then later have a jolly good pump using my wireless, custom-made double breast pump (absolutely top-of-the-range – and store the milk in the fridge.

Sue arrives at 9.30 and plays with the baby, takes him for walks, feeds him and puts him down for his nap in front of the washing machine. She has found that as well as Status Quo, he responds well to hoary British rockers Deep Purple, likes a bit of early Led Zeppelin and has even nodded off to AC/DC. I made the mistake of trying a bit of Coldplay last week, which led to frenzied howling. You can't win them all.

Having three days where I can work solidly from 9.30am to 3pm has made all the difference. The baby has taken to Sue, who has a God-given ability to work with tiny wailing people.

The piece in *Cursive* magazine has caused quite a stir! Several lifestyle editors have been in touch with Mimi, begging her for interviews with the woman whom Katie Moran called, 'One of the most noteworthy and influential influencers writing in Britain today.' *Cursive's* photographer produced a range of shots that I myself would not have been ashamed of. I particularly liked the one of me gazing out of the dining room window. The lighting accentuates the curve of my body and the shadows are masterly.

It was a proper think piece, quoting from many of my works and calling my writing 'fluid, entertaining and witty'. Ha! Take that and shove it where the sun don't shine, Lavinia! **#revengeissweet #noteworthy #influential**

Finn is off for a week on the school residential. They'll be abseiling, caving, canoeing and doing all manner of thrilling things. It will just be me and the girls (and the baby, of course) in the house.

Parents' evening, which I attended with the baby strapped to me (so inconvenient, but at least he went to sleep, his head nestled into my capacious bosom), was encouraging. Young Mr Rycroft gave Chloë a glowing report and suggested that I might like to look into some drama or theatre classes after school. Mr Cresswell praised Finn for his perseverance and hard work, and chatted at some length about what he called 'the Year Six issues'. These mainly centre around hormones, it seems, and there is very little anyone can do about them.

Mrs Jenkins is her usual elegant self, and apart from a slightly awkward moment when I greeted her with exactly the wrong words ('Ah, Mrs Jenkins! We meet again,' like a Bond villain), she gave my little Elsie a lovely report, praising her cheerfulness, ability to make friends and excellent work ethic.

Surely I must be doing something right.

I ran into Hayley who was accompanied by a weedy little man I assumed was her husband. I made a point of saying, 'Hello! How are you?' in a loud, cheerful voice and was rewarded with a pallid, 'Hello. Fine.' Walking past the Year Two classroom en route to Year Six, I overhead her saying, 'But Lysander is such a naturally gifted child. We can't understand it.' I smiled grimly to myself as I powerwalked past elderly trolleys stocked with dog-eared books. Perhaps the munificent hand of Isabella M Smugge is required in this department too. We'll see. **#generosity #givingtomycommunity #loveliteracy**

I now attend two toddler groups, the one at the village hall and Claire's group at the church hall. As luck would have it, they're held on the days when Sue doesn't work, giving me a chance to relax, enjoy a hot beverage and chat to people while the baby is passed around from person to person. He seems remarkably sanguine about it all, which is just as well.

Lauren was right to encourage me to go to toddlers. I'm making new friends and meeting the people who are going to be in Milo's class. It's rather fun, actually. The only cloud in my sky is Hayley, who comes to both groups. I am very careful about what I say and to whom when she's around. You just never know.

My policy of taking life one day at a time was working very well until I glanced at my calendar for June and realised that it was full of painful memories and hard work. Rafe and Xenia had their first wedding anniversary last month, which made me remember how, just over a year ago, I had been quite unaware of what was going on under my nose. It's my fortieth soon and Johnnie and I had planned a wonderful trip away. That won't be happening. I've got to decide when to have the baby christened (it may have to wait until the autumn), and perhaps worst of all, the Bloggers' Awards are nearly upon us. How I am meant to attend looking dewy, fresh and successful with an incontinent vampire in tow I do not know.

At my Zoom with Mimi on Monday, I shared my concerns.

'Darling, if anyone can be cheated on blatantly by her husband, get accidentally pregnant and be left as a single parent, yet still come up smelling of Comtes de Champagne roses, it's you.' She inhaled deeply on a plastic tube which, when I peered more closely at the screen, turned out to be what I believe is called a vape. Her soignée head was enveloped in a cloud of steam, giving her an alarming other-worldly appearance.

'Is that supposed to cheer me up, Mimi?' My voice came out rather more peevishly than I had intended. 'No need to rub it in. I'm just about managing to keep all my plates in the air and pretend to my followers that everything's peachy. How on earth am I supposed to rock up at the Awards looking like this?' I indicated the dark circles under my eyes.

'Sweetie, you look fine. Nothing there that a gifted make-up artist can't disguise. In fact, you look better now than you did when Mr Smugge was in residence. That extra weight suits you. I know, I know (she laughed, raspingly), as dear Wallis used to say, "You can't be too rich or too thin." Hit forty, though, and you need to have a bit of meat on your bones.'

I was yet to be convinced on that one. 'I suppose I could invite my mother-in-law up. She could look after the children and I could pump enough milk off to feed the baby while I'm away. I won't be able to stay over, though, Mimi.'

My agent waved her hand and coughed loudly. 'Listen, sweetheart, I'm just happy you're coming and won't be snatched away by your jealous husband just as the fun's starting. You have to be there. You're up for Best Photography again, Most Inspiring Influencer, Mumfluencer of the Year, Best Spin-Off Series and Outstanding Guest Blogger. You'll be the star of the show. I wouldn't be doing my job if I didn't encourage you to drag yourself there over broken glass if need be. Not that it should come to that.' Here she wheezed with bronchial laughter and took a swig from her flask.

I sighed. 'I'll be there, Mimi. Don't worry, you can count on me.' #bloggerawards #hardwork #reapingtherewards

I got my head down and worked as I have never worked before. I whipped through my to-do list, inviting Silvia up for the week, pencilling in October for the baby's christening (I really want Davina and Toby to be there, and she needs to get over baby number two) and asking Tom, Claire and Lauren to be godparents, reading and correcting the proofs of my latest book and scheduling interviews with two more broadsheets for lifestyle interviews. The local radio station has also been in touch, asking me to come and do an interview on its flagship afternoon show and its evening show. I've said yes to both. I like radio.

I batted away the many issues lurking at the edge of my mind. Would Johnnie ever come back, and did I actually want him to? What did Sofija know about the murky goings-on surrounding Milo's conception? When would Lavinia next strike? And most of all, how was I going to appear to be perfect and yet honest and transparent at the forthcoming Bloggers' Awards? #somanyquestions #keepsmiling

Johnnie appeared on Friday night to do his fatherly duties. His elegantly shod foot was barely through the door before I'd handed over the baton. Thrusting a bottle of milk into his hand, I instructed him to take care of the baby and the other three and on no account to disturb me as I took a long, candlelit bath. Fair's fair.

Barely had I sunk beneath the fragrant foam (white tea and cucumber, so calming) than there was a timid tap at the door.

'Daddy says is he supposed to heat the milk up?'

I told Elsie yes and to test the temperature on his wrist before administering it to the baby. Ten minutes later, there was another tap. Chloë this time. Daddy couldn't find a clean muslin. Was it normal for the baby to bring up quite so much milk? I sighed and gritted my teeth.

'In a pile on the island. There are three of them. And yes, it is. Tell him to put the muslin over his shoulder and walk about. And not to jiggle him, whatever he does. The baby hates that.'

After ten minutes' blissful marinating, I could feel my knotted muscles starting to relax. Any thoughts of peace and quiet, however, were shattered by yet another visitor.

'Sorry, Mum. Milo keeps yelling and he's gone red in the face and been sick on Dad's leg. I told him to put the washing machine on and find some Led Zep on your playlist but he told me not to be so silly.'

I sat up and said a naughty word under my breath.

'Darling, can you go downstairs and tell Dad to come up here?'

After a few minutes, I heard Johnnie's step on the stair. Wrapped in one of the surviving Egyptian cotton smoke-blue bath sheets, I confronted him, fragrant and steaming, eyes narrowed, toe tapping.

'Iss, he won't stop crying. Can you just…'

I interrupted. 'Johnnie Smugge! I have been looking after *your* children day and night, while working full-time and managing the household, and have I complained? No. I have simply sucked it up as I always do. Here's what you're going to do. Go downstairs and cuddle the baby. He likes his bouncy chair and he also likes sitting in front of the washing machine listening to British rock bands from the seventies. Look on my playlist. It's under "Go to Sleep Milo". If it doesn't work, I don't care. If you come up here, or send the children up one more time, I swear I won't be responsible for my actions. You're doing bedtime for all four of them. You're cleaning the kitchen and leaving it spotless. And if you have a shower upstairs, put the towels in the laundry basket and don't leave the floor swimming in water like you did last time. I am not your mother. Goodnight.'

And with that I banged the door in his face and returned to the steaming depths of my bath. #whatssauceforthegoose #bubblebath

Milo obliged me by sleeping through the night for the first time, God bless him. I awoke at half past seven, upper regions rock hard and in dire need of relief.

Perhaps for the first time since he was born, I found myself gazing down at the baby's fluffy little head and chubby limbs and feeling real affection for him. After twenty minutes of determined slurping, all was well. He belched in a meditative fashion, filled his pants and beamed at me. I picked him up and cuddled him, not to stop him crying, not because someone was watching, but because he was looking up at me with his dark-blue eyes and I wanted to. I found myself singing him a little song and walking around my room gently kissing his head. It was rather nice.

After a few minutes, the aroma from his pants reminded me that, for this weekend at least, Isabella M Smugge was not a lone parent. Smiling to myself, I grabbed a nappy and some wipes and ambled up to the second floor where my husband was sleeping peacefully. **#haha #sharingiscaring #smuggecontrol**

My fortieth birthday is coming up fast. Lauren and the girls are taking me out for a meal and dear Silvia is coming up for the week to look after the children as I've also got the Bloggers' Awards. Lavinia has been dipping her pen in bile again.

> *Over the Hill? Bragging Blogger Faces up to Milestone Birthday Alone*
> *Grande dame* of the blogging world, Isabella M Smugge, has been around for what seems like forever. This month, the self-satisfied scribbler turns forty, without her handsome husband by her side. A source who didn't wish to be named told me, 'It's a real slap in the face for

her. She makes such a fuss on her socials about birthdays and she'd planned a typically lavish trip to celebrate her fortieth. The way things are going, she'll be sitting at home by herself in front of the telly having a ready meal for one.'

And that's not all. The Old Lady of Instagram, as she's known, has been letting her standards slip of late. You'd never know it from reading her sugary posts, but the wheels are coming off the ageing influencer's carefully crafted social media wagon. 'She's piled on the weight,' a source told me. 'She looks as if she's just fallen out of bed most mornings and even though she still wears designer clothes, she looks a mess.'

The narcissistic natterer is desperately trying to appear relatable by taking up much-needed spaces at the local toddler groups. 'It's infuriating. She's sucking up to all the other mums and trying to get herself in with the popular ones. She can't see that they're laughing at her behind her back.'

If Smugge has any sense (which this writer doesn't believe she does), she'll quit while she's (just) ahead and give us all a break. Happy Big Four-Oh, Issy Smugge.

Well! Narcissistic or not, I've learned quite a few valuable lessons this year. I hosted a post-drop-off coffee session at mine and we went through Lavinia's poisonous prose with a fine-tooth comb.

'*Grande dame*. Well, that's OK. Meryl Streep's a *grande dame*. So's Judi Dench. I can live with that.'

Kate took up the cudgels. 'A ready meal for one? I bet you don't even know what one of those is! And anyway, little do she and her source know that we're taking you out for a wild night at the Greedy Pig at Metfield Parva.'

'Her *source* (here Lauren indicated quotation marks with her forefingers to howls of laughter) is talking out of her bottom. The self-satisfied scribbler's going to be caning it down the pub with us. Sitting by herself in front of the telly, indeed!'

The baby, being cuddled by Lovely Lou, seemed to be enjoying the laughter and clinking of coffee cups enormously. He appears to be of a rampantly social disposition.

'The Old Lady of Instagram? *Are* you known as that?' Claire was laughing and shaking her head.

'Of course not! She just made it up. As for piling on the weight, sadly, she does have a point there.' I looked ruefully at my stomach, still doughy and untoned, a whole two months after the baby's egress.

'That's a load of old waz!' Lauren was righteously indignant. 'You look amazing! And I think a bit of extra weight suits you. You were looking scrawny before you had Milo.'

'So who does the *source* think is laughing behind my back? I've been trying to get on with everyone. Liane is being quite nice to me, in a rude way. And I've met loads of people. What have you all heard?'

The girls assured me that no one was laughing at me. Quite the reverse, in fact. We agreed that Hayley was paying for her kitchen with blood money and was welcome to it. Claire was all for having a chat and trying to talk it out, while Kate and Maddie suggested cutting her dead in the playground. I haven't got the energy, to be honest. **#granddame #illgiveyounarcissistic #fabulousandnearlyforty**

Wonderful news! Suze has set up a phone call with Nanny. I handed the baby over to Sue and ran upstairs for one of the most important conversations of my life. When I heard Nanny's gentle Scottish tones, I could have wept. We talked for about half an hour and I could almost feel the wounds in my heart healing. Suze had sent her pictures of the two of us and our families. Nanny is semi-retired now, not in the best of health, but still her old self. I had a little cry when I put the phone down and lay on my bed for twenty minutes or so, staring out of the window. I couldn't exactly tell you how I felt. Meditative.

Thoughtful. Sad. Happy. A real mixture of emotions. #wonderfulmemories #pasttopresent #love

Famine to feast! Not only do I have the Greedy Pig and the Bloggers' Awards to look forward to, but Suze has contacted Minty and Penny Pryke-Darby! Mummy was so bitter and angry after Daddy and Arabella ran away together that she cut us off from our best friends without compunction. Poor Bertie, Arabella's husband, was such a kind, sweet man, and such a huge part of our childhood. I haven't let myself think about him or my friends very often since then because it hurts too much.

'Minty's getting married in August, Bella! Second time around. She wants us both to go to her hen night next month and come to the wedding! She hasn't changed a bit. What do you think?'

What did I think? I thought this Old Lady was more than ready to party her slightly ample derriere off. In your face, Hayley! Take that and stay fashionable, Harcourt! #fabulousatforty #oldfriends #weddingbells

I have decided to kill Hayley with kindness. That'll confuse her. Every time I see her, I suck my stomach in and grin at her like a Cheshire Cat. Claire says it's a start and do I want to think about forgiving her? No. I don't. **#thanksbutnothanks**

Isabella M Smugge is no stranger to haute couture and can put together an Insta-ready on-trend outfit at a moment's notice. To my horror, however, two months post-birth, I was infinitely more ample than expected. Standing in front of my full-length mirror, I turned and pirouetted, gazing at myself from every angle and critiquing my look. I'd selected a monochrome dress with chunky bangles, a messy updo, lilac nails (so desperately now) and a pair of heavy metal pressure earrings. I looked as good as a woman can in the situation I found myself in.

I floated downstairs to show myself off to Silvia. No sooner had she approved my look than my car pulled on to the drive. I lifted my skirts and walked out, head held high, for my first-ever solo awards' ceremony. I should have been scared, but I wasn't. If I can allow an 8lb 8oz person to emerge from my lady bits and bring up four children by myself, I can do anything.

One of the few good things about being a new mother is the effect it's had on my upper regions. Pre-Milo, I would say coffee cup. Post-Milo, it's challenge cup all the way. I never wore anything even a little low-cut when Johnnie was around (he hated it when other men insulted me by staring), but this dress is beautifully made and accentuates my curves, if you know what I mean. As long as I pump regularly, everything will be fine.

Being driven back to Suffolk, glowing with joy at being not only crowned Best Photographer *again*, but also Mumfluencer of the Year and Outstanding Guest Blogger, I pondered the evening's events. It was my first public outing without my husband and I was surprised at how much I'd enjoyed myself.

Arriving fifteen minutes early, I received my lanyard and goodie bag from the smiling girls at the door ('We just *love* you, Mrs Smugge! What a year!') and headed into the ladies' to check on my upper portions and general look. Pleased with what I saw, I walked into the suite to be met by a phalanx of agents.

A lesser woman with fewer years under her belt would have quailed at the sight of so much power and influence. There was Venetia Portarlington, founder of VPT who manages Daisy Finch the cleaning blogger and a whole host of other successful influencers; Denizia de Browning who spotted Bendy Wendy the Fitspo Queen when she was just a parkrun mum, and has taken her to dizzy heights; Mandeep Singh who made his pile with Vegan Megan, Peashoot Poppy and by cornering the burgeoning market in wellness and plant-based cuisine and, of course, the queen of them all, my very own representative rottweiler, Mimi, who was propping up the bar and drinking from a small silver flask.

'Sweetheart! How's my absolute favourite client in all the world? Mwah! Mwah!' She kissed the air adjacent to first my left and then my right cheek and patted my shoulder. 'Looking utterly radiant, may I say!'

'You may!'

I beamed at Mimi and accepted her offer of a flute of organic rosé cuvée champagne. Delicious. Soft notes of peach and berries. I can pump it off later.

I glanced around the room. Bressumer Beams, the historical property blogger, aka Portia Waldegrave, and her creepy husband, Nigel, were sitting glumly at a table, quaffing fizz. Bendy Wendy was chatting to Daisy Finch, Fantastically Fabulous Fiona and a girl I didn't know, and a furtive-looking woman with a suspiciously large handbag (clearly last season!) was lurking near them. I consulted the oracle.

'Mimi, who's that talking to Daisy and Fiona? And I don't recognise *her* – the one eavesdropping and staring at me. She's not a blogger, is she?'

Mimi filled me in. Daisy's friend Abz wrote *Neat Freak: My Life in Tidying* and has become an overnight sensation. I hadn't realised that putting stuff in the place it's meant to be was a thing, but so it would appear. 'Book rocketing up the charts, just got her blue tick, had a baby last year, big news. I suspect that *she* is one of Lavinia's runners. Watch yourself. She'll be after anything to make you look bad, darling. I'll see if I can brace her in the loos.'

Duly briefed, I walked over to Daisy and was introduced to Abz. I've always wanted to know Daisy better and, with no

Johnnie at my shoulder, now was the time. She's a sweet girl and has always been lovely about my content.

'Can I just say how inspiring I think you are, Isabella?' Daisy was gazing at me as though I were some kind of icon. Not so bad for the Old Lady of Instagram! 'I had my second baby just before Christmas and I struggled so much. I thought it would be easier second time around, but it was harder! I felt like I was in a fog, but I'd signed the book deal and I felt I had to keep on posting more and more content to keep my followers happy. When I read that piece you did on sleep deprivation, I realised I could be honest. I've had more interaction and more followers ever since and it's all down to you!'

I felt ridiculously pleased that my step into the unknown world of honesty and transparency had had such a beneficial effect. I took a seat at the bar and we talked babies, nappies, feeding, stretch marks (not that I have any – a proprietary blend of coconut oil and lavender extract is my secret) and relationships. It felt pretty good, I have to say. I found myself dishing out advice to Daisy and Abz, which they seemed to be very grateful for. Who knew?

Glancing over my shoulder, I saw the furtive-looking woman scribbling notes. I warned the girls to stay away from her and worked the rest of the room.

'Mandy! Darling, how *are* you? Congrats on Megan's book deal and that great new range of vegan yoghurt. I tried the hazelnut one – delicious!'

I've always been very fond of Mandeep. Before he set up on his own, he was married to Mimi, which deserves a special award all of its own. He was her second, I think. Lovely man.

As I was about to approach Denizia, the lights dimmed and inspirational music started playing. It was time for the fun to start. I glanced down to see how things were looking in the northernmost reaches of my outfit (generous, but manageable), checked my phone for texts from Silvia (none) and glided over to my table. Someone had decided it was a good idea

to place me next to Portia and Nigel. Great **#creepynigel**
#amplebosoms #keepsmiling

Ever since I met Claire and realised that it's possible to be nice
and yet still get on in life, I have been trying to be a better
person. However, after a night spent with the dullest woman in
blogging and her pervy husband, I'd like to go on record as
saying that they are both *awful*.

Portia kicked things off by leaning over and whispering, 'Still
not back with Johnnie? Nigel and I were so surprised to hear
you'd let him slip through your fingers. Such a charming man.
Is he still with your little nanny?'

Hard on the heels of this tactless conversational opener,
Nigel put his hand on my leg, leaned over to get a better view
of my cleavage and opined that Johnnie was a fool who didn't
know a good thing when he saw it. I slapped his hand off and
discreetly ran my fingers over the tines of my fork. Nice and
sharp. Good.

Thank heavens for Bendy Wendy and Denizia who were
seated on my other side.

Once the opening presentation was over, the lights went up
and dinner was served. We started with hand-dived scallops
with roasted chicken butter (delicious), then enjoyed
Vietnamese lime leaf chicken, smoked new potatoes with caper
and basil dressing and crunchy Asian slaw. I could feel the
contents of my elegant black lace-trimmed *Je T'Aime Maman*
throbbing, a bad sign. There was plenty of room in there for
expansion, so I decided to go and have a pump after dessert.

As I nibbled on my miniature gooseberry crumble, I felt
rather than saw Nigel's lecherous gaze lighting upon my upper
portions once more. I flicked my eyes sideways and saw Portia
scowling at him. 'Close your mouth, dear,' she hissed. I took the
opportunity to drive my dessert fork into his hand, lying like a
limp rag on his leg, while smiling radiantly into his eyes. He let

out a muffled yelp and that, I would say, was a blow for women everywhere. **#stopstaring #notanobject #perve**

It was a wonderful night and I think my favourite bit was not winning all those awards, but listening to Daisy's emotional acceptance speech for Best Blog-Related Book. She namechecked me not once, not twice but thrice and referred to me as an important and supportive member of the blogging community. I got a standing ovation.

I could see Lavinia's runner making frantic notes, but I didn't care. I had won more than awards. The respect and affection of my peers, victory over pervy Nigel and the realisation that I can do this on my own. I stayed until midnight and talked to everyone, and I can honestly say that I had the best time ever. **#happy #itsnotjustaboutwinning #lifelessons**

July

I have vowed to be spontaneously encouraging and inspirational more often. When I woke up, however, I had a bit of a head. I took a long, hot shower, gave my hair a deep condition, and exfoliated. By the time I ran downstairs, I was feeling young and perky. The baby was fast asleep in front of the washing machine, Deep Purple playing in the background. Silvia had loaded the dishwasher and hung out a wash, as well as getting the children off to school. **#solucky #routines**

It's been exactly a year since I found out that my husband was cheating on me with my au pair. I've gained one child, three-quarters of a stone and some cellulite I have no use for. In spite of that, I feel more confident, have an exhibition at a gallery coming up and my new book is doing really well. They're calling it my best yet.

But I'm racing ahead of myself. I haven't told you about my birthday, which was excellent. I still had lingering feelings of regret about being parted from Johnnie on such an important date, but those feelings took a bit of a battering after school on Wednesday. I was still on cloud nine from the Bloggers' Awards and was walking along the landing en route to my room to dig out a rather gorgeous ensemble from my dressing room for a fashion piece when I heard whispering from Elsie's room. Is it bad that I find out most of what I need to know about my children's mental states by eavesdropping outside their doors? **#dontjudgeme**

'… mustn't say anything in case you upset her.' It was Finn's voice. 'She's been crying a lot lately. You can always tell because she puts on that special big smile and the happy voice.'

'But if Daddy's sleeping in our house again, he must be coming back soon. And maybe that means Sofija is too. I miss her.' Elsie sounded suspiciously close to tears. I wanted to rush in and hug her and tell her it was all going to be all right, but that would have been entirely the wrong thing to do.

'Don't be such a baby, Elsie. Mum will never let Sofija come back, and if Dad was going to leave her, he would have by now. We have to get used to it. Loads of people in my class have got divorced parents. They all say it's good because you get extra presents.'

I could hear sniffing. 'But I don't want Daddy to live in London and Mummy to live here. I want everyone to be together again like they used to be. I don't like it like this.' Elsie was sobbing. I felt my heart break in two. What a mess. I walked noiselessly to my bedroom and texted Johnnie.

'Stop coming up here to see the children. Sort it out or you won't be seeing them at all. You've already caused enough damage. Don't forget this weekend coming's my birthday, so you're not needed.'

Ha!

I had a lovely week with Silvia, and I made an extra special effort to spend time with the children. I went to the park, I pushed Elsie on the swing, I bounced on the trampoline with them, we went for walks, we swam together and sometimes they talked to me about the stuff that matters to them. Maybe that's what good parenting is.

Naturally, that vicious reptile Lavinia couldn't resist writing a horrible piece about my triumph at the Awards.

Overweight, Overbearing, Overconfident: How Much Longer Must We Listen to this Nonsense?

Bragging blogger Isabella M Smugge has built her success on family values. Married with three unfortunate children whom she used, shamelessly, on her social media posts, the boastful bore exhausted everyone in London and fled to the country to chase after more followers.

As regular readers will recall, this was a mistake. For a year now, handsome Mr Smugge has been in the arms of a much younger, prettier woman and shows no signs of ever leaving.

When she was still married, Smugge wrote a particularly nauseating book, called *Issy Smugge Says: Turn the Lights Down Low*, in which she instructed the rest of us on how to keep our relationships healthy. Oh, the irony! If only she had followed her own advice, perhaps she wouldn't be sitting alone in her echoing mansion, a congealed TV dinner for one sitting at her elbow.

Not content with clogging up the internet with her unwanted advice, the sickly scribbler recently attended the Bloggers' Awards in London. A source close to the organisers told me, 'She spent most of her evening drinking heavily and schmoozing with younger, edgier bloggers. It was pathetic. Obviously no one really wanted her there. The organisers gave her some awards, presumably to keep her quiet. She's pushing forty yet still squeezing into fashionable clothes which really don't suit her.'

For everyone's sake, Isabella M Smugge, take the hint and turn off your laptop.

The piece was accompanied by a blurred photo of me with my mouth open holding a champagne flute. I am going to have to do something about Lavinia Harcourt. And soon.

I was restless on Thursday morning. I couldn't seem to settle to anything. I took a turn around the garden, which is looking particularly lovely, and ran into Ted.

'Morning, Missus. Raspberries have got cane blight. Gooseberries looking good, though. Are you picking them and making jam again this year? For the babies in Africa?'

I confirmed that I was and shared the news that Jess and Andy, the people who look after babies in Kenya, would be coming to stay for a fortnight later on in the month. I followed my gardener into the fruit cage where I was given a guided tour of the redcurrants, blackcurrants, gooseberries, rhubarb and the blighted raspberries. 'They wants a good prune, they do, Missus. I'll be at them with the secateurs soon.'

What a delightfully simple life Ted leads. How wonderful it would be to spend my days snipping bits off plants and mowing the lawn. Chance would be a fine thing. My phone beeped. A direct message on Twitter from Daisy Finch. *'Hey Isabella. How are you? Was chatting to Abz and we hated what Lavinia wrote about you. How about a bloggers lift tomorrow? We'll start it. Got a hashtag too. #weloveissysmugge xx'*

I took a deep breath of fragrant summer air and thanked whoever was listening. Yes! A bloggers lift and a new hashtag. Maybe this was just what I needed to get Lavinia off my back.

Even though it's my fortieth, I haven't really allowed myself to think much about it. I know it's the new thirty and all that, but it's still an awful lot of years for a person to accumulate. A huge bouquet of flowers arrived this morning with a card from Johnnie saying nice yet shallow things. Just a few weeks ago, I'd have taken it as a good sign. Now I'm not so sure.

The plan had been for me to be driven to the Greedy Pig at seven on Saturday night. However, Davina suddenly got in touch asking if she and Toby could treat me to a stay in a gorgeous local boutique hotel and spa. They want to take me there on Friday for afternoon tea and have booked us in for hot stone massages at 3pm on Saturday. I say us. I mean Davina and me. I can't imagine Toby supine on a massage table covered in essential oils. No offence.

I texted Lauren to ask if that wasn't cutting it a bit fine. She replied saying it was no problem. She's invited Davina too. Which is nice as she doesn't know her from Adam.

I've asked Ali to make up the second guest suite for Toby, Davina and Baby Matthew. Silvia is staying until Monday lunchtime then going home with them. She is the best grandmother in the world. I took the plunge and invited Mummy (it is a milestone birthday, after all) but she declined, none too politely, telling me she's far too busy with settling herself into the new house to come up to Suffolk again. Oh well.

I awoke on Friday morning to the baby crying. Sighing, I changed and fed him and wandered down the stairs in my dressing gown with him over my shoulder. It was only 6.30 so I took the risk and went for an early morning swim in my lovely heated pool. I strapped the baby into his pram and put some Hawkwind on the sound system. He was asleep in minutes and I powered up and down the pool at top speed, driven on by the pounding rhythms. I felt incredibly energised as I showered and dried myself – this is what has been missing from my life! Regular exercise. I made a note to myself to build swimming back into my routine. That and getting revenge on Hayley and Lavinia. And getting Johnnie back. And losing three-quarters of a stone. Honestly. A woman's work is never done.

Ali had made and dressed the beds in the two guest suites and sorted out clean towels, but I always do the flowers. I ambled out to the flower garden to select the correct blooms, but was surprised to see that the Sweet William had been severely denuded and that there were virtually no pinks left. Had there been an outburst of mollusc activity? Ted was off, so I couldn't ask him. I used my initiative and harvested some foliage from various shrubs plus a small bunch of roses. That would just have to do.

I had the most marvellous time at the hotel. Davina was unsure about leaving the son and heir with Silvia, but I assured her that our mother-in-law was more than capable of looking after babies. She's looking very squat, carrying to the front and suffering badly from heartburn. I was heartened to see that she'd kept her hair nice. We both texted Silvia for updates and were assured that Baby Matthew and my little Milo were having a perfectly splendid evening.

Nestling into the crisp white sheets of my hotel bed, I breathed a long sigh and let my mind empty. I find it almost impossible to let myself be in the now and, of late, have been trying very hard to be more relaxed and present. I resisted the impulse to check my phone. Daisy and Abz had been as good as their word and **#weloveissysmugge** was trending. Messages of support were pouring in and a new hashtag had emerged. **#shutupharcourt** Ha!

I had a leisurely breakfast with Davina and Toby, we all went for a swim and steam and then a walk in the hotel grounds. I was a bit concerned about fitting in my hair and make-up post-massage, but Davina assured me there would be plenty of time. Although what does she really know about appearance, God bless her.

I'd had my nails painted an achingly on-trend cornflower blue. Feeling delightfully chilled after my massage, I put my hair up, applied a light make-up and spritzed myself with perfume. I had to keep reminding myself that I was only going to a Suffolk pub with the girls and that there was no need to dress myself up to the nines. I slipped into a cotton-knit ribbed sweater dress and a pair of nude heels and accessorised with a pair of chocolate metallic hoop earrings and a chunky bangle.

Davina appeared, dressed in absolutely the wrong colour and style, but beaming. I have grown so fond of her over the last year. Her good nature is infectious and she and Toby have been an absolute tower of strength. I found myself beaming back as she said she'd be driving us to the pub. 'I'm not drinking, so I might as well. Your friend Lauren said she'd meet us there.'

The table was booked for 7pm and I estimated it would take nearly an hour to get to the pub. I was a little surprised that the girls had chosen a pub on the other side of the county, but it wasn't for me to ask questions. Gorgeously dressed and fragranced, I climbed into Davina's battered Land Rover and we drove Toby back to the Old Rectory.

'Drop me at the gate, darling. I don't want you being late. Have a super time.'

We'd been driving for about ten minutes when Davina's mobile rang. It was Silvia. I picked it up and put it on speakerphone.

'I don't want to worry you, but little Matthew is running a temperature and won't have his teatime bottle. I've given him some medicine but he's quite distressed. Toby didn't want to ruin your evening, but is there any chance you can pop back just to see what you think?'

Poor Davina was distraught. I assured her that we had time and she executed a surprisingly tight three-point turn and sped back in the direction of the Old Rectory. We were about five minutes away when the phone rang again.

'Darling, I am so sorry, but poor little Elsie has taken a tumble and banged her head. She slipped on the stairs. Do you mind popping in too just to check on her?'

Honestly. My one chance at a girls' night out and it was being ruined by bellowing babies and careless footwork. I tried to hide my annoyance from Davina, who is a far better mother than I will ever be. We screeched to a halt on the drive. Davina galloped up to the front door and I wasn't far behind her.

I couldn't hear any crying, or in fact any noise at all. For a house containing an overheated baby and a severely bruised seven-year-old, it was remarkably quiet. I walked through the hall and pushed the kitchen door open, only to be struck dumb by the sight of what seemed to be hundreds of people clustering around my island shouting, 'Surprise!'

I've thrown plenty of surprise parties in my time, but no one has ever done one for me. I was so taken aback that I just stood there, my mouth open, gazing at the balloons, the posters, the flowers and my mother, who stood in front of me with Milo in her arms. Lauren and the girls were grinning all over their faces, the children were jumping up and down and, far from running a temperature, Baby Matthew was safe in his father's arms, beaming and showing off all four of his teeth.

'Does this mean we're not going to the Greedy Pig after all?' I enquired, a perfectly reasonable question, but one that was met with gales of laughter. I was furnished with a flute of champagne and invited to take a seat and be filled in.

The whole thing had been in the planning for weeks. Lauren, Claire, Maddie, Kate and Lou had wanted to take me out, but then had come up with the idea of a surprise party. A WhatsApp group had been formed and my sneaky mother-in-law had been the driving force. The reason that the flowerbeds were half-empty was because the entire second floor was decked out for my guests.

It seems that I have my mother, my mother-in-law, Davina, Toby and Baby Matthew, Rafe and Xenia, Suze, Jeremy and Lily and the Hartingtons staying tonight! Seeing nearly all of my family and most of my friends gathered together in one place was wonderful. Davina had been in on the plan for weeks and the whole hotel thing was a ruse to get me out of the way. In the back garden, fairy lights were strung in the trees and music was playing. It was perfect. Absolutely perfect.

Also, **#shutupharcourt** is trending. And I'm a meme. Hooray! Maybe having racked up quite so many years isn't so terrible after all. **#happybirthdaytome #issybouncesback #fabulousatforty**

I don't know about you, but sometimes the most profound thoughts pop into your head at the strangest times. I was dancing, hands in the air (and I absolutely did not care, let me say), looking up at the blanket of stars above me and I suddenly realised that thinking of Johnnie was OK. The stab of pain to the heart that normally accompanied such thoughts had gone. Here I was, surrounded by people who loved me and cared about me, no one was telling me to stop dancing and making a show of myself and I hadn't had to organise a single, solitary thing.

I am the luckiest girl in the world to have such wonderful, supportive friends. We had a scratch lunch in the garden on Sunday and it was lovely to see different people from different parts of my life getting to know each other. Charlene came with Jake, which made me very happy. She's been seeing a counsellor about her anxiety, and while it's early days, she's definitely improving.

On Monday morning, I floated into the playground with the children, pushing Milo in his pram and actually looking forward to the week. I can't remember the last time I felt like that.

Actually, I can.

It was the day before I found out.

Back at home, Milo fed, changed and parked in front of a hot wash, I stood at the island opening the post. A small hand-tied bouquet of flowers had been delivered while I was out. I didn't have to open the card to know who it was from. Who else would have taken the time and trouble to choose each and every one of my very favourite flowers? I closed my eyes and inhaled the delicate fragrance, brushed my cheek against the soft petals then dropped it into the bin.

Over the years, people have often told me that they envy me. 'You're so lucky to be able to work from home,' they say. 'I wish I could make my living just sitting at my desk writing things and taking photos of my house.' When you work from home, you're never not at work. My phone is constantly pinging with notifications and while many of them can be ignored, often they are telling me that something really important has just happened. This was the case today.

I was halfway through a piece I'd been dreading on coping with difficult situations. My new honest style has really hit the spot, and gradually, I've been revealing more of my struggles to my followers. Most of them are responding with huge empathy and compassion, God bless them, and Harpreet is over the moon with the stats and the engagement. I even took a picture of my bedroom with the bed unmade and nappies and wipes scattered over it the other day. Believe me, that might not sound like much, but for Isabella M Smugge, doyenne of inspirational lifestyle bloggers everywhere, it was a huge step.

People talk about the tyranny of the blank screen and I can tell you, it's a thing. I had taken an hour to produce three paragraphs and had just hit my stride when my phone went mad. I turned it to vibrate and carried on writing, but after a few minutes, the incessant buzzing was driving me crazy. Three texts, an email and a missed call from Mimi. This probably wasn't good.

'Sweetheart, call me. Lavinia's posted a really nasty piece and you need to see it.'

I clicked on the link Mimi had sent and read the words with a mounting sense of panic. I couldn't blame Hayley for any of it. This was coming from someone else, and as my heart sank into my boots, I realised who.

A Friend in Need: No Indeed. The Dark Side of Isabella M Smugge

How does it feel to have to watch a woman who claimed to be your friend babble about love and friendship and forgiveness every day and feel powerless to do anything about it?

Annoying Bragstagrammer Smugge has been taking a different tone since her dashing hedge fund manager husband left her for a younger woman. It's all about honesty, she says, sharing nauseating snaps of her perfect life and dropping in the odd disingenuous remark about unmade beds and takeaways.

The selfish scribbler never posts anything without an eye to what she can gain from it. Whether it's more followers, better engagement or selling more of her frightful self-help manuals, she only cares about herself.

And no one knows this better than a former friend, who doesn't want to be named, for her own protection. 'We were so close, Lavinia,' she confided to me. 'I thought we'd be friends forever. We holidayed together and had so many shared passions.'

It all went wrong when the blogger's husband did a dodgy deal at work. 'I confronted her about it, of course, but she totally took his side. It broke my heart when our friendship ended. Looking back, I can see that they were both users. They only cared about us when we were useful to them. It's hard to have to watch her bragging about her wonderful house and children and to know the truth.'

I asked this poor betrayed woman if she had a message for the arrogant author. 'I'd want to say to her,

"Watch your back, Issy." I fear for her new friends in the country. They don't know who she truly is. I hope they don't feel the bitter sting of betrayal as I did.'

Two-faced schemer? User? Bad friend? Lavinia Harcourt Says It Like It Is.

Mimi and I were on the phone for an hour talking damage limitation. This is all Johnnie's fault and I'm paying the price for it. What I want to know, though, is why now? After all these years? What has brought this on? And what, if anything, can I do about it? **#pastpain #sadface #oldfriends**

When Johnnie and I were first married, we had a couple of really close friends called Josh and Kat. He worked on the same trading floor as Johnnie, she was in music PR. We got on brilliantly, went on holiday together, thought we would be friends for life. Kat and I were like sisters, which was just as well since my actual sister was hardly speaking to me at the time.

We'd just got back from a mini-break to Crete when Johnnie came home from work one night with that look on his face I'd come to dread. 'What's the matter, darling?' I asked, pouring him a glass of fizz. 'Bad day at the office?'

His face darkened. 'I'm not in the mood for jokes, Iss. Josh has completely lost his sense of humour. Pulled me up on a deal in front of everyone. I can't believe it.'

He drained his glass and waved it at me.

'Would sir like a little more?' I gave him a cheeky grin.

'Shut up, Iss! I told you, I'm not in the mood.' He snatched the bottle from me and poured himself another drink, leaving my glass half full. 'I'm going to have to spend what's left of tonight working and sorting out the mess Josh made.' He walked out, slamming the door, leaving me feeling as though I had been slapped in the face.

I texted Kat. *'Hi, boys have had falling out at work. Are you OK? xx'*

Nothing for ages, which was unheard of, then just as I was taking my make-up off and getting ready for bed, she replied.

'Hi. They have. Josh is really upset, thinking about leaving. Johnnie has behaved in such a dishonourable way. Sorry to upset you, Issy, but we can't believe it xx'

I suggested we met for a drink after work the following day and left it at that. Johnnie came to bed at two and was up and out again at six, leaving me to shower and get ready for my own day alone.

Nursing a Cosmopolitan and nibbling on some organic cashews, I waited for Kat at our favourite bar. She was ten minutes late and looked unhappy and confused when she arrived. Even now, I can't remember our conversation without pain. I felt torn between Johnnie and my best friend. That wrenching feeling of divided loyalties hurts my heart to this day.

We talked and talked and tried to come to an amicable conclusion, but Kat kept on coming back to what she called Johnnie's dishonourable behaviour. 'He's put Josh in an impossible position. Everyone knows Johnnie's the golden boy at work and can do no wrong, and people are questioning Josh's motives. Someone accused him of trying to get Johnnie's job, but honestly, nothing could be further from the truth. Josh looks on him as a brother.'

I ordered us a couple more drinks and assured Kat that I would get to the bottom of it. As I came back from the loo, I saw my friend texting with an earnest expression on her face. She jumped as I pulled my chair back.

'That was Meredith. I hope you don't mind, but I told her what happened.'

I did mind but of course didn't say anything. The night came to an end inconclusively and the next morning I had a headache from one Cosmopolitan too many. **#sadmemories #friendshipsplit #onetoomany**

We never did make up. Johnnie got offered a fantastic job with more pay and benefits, which of course he took, and Josh carried on toiling away on the trading floor. I check him out on LinkedIn from time to time. He's a financial consultant these days. Johnnie was wrong. I knew that at the time, but what could I do? I'd given up so much to be with him and he valued loyalty above all other qualities. I stayed friends with Meredith, and for all I know, so did Kat. In fact, reading Lavinia's poisonous prose, I would imagine that she had urged Kat to take my old enemy's blood money and stir up painful memories.

Sitting on my bed, sobbing helplessly, I looked up and saw my face in the mirror and, for a split second, it was like looking at little Bella Neville, locked in the loo at St Dymphna's, crying without sound and yearning to be back at home.

These days, I would have stood up to Johnnie and made it right with our friends. Back then, I was far too afraid of losing him. I took some deep breaths, cleansed, toned and moisturised, applied more make-up and got myself ready to walk down to the school. My heart was banging in my chest and my palms were sweating with fear.

Once upon a time, I would march onto the playground, head held high, and brazen it out. The new me is terrified that my lovely friends will read the article and believe it. It's only now, with those spiteful words ringing in my ears, that I truly realise what a blessing they all are to me. I donned my biggest sunglasses and sidled onto the playground, trying to be invisible.

Liane Bloomfield and her foghorn voice put a stop to that.

'Oi! Smug! What's going down? Tell us the goss!'

Heads turned as she barrelled towards me, resplendent in her shocking-pink smock.

'Nothing much, Liane. Just some made-up nonsense from the past.' I spoke in a breathy whisper, hoping that my frenemy would pick up on the cue. No such luck.

'The bitter sting of betrayal? What did you do to her, Smug? I'd better watch my back at toddlers! You'll have all the chocolate digestives away if I'm not careful.'

She appeared to be laughing at my pain. I still don't really know how to handle her. Just then, Claire and Tom appeared at my elbow. They seemed to be pleased to see me, but that could be because they are good and holy people who don't believe what they read in the newspapers. Or that they don't have time to read the newspapers. Or that they have read them, believed what Lavinia wrote and wanted to have a quiet, non-judgemental chat with me back at the vicarage.

'Hello, Liane. How are you? How's the new job?' Tom was smiling at Liane and rocking Ben gently in his pram.

'Can't complain. It pays better than cleaning and I like working with the oldies. Just having a chat with this two-faced schemer here. The bad friend.' She chuckled and started rolling a cigarette.

I could feel my cheeks flaming.

'How do you mean?' Claire was looking puzzled.

'Hang on, let me get it up on my phone.' Liane started scrolling through her feed and I felt my eyes fill with tears as I faced up to the end of my lovely friendships.

'Is everything OK, Isabella?' Claire laid her hand gently on my arm. I felt a tear trickle down my cheek.

'Here we go. *A friend in need* blah blah blah, *unmade beds and takeaways* (get you, Smug!) the *selfish scribbler* blah blah blah. Oh, here it is. *I fear for her new friends in the country. They don't know who she truly is. I hope they don't feel the bitter sting of betrayal as I did.* She fears for us! That's nice of her.'

I couldn't speak. Thank goodness I've let my hair grow since I had Milo. I looked at the ground, letting my well-conditioned locks cover my face, hoping that no one could see the tears running down my cheeks.

'What are you talking about? Who's saying those things about Isabella?' Claire sounded quite cross.

'That woman she was at school with. The one who bullied her sister and then Isabella cut off one of her plaits. She's written a piece about her. Someone else has come forward to say how horrible Smug is. Fame at last!'

I managed to stutter out a few words. 'I can explain. She's made it sound so awful, but it honestly wasn't like that.'

To my amazement, I was enveloped in a hug. 'Don't be so silly! We know you well enough for that kind of spiteful nonsense to make no difference at all. Please don't let it upset you. Is there some way we can get in touch with the paper to put our views across?'

I love Claire. I sobbed moistly on her shoulder while Liane read the rest of the article out to Tom. To my embarrassment, we were joined by Kate and Lauren who also wanted to know what was going on. Liane explained at the top of her voice and slapped me on the back.

'Don't be so wet, Smug! We know it's rubbish. And if it isn't and you really are a bad friend, at least we've got the heads up. Gotta go. See ya!'

And she was off, leaving me with my cheeks tear-stained, my hair a mess and my mascara running.

My friends clustered around me, assuring me that they were on my side and didn't believe a word of Lavinia's poisonous prose. The whole thing had really shaken me, so I accepted Claire's offer of a coffee. I let Finn run home with Harry (playdate tonight) and trundled towards the vicarage, safe in the knowledge that at least there I was not thought of as a two-faced schemer. #truefriends #blastfromthepast

My new book is out! They're calling it a triumph, which it jolly well is! I am in a whirl of marketing and media, which is just as well as I need something positive to drive those painful memories from my mind. Three radio interviews this week. Hooray!

Sitting in the green room at the local radio station, about to launch myself on the airwaves with Lucy Salmon's flagship show (*Salmon's Super Suffolk*), I engaged in light chit-chat with the researcher, who told me she was one of my biggest fans. 'Your books are amazing! I've got them all. Can I be cheeky and ask you to sign this one?'

I was delighted, of course, and we chatted about my concept of elevating the everyday and giving your home a touch of instant elegance. As I always say, you can turn even the most mundane meal into an occasion with runners, fresh flowers and candles. Switch up your interiors with a new lamp, rugs and throws and even by changing the angle of your furniture. It's not hard when you think about it, but so few people do, and that's why my books are bestsellers.

On the sofa with Lucy Salmon, we chatted at length about my move to Suffolk, what I think about the county and how my work has been affected by it. We were doing really well, talking about room refreshes and how to dress a bed properly, when she cut to traffic and asked me if I minded talking about Lavinia Harcourt.

Naturally concerned that traffic was heavy at the Copdock Interchange and that there were long delays on the A140 owing to roadworks, the traffic person went on a bit, giving me a chance to take some deep breaths and think about what to say. For some reason, a sermon I'd heard Keith preach a few weeks ago popped into my head. 'Pray at all times, wherever you are, and for whatever you need. On a bus? Pray. In the loo? Pray. At work? Pray. The more you do it, the more coincidences will start to happen.'

At the time, I'd thought it all sounded a bit crazy, but I like Keith and he seems to know what he's talking about, so as the traffic person rounded off with heartening news about the burst water main in Felixstowe, I addressed the good Lord.

'Isabella Smugge here. Can You help me to say the right sort of things about Lavinia, please? I'm tired of her attacking me all the time and I want it to stop. Also I am very upset about Josh and Kat. What should I do? Thank You. Amen.'

I waited for an answer, but all that happened was that the word 'forgiveness' popped into my mind. Nonsense, of course. I knew that Lavinia would never forgive me.

Lucy played an uplifting jingle and reassured her listeners that she was back.

'I'm on the sofa with Isabella M Smugge, lifestyle blogger and bestselling author. Isabella, you've got millions of followers, your books sell like hot cakes and you're generally considered to be at the top of your game. How do you feel about the constant attacks in the national press via Lavinia Harcourt's column? From where I'm sitting, it looks pretty personal.'

When on the radio, it's vital not to gabble. Speak more slowly and at a lower pitch than you normally would, and if a question throws you off, counter with, 'Hmm. That's such an interesting question.'

I applied this rule and replied to my hostess in a calm and measured manner.

'What most of your listeners won't know, Lucy, is that Lavinia and I were at school together. She was a couple of years below me. I can remember the first time I saw her. Such a pretty girl with blue eyes and long blonde plaits.'

I smiled graciously. So far, so good. A plan was forming in my mind.

'Were you friends at school? Did you have some kind of spat on the hockey field?'

I shook my head. 'Oh no. We weren't friends. Then, as now, Lavinia was a powerful personality, someone who was able to engage with people. My younger sister was in her year and she suffered intense bullying from Lavinia and her friends. As her older sister, I'd always felt very protective of her. I wonder what you would do, Lucy, if your little sister bit her nails until they bled and told you that she would rather die than go back to school? How would you react, do you think?'

'So you're saying that Lavinia Harcourt was a bully?'

'She was, and she is, Lucy. I took decisive action to protect my little sister. Lavinia was very proud of her hair. One night, I sneaked into her dorm and cut off one of her plaits. She knew it was me, although nothing was ever proved. The next week, we came to blows over it. She vowed to get revenge and this is it. A forty-year-old woman locked in deadly enmity with a thirty-eight-year-old woman.'

'Goodness. That's quite a story. Are you saying that one of the country's most successful journalists still holds a grudge from thirty years ago?'

Well, duh, as the kids say.

'Yes. That does seem to be the case. I understand that she has even been paying someone in my village, right here in Suffolk, to spy on me. It's hard to read such vitriol, especially knowing that someone you see every day is reporting back on your every move.'

Lucy Salmon seemed taken aback. I don't suppose she gets internationally acclaimed lifestyle bloggers sitting in her studio every day, and certainly not ones who have a vendetta against them. She decided to play a song, giving me the chance to regroup and take a bold decision about what to say next. It was a huge risk, but maybe the time had come to step out into the abyss. I double-checked with God and seemed to hear a quiet voice whisper, 'Try it and see what happens.' Sleep deprivation, probably. Aural hallucinations. But it was worth a try.

As the final notes died away, we were back. I took a deep breath. Show time!

Who knew that so many people listen to local radio? I was mobbed in the playground and Claire gave me a huge hug.

'I am so proud of you! You did exactly the right thing and it can't have been easy.'

'Babes, you are the biz.' Lauren was grinning at me. 'You really have been listening in church!'

They all seemed hugely impressed by the fact that I'd been on the radio. Issy Smugge is no stranger to broadcast media and has been featured on all the major TV channels in her time. However, an interview with a woman in a studio in Suffolk seems to have been pivotal in a way the others haven't. Strange.

I could see hirsute Hayley lurking by the veranda, staring at me. I smiled radiantly and waved at her. Hopefully, her kitchen is all bought and paid for, otherwise she's going to be living on a building site for the rest of her life.

I have been up and down to the high school with Finn any number of times, attended talks and orientation meetings, bought all his new school uniform, met the girls' teachers for next year, gone to Sports Day (surprisingly good fun), accompanied the children to the school disco, where I sat in the dark for two hours giving them money for glow sticks and cheap sweets, and made a donation to the school library.

Silence from Lavinia. I expect she's sharpening her quill and harvesting the blood of slain fawns, or whatever it is she writes with.

I've just read Daisy Finch's autobiography, *Daisy, Daisy*. It's a strangely moving read, very honest about her various struggles and rather touching. We bloggers have got the top five spots in the *Sunday Times* Bestsellers List. I'm at Number One, Daisy is Number Two, a rather annoying braggy fitspo woman from Australia has bagged the Number Three spot, Abz's first book is at Number Four and the reissue of *Issy Smugge Says: Let's Move to the Country* has come in at Number Five. All the literary types are backed up from Number Six onwards. I take my hat off to anyone who can write fiction. I don't know how they do it.

This weekend, the children were collected by Johnnie and taken to a hotel in Essex. He plans to take them to one of those places where you swing on ropes and walk along high platforms through the trees. I assume Sofija will be there. None of my business, really.

I took the opportunity to get everything ready for Jess and Andy, who arrive on Tuesday. I'm putting them in my beautiful guest suite and am hoping that enough flowers will have grown back in the garden for me to decorate accordingly. I'm feeling a little nervous about having two such holy people living in my house. What will I talk to them about? What if they judge me for not going to church every week or being unsure about God and stuff? I've been reading a chapter of the rebooted version of the Bible every night on my phone, just so I'm up to speed. I started with the Old Testament, but it didn't really do it for me, so I am currently ploughing through Luke. Not as boring as I thought it would be. Quite a good narrative flow.

A text from an unknown number. A question. Just five words. I knew who it was, of course. I sat down on my bed and thought long and hard before replying. This is huge. Life-changing. I hope I've made the right decision.

I went to church on Sunday. Several people hugged me and said they'd heard me on the radio. I seem to have done the right thing. It feels good.

They read out some stuff from the traditional Bible which I liked. 'Take delight in the LORD, and he will give you the desires of your heart.'[5] I'm not quite sure how to do that, but the desires of my heart aren't what they used to be.

---

[5] Psalm 37:4, NIV.

My social life has gone insane! Liane has invited me to the toddler girls' night out at the beginning of August.

'Dress up, go to the Grasshopper for some food to line our stomachs, then off to Fluid till 1am, back home via the squirt wagon.'

I was quietly distressed to realise that I had no idea what she was talking about. Liane rolled her eyes. 'Where have you been, Smug? Grasshopper. Pub in Ipswich that does cheap food. A night up Fluid's. Best club around. My cousin's the doorman. He'll let us in half price. Try not to show yourself up.'

I wasn't at all sure that it was up my street, but I felt rather privileged to be asked. Lauren will be there, as an honorary former member of toddlers, but it's mostly people I don't know that well. 'Is Hayley coming?'

'Probably.' Liane curled her lip. 'She doesn't drink and she hates dancing, but she can't bear the thought of missing out. Watch yourself, she'll be ready to spill the beans on anything she thinks that woman might be interested in.'

Liane Bloomfield clearly doesn't listen to the radio.

Jess and Andy are nothing like I expected! They seem completely normal, even though they are top-notch Christians who do good things 24/7. I did a low-key supper of baked mango chicken with spicy Asian noodles which I thought might hit the spot. They seemed rather overwhelmed.

'It's nothing to do with the meal, Isabella. It's delicious. You're so kind to put yourself to all this trouble on our account. It's hard for us to get back into Western culture after so long in Kenya. We live very simply and eat a very basic menu.'

This had not occurred to me. I made a pot of tea and invited them to sit out in the garden with me. The birds were singing, the sky was a beautiful pink and the fragrance of flowers drifted across to us on the terrace. We talked until it was late and I went to bed pondering on the things they'd told me. What a useless, shallow life I have led! I must give more to charity and do more good things.

Keith wasn't wrong. Jess and Andy are out nearly every night. Over a leisurely breakfast in the garden (toasted Suffolk trencher, butter and some of Wendy's delicious jam), I asked why they were dashing about the county to such an extent.

'We're visiting all our supporters and that means a lot of travelling. Quite a few churches support us, we've got our prayer and support team, the fundraising group and various people who are key to what we do out in Kenya. Without them, we couldn't do even a tenth of what we want to.'

I was impressed with their drive, but couldn't help wondering why they'd decided to take such a difficult path.

'Couldn't you have stayed here in Suffolk, kept your jobs and just given money? Call me shallow, but that's what I would do. And don't you miss your children and all the home comforts?'

I saw a shadow pass across Jess' face and regretted my words immediately.

'I'm sorry, that sounded crass.' I poured her another cup of English Breakfast tea.

'Not at all, Isabella. We do miss our children very much, but our youngest started uni the year we left and they're all pretty much independent now. Even considering that, I can completely understand that our decision might look a bit strange. We both felt a nudge and heard a little voice, quite independently of each other. We prayed it through and then met up with some of our closest friends to investigate. I suppose we met about six times to pray and then people started getting words from God about what we should do.'

We were back on shaky ground as far as I was concerned. I chewed my toast and washed it down with a gulp of single-origin decaf coffee.

'See, I've heard this kind of thing at church. What do you mean, a word? How you can hear what He's saying? It's not like texting or Snapchat. That I get.'

Andy explained at some length how the good Lord communicates. He's got a lovely way about him. At no time did I feel as though I were being lectured, although perhaps the fact that Milo, who was asleep on his lap, let out the most enormous gust of wind halfway through the explanation added to the informal tone. I still wasn't sure, though.

'I don't mean to sound cynical, but I don't understand a lot of the stuff they talk about at church. Can you give me an everyday example? Some kind of proof that it really was God talking and not your imagination. Sorry, I don't mean to be rude.'

Jess told me that for the first year out in Kenya, they were living hand to mouth. They had no funds, no grants and the government gave them nothing. Every time the local children's officer referred a pregnant girl to them, they prayed and then said yes. Soon, they had two fifteen-year-olds, a fourteen-year-old and three babies living with them. One of the fifteen-year-olds was HIV-positive.

'We prayed about everything and asked God to provide for us. We always had just enough, although often the figures didn't seem to add up. The first time we flew back to England, we met up with our fundraising group. We looked at the accounts and found that each month, we needed a further £200 to make ends meet. When we took the amount the group had raised throughout the year and divided it by twelve, it came to £200 exactly. We took that as a sign.'

I meditated on this as I chewed thoughtfully on my toast. Maybe there was more to this religion lark than I had realised. **#newideas #spiritualrealms**

I waved Jess and Andy off with genuine regret. They are absolutely delightful and also (and I think this is key) seem like the kind of people you meet in everyday life. I was expecting them to float in with harps in their hand luggage, clad in white raiment, but apart from the fact that they genuinely think God told them to go to Kenya, they could pass for ordinary, everyday folk.

Still nothing about me in Lavinia's column, but I am everywhere else! Snippets about my blog, book reviews (all very positive), think pieces – I am hot news! A text from Mimi.

'Darling, how do you feel about doing a double page spread in Lavinia's rag? Her editor's practically on bended knee to me. Your take on the whole bullying thing, photos, pull quotes, the lot.'

As I'm sure you know if you read the papers, many of the nationals enjoy setting their top columnists against each other from time to time. Lavinia is queen bee at her paper, but Debbie Bosworth ('Bosworth Beholds') isn't far behind. They don't get on at all, hence the editor's brilliant idea to sell a few more copies by getting Debbie to interview me.

I gave Mimi the green light and settled down to write some content. I must start selecting photographs for the upcoming exhibition too. It's all go!

I have lost 5lb! The joy of it. The time I used to spend writing about relationship enrichment is now spent swimming. Milo is still feeding like a vampire with a tapeworm so we must hope that his voracious appetite is having a reductive effect on my cellulite. At Finn's class assembly, Liane Bloomfield caught my eye across the hall and almost smiled. I have arrived!

Lavinia has struck back, as I knew she would. Today's edition of her frightful rag featured me and only me. I suppose I should be flattered. I'm not, obviously.

Delusions of Grandeur. Who Exactly Does Isabella M Smugge Think She Is?

As my dear mother used to say, 'Lavinia, you can't make a silk purse from a sow's ear.' However, that's exactly what hypocritical horror Isabella M Smugge has been doing for the last ten years, and those ears are lining her bottomless pockets. While most people would see sense and call it a day when dumped by the husband they've featured in nearly all their nauseating posts, Smugge is soldiering on all the way to the bank.

The manipulative mumfluencer has made her fortune by tricking her gullible followers into believing that they can mimic her lavish lifestyle. Smugge was born with a silver spoon in her mouth, benefited from an expensive private education and launched herself upon an unsuspecting world buoyed up by a trust fund. So far, so entitled. But there's more.

Since moving to the country, the two-faced troublemaker has allied herself with the local church in an effort to make herself look holier-than-thou. Her latest stunt was to go on a local radio station and deign to forgive me, Lavinia Harcourt, Journalist of the Year more times that I can remember. Smugge claims I bullied her sister at school. What she forgot to mention is that she, a much older and bulkier person, battered a defenceless nine-year-old without any provocation. That helpless child was me.

Sometimes, I dream that I am back at St Dymphna's, lying on the muddy lacrosse field and pleading with my attacker. My cries of pain go unheard as her fists rain blows upon my defenceless form.

Have I had flashbacks? Yes, I have. Has her violent attack mentally scarred me? Of course. Am I considering suing her? You read it here first.

Violent, greedy and manipulative, now Smugge adds double-dyed hypocrisy to her less-than-attractive qualities. This reporter's question to her is, 'How can you *ever* forgive yourself?'

I suppose it's a measure of how far I've come that rather than swooning on a convenient couch and then ringing Mimi for advice, I laughed so much that some of my coffee went up my nose and exited in a rather undignified fashion. As I remember it, that nine-year-old was far from defenceless! My bruises took weeks to fade completely.

It was a Sue day, so I pulled on my trainers and went for a refreshing three-mile run before coming back for a long, hot shower and a chat with Mimi. Sue me indeed! I'd like to see her try.

What a week! I fell into bed on Friday evening absolutely exhausted but with a sense of enormous well-being. I've been featured in any number of magazines and newspapers, trended on Twitter and all my stories on Instagram have gone viral.

Lavinia's spiteful comments caused a bit of a hoo-hah on Twitter, but that's only to be expected. Mimi and I agreed that ignoring it was the best thing to do. Mimi had a quiet word with Lavinia's editor and confirmed that her threats were groundless. Ha! Success is the best revenge. Not that I should be seeking revenge on my old enemy. I have had to put a reminder on my phone to forgive her every morning. It's not easy, I can tell you.

I am so excited about seeing Minty Pryke-Darby again! A wonderful weekend away for her hen party should take the nasty taste out of my mouth. Suze is staying over on Friday night, then we're driving up to a beautiful barn in Norfolk. Lauren, Scott and the girls are house-sitting and looking after the children for me. They are true friends.

Having settled Milo (the fridge is full of pumped milk), made sure that Lauren knows where everything is and told the children to be good, we departed. The SatNav assured me that our destination was only forty miles away, but seemed to be suggesting that it would take nearly two hours to reach it. Wide roads are a concept that has not yet reached Norfolk, it seemed. Suze and I talked non-stop all the way, and by the time we pulled on to the gravel drive by the barn, I was more than ready for a wee and a cup of tea.

I must confess that I was feeling a bit nervous about seeing Minty and Penny again. It had been twenty-eight years since we'd last met, and that was a lot of sparkling lime-infused water under the bridge. What if we no longer had anything in common? What if there were awkward silences? What if Minty's friends didn't like us? What if…?

My internal monologue was interrupted by the sound of footsteps and a person hurling themselves at me.

'Bel! Is it really you? Oh my goodness, I can't tell you how happy I am to see you! Zan! You haven't changed a bit!'

Same old Minty, except with a nose piercing and several tattoos. We were the first to arrive, so we sat outside in the courtyard and talked nineteen to the dozen. It was as if not a minute had gone by. Penny is married with a daughter and lives in Hampshire. Minty runs her own artist's studio and gives workshops on the Essex/Suffolk border. All this time, and I didn't know how close she was. Her husband-to-be is ten years younger than her, a silversmith who met her at a workshop.

I sat in the sun and gazed at my old friends. Minty looks so alive, so vibrant. I've missed her whole life because of Mummy's anger and bitterness. Not that long ago, I would have been harbouring feelings of rage, but I'm starting to realise that my mother did the best she could with what she had. And really, who can do more than that?

I feel that I'm getting my life back when I didn't even realise I'd lost it. Minty had imported her favourite DJ who did a couple of sets (smoke machine, bubbles, the works), we sipped espresso Martinis and nibbled on delicious street food. It was heaven. Her friends were lovely too, the most interesting bunch of people. Artists, photographers, cooks and even a trapeze artist who was absolutely delightful. Minty says she's performing at the wedding.

After breakfast on Sunday, Minty and I sat for ages chatting about the past. Even though her father, Bertie, was heartbroken when he found out about Arabella and Daddy, he didn't allow bitterness and anger to ruin his life, as Mummy had done. He had begged her to let us all stay friends, but she refused. 'He still talks about you to this day, Bel. I'm so glad you're going to see him again at the wedding. He hasn't been in the best of health and... well, I wouldn't want much more time to go by before he sees you again.'

I hated saying goodbye, but it was time to head back to Suffolk, land of the A12 and roads that are straight much of the time. Which was a relief.

In the playground on Monday morning, I consulted Claire.

'I don't think I'm doing a very good job forgiving Lavinia. It might be easier if there was something I could download. You know, like Couch to 5K. Is there an app, do you think?'

Claire looked amused and broke the news that as far as she was aware, no one had yet come up with such a piece of software.

'I'm not saying it's easy, Isabella. It isn't. If it was, everyone would be doing it. Some days you don't feel like it and you don't mean it, but that's when saying that you *choose* to forgive is so powerful. The natural human impulse is to carry on hating that person and seeking revenge, but that isn't what God wants for us. I've had to forgive so many people and it doesn't get easier.'

I shared the news of Lavinia's angry piece. The irony was that my publicly trumpeted forgiveness seemed to have made her even crosser. I shall keep at it. Perseverance pays off, as they always told us at St Dymphna's.

At our regular Zoom meeting, Mimi reported that Debbie Bosworth was ready to book a visit to the Old Rectory for a heart-to-heart. As I said, she's no friend of Lavinia, and the temptation was to do a hatchet job. Loathsome though my old enemy was, though, mindful of my chat with Claire, I wasn't going down that route. We fixed on a day and the deed was done.

I am a bit worried about Mummy. Suze and I were chatting on the way back from Norfolk and we both agree she isn't quite herself. Suze had a quiet word with her at my party and entreated her to see the doctor, but of course she refused. Walking back into the kitchen at the party to pour myself another drink, I saw her sitting at the island, gazing into space, her eyes vacant and her face blank. She seemed to be many miles away. She wasn't even cross when we told her we were meeting up with the Pryke-Darby girls. Age is creeping up on her. #gettingolder

July slid by, a haze of children's assemblies, playdates, work, interviews and parenting. I had a chat with Mimi about the direction I'm headed in. I don't want to carry on like this for much longer. I'm at the top and I'd rather diversify now than

slowly slide down the greasy pole. Who wants that? I'm genuinely excited about the photography exhibition at Nicki's gallery and I'm concentrating much more on my images at the moment. I'm even thinking of writing a photography book – not one in the *Issy Smugge Says* series, more of a 'how to' with examples.

I can't believe that Finn is off to high school in September. I sat proudly in the front row and watched him in the Year Six production. Jake's mum, Charlene, sat next to me, with only the very slightest tremor in her hands, if you looked closely. No one did. We had the leavers' assembly at the end of term, which I was surprised to find was extremely emotional.

Through gritted teeth, I invited Johnnie to both events and he came. He actually came. Sitting in the darkened hall, surrounded by parents and grandparents and holding my little Milo on my lap, it felt like we were a united family again. But when the lights came up and I turned to see him texting furiously, that illusion was shattered. Oh well. The children were pleased to see him and maybe that's all that matters.

I've got a lot coming up in the summer holidays. Minty's wedding, the toddler girls' night out and a holiday! I've invited Silvia to join us and we're off to a delightful cottage in the Cotswolds for a week. It's got a hot tub and I simply cannot wait.

I've blocked out days to be spent with the children and days to be spent working. I've told Mimi that I'm cutting back and that summer holidays won't all be about work. She was rather taken aback, but that's just too bad. I've discovered a snow park in Norwich which looks rather fun, and of course we'll be hosting lots of camp-outs and sleepovers. Mummy has booked to come up for a week in August, which I find I don't mind. Dear Silvia is looking after the children (including Lily) when Suze and I go to Minty's wedding. She says it will be nice to have my mother for company. We'll see. **#tryingtobeabetterparent #endofanera #highschoolboy #micdrop**

August

To my amazement, I am enjoying the summer holidays. I have cut back on work a fair bit and reminded myself that I am the boss, not Mimi. Neither of us had realised this.

Lauren and I took the children to the beach and had a wonderful day. I don't think I've ever met a woman who is so down to earth. As I dug a pool in the sand for Milo to sit in (ruining my nails in the process, I might add, but such are the sacrifices we working mothers must make), I quizzed her about the whole forgiveness business.

'Look, babes, when Claire started talking about it at group, I thought she was mad. Why should I forgive people who screwed up my life? They don't deserve it. It took me ages to get my head around it. Some days I just shout at God and swear loads, but I always say that I choose to forgive whoever it is.'

I was shocked.

'You swear? At God? Is that even allowed?'

Lauren tapped the top of her bucket and pulled it up, revealing a perfect sandcastle into which Milo plunged his fat little hands with chuckles of delight.

'Claire says it's OK. She does it sometimes. God doesn't mind, apparently, as long as you say sorry at some point.'

Well. This was news to me. I had never, ever even considered the possibility of using naughty words in the presence of the Almighty. I had assumed that it was a bit like breaking the rules at St Dymphna's and being sent to the head's study. Why would you?

My thoughts were rudely interrupted by what looked like an oil slick making its malodorous way across the limpid pool I had constructed for my child.

'I think the baby's swimming nappy might be full, babes.'

Lying back on the warm sand, my eyes squeezed shut and my shoulders shaking with helpless laughter, I sent up a silent prayer.

'Thank You. I will try to be good and mean it when I forgive Lavinia. Amen.'

Speaking of unexpected ordure, Meredith called the other day. She'd sent me an insincere card and a gift certificate for a facial when Milo was born and a somewhat battered orchid for my birthday. Apart from that, nothing. She hasn't changed a bit. As two-faced as ever.

'Isabella! Darling! How *are* you? How are you coping? How's the baby? Oh my goodness, what an utter *nightmare*. I was just saying to Hugo, how on earth is that *poor* woman managing *alone* as a single parent?'

Well, I wasn't having that.

'Hello, Meredith. This is a surprise. I'm very well thank you, coping just fine. I'm very fortunate to have such a supportive group of *real* friends around me. Such a blessing.'

'And now you're forty. I don't care what *anyone* says, it all starts to head south as soon as you hit the big four-oh. Hugo gave me a tummy tuck and Botox for my forty-first. He's a *doll*. How are you and Johnnie getting on?'

I certainly wasn't going to let Meredith know anything about my private life. 'Hang on a sec, the baby's crying.'

I left my mobile on the island and walked around clenching my fists until I felt ready to speak to her again.

'Congrats on the tummy tuck. They say it's one of the most painful procedures there is. And nothing says "I love you" like an injection of poison to the face, Lucky you.'

Fight fire with fire, that's what I say. I could hear Meredith bristling at the other end of the line.

'I've had Johnnie and Sofija over for supper quite a few times. No offence, *darling*, but they make such a lovely couple. Sometimes you've got to move on, stop holding on to the past.'

'Oh, really. Move on? Stop holding on to the past? Thank you so much, Meredith. Thank heavens you rang. Here was I thinking that I should try to save my marriage, but you think not. Wonderful! Do feel free to ring again if you've got any more advice for me.'

There was an affronted snort from the other end.

'No need to take that tone with me, *darling*. Just trying to help. Sofija is an absolute sweetie, so young and perky. I always think it's a mistake to marry someone the same age as you. Hugo is nearly a decade older than me and he treats me like a princess.'

Issy Smugge is not one to be rude or coarse. Nanny taught us to be perfect little ladies and it's rare that I lose my rag. However, if ever there was a time to lose it, this was it.

'A princess? A princess? He treats you like a pincushion, Meredith! Breast implants, eye lift, tummy tuck, Botox – what next? And if he's a decade older than you, I'm Kim Kardashian! Four years and that's being generous!'

I could hear heavy breathing from the other end. I tried to visualise Meredith's features, but with all the surgery, she probably looked like a completely different woman these days.

'I meant it kindly. No wonder Johnnie ran off with Sofija. *Such* a sweet girl. She doesn't have that edge that you've always had.'

I thanked her for her time and cut her off. I do miss landlines. Nothing says, 'Never contact me again as long as you live, you hypocritical silicone-filled old trout!' like the crashing of a receiver back into its cradle. **#hangingup #pushoff #plasticnotsofantastic**

A text from Mimi alerted me to the fact that Lavinia's rage had not yet fully abated.

Empty Vessels: Who Does Saint Isabella Think She Is?
Hypocritical lifestyle blogger Isabella M Smugge has apparently made it her life's work to act as an irritant to hard-working folk. Hot on the heels of her recent outburst on a tinpot radio station, now she's posting nauseating images of what she calls 'carefree time on the beach with my family'. Not content to clog up the feeds of the unwary with her endless ramblings about trends, interiors and fashion, the droning diarist is back on the family values wagon.

Handsome hedge fund manager husband, Johnnie, was conspicuous by his absence as the Smugges frolicked in the surf with an unnamed companion and her children. A source close to the shouty show-off told me, 'She's been sucking up to loads of the girls in the playground. Several of them have fallen under her spell. I think it's because they like going to her house and seeing all the expensive stuff she's got. She doesn't have any real friends.'

Smugge has got where she is today with a combination of pushiness and pretence. She's weaponised every aspect of her life to present a picture of utter perfection. I doubt she's capable of visiting the smallest room without posting it on Instagram. Lavinia Harcourt says, 'You're full of it, Issy Smugge. Stop pretending to be so perfect. You're a hollow hypocrite.'

Charming. I emailed Mimi and asked if I could sue Lavinia for libel before remembering that I was supposed to be forgiving her. Old habits die hard.

I organised Debbie Bosworth's visit on a day when all the children had friends over. The old Isabella M Smugge would have packed them all off with Sofija and had the house dressed and ready. The new one was using honesty and authenticity as her two main weapons. Jake, Finn and Harry were playing on the Xbox. Chloë was in the garden with Maisie. Elsie and Becky were upstairs playing teachers and Milo was crashed out in front of the washing machine working his way through Led Zep's compilation album, 'Mothership'. The chatelaine of the Old Rectory had no intention of giving her interviewer even the least little chance to accuse her of pretending to be perfect.

I'd loaded the dishwasher and put a vase of fresh flowers on the island, naturally. I haven't changed that much! But the family room was just that – a place for family, with books and board games on the floor and some of Elsie's drawings pinned up on the wall. There was a faint aroma drifting from Milo's pants, but that's life. I certainly wasn't going to rouse him to change his nappy.

The crunch of tyres on the drive indicated that my guest had arrived. I opened the front door and smiled charmingly.

'You must be Debbie! Welcome to the Old Rectory. I hope you had a good journey?'

We engaged in a little light chit-chat and she introduced me to her photographer, Dave. They're always called Dave.

I'm getting a double-page spread with photos, and if it goes well and I bond with Debbie (as much as you *can* bond with a journalist), it's been intimated that Issy Smugge may well feature again. I can just imagine Lavinia writhing with ill-concealed rage. But this is not about revenge.

I took my guests for a wander around the grounds. It was the perfect day for a national paper to visit my abode and take pictures. The sky was cerulean blue with tiny puffs of white cloud, birds were singing loudly and harmoniously, the fountain was tinkling melodiously on the pond and Maisie and Chloë were playing on the big swing suspended from a branch of the oak tree. It was a scene of utter pastoral bliss.

We walked and talked, and if it hadn't been for the fact that Debbie was recording every word I said and Dave was snapping away, a casual passer-by would have seen nothing but three friends examining the dahlias and gazing out over the open fields beyond the tennis court.

From the start of my glittering career, I've focused on appearing authentic and relatable. Now, after probably the most difficult and painful year of my life, I want to *be* authentic and relatable. There's a difference. Lying awake late into the night working out what I was going to say, the words, 'You're a big, fat show-off,' kept coming into my mind. I hated to admit it, but it was true. Or at least, it had been. I suppose you could say I'm a show-off for a living, but is that really the way I want to go?

Sitting on the rustic bench in the reclaimed Edwardian gazebo by the pond, Debbie asked me the big question. 'Isabella, did you mean it when you said those four little words on the radio? How can you possibly be sincere?'

I took a deep breath and smiled.

'Debbie, I really meant it. I was being completely sincere when I said, "I forgive you, Lavinia." It's not a fashionable concept, and lots of people see forgiveness as a sign of weakness. But a dear friend of mine often says it's the hardest thing we can do. And she's right. Every morning, I wake up, and before I even open my eyes, I say, "I choose to forgive you, Lavinia." Every single morning. Some days I don't feel like it, I have to be honest. But by making that choice, I am releasing Lavinia from what she did. She was wrong to bully my sister, but I was wrong to react in the way I did. So I would hope that she could find it in her heart to forgive me too.'

I glanced down at my lap and smiled in a thoughtful fashion. *Click!* Dave's camera went off as I knew it would. If a black and white image of Isabella M Smugge looking pensive, backlit by the summer sunshine in her beautiful garden isn't the main photo in my double-page spread, then I'm not the five-time winner of Photographer of the Year.

I might be a lot more sincere than I used to be (and I can assure you that I am), but I still make my living in the public eye, and a picture paints a thousand words. #trueforgiveness #monalisasmile #thatshoulddothetrick

For a woman who lives in such a beautiful place and has people doing all the boring stuff for her (for which I am eternally grateful, let me say), my life is shockingly short on fun. Even with whole days blocked off for child-based activities, this hit home when Kate texted to ask if I fancied going to the country park for the day. Obviously, I couldn't drop everything and go at a day's notice. Everyone else was chilling out, enjoying their children's company, but I had to work. I was just about to hit send on my regretful text, when I paused.

Would the world stop spinning if I didn't write a long-awaited piece on spontaneity? Would civilisation as we know it grind to a halt if I didn't finish off my blog on summer dining today?

No. It wouldn't. I texted back to say I'd love to come and what could I bring? Then I texted Mimi and told her I'd be late on both pieces and turned my phone to silent. I heard the tinny music of the ice-cream van and legged it to the front gate to surprise my children with a ninety-nine with raspberry sauce and sprinkles.

Because really, what's the point of it all? Why have I worked so hard and achieved so much if I can't have fun with the four people who seem to love me unconditionally, however many mistakes I make? What a year it's been. **#lifelessons #betterperson #beachfun**

Debbie Bosworth's piece has turned out to be even better than I hoped. It's a love letter to me, my house, my parenting and my influence on the wider world. As predicted, the picture of me looking thoughtful is the main one, along with a lovely one of the girls swinging on the oak tree (blurred, naturally, to preserve privacy) and some nice interior shots. Dave the photographer knows his stuff. We had a chat over lunch (homemade beetroot, feta and spinach tart with a mixed leaf salad and Moroccan couscous) and bonded over the art of photography.

'I love your images. You've got a really good eye. Have you thought about diversifying?'

I shared the exciting news about the upcoming exhibition and he promised to try to come. I'm so excited! I haven't felt like this since my final year project. I spent ages on it, taking artful shots around London and won the Third Year Prize. Have I ever mentioned that?

On the day of the toddler girls' night out, I was up at 6am, managed to get in forty lengths of the pool, made bread and then settled down to a solid day of writing. Ever since Debbie's piece came out, I've felt subtly different. Not so much showing people what I've got, more telling them how I feel. I found a lovely quote and shared it on my Insta, accompanied with a beautiful shot of Milo lying on his back gazing at Elsie.

'Be thankful for what you have today. Work hard for what you want tomorrow.'

True dat.

It's years, literally, since Issy Smugge threw a shape or strutted her stuff. I've probably forgotten how.

Lauren came over early to help me select my clothes. 'There's enough here to start a shop! What do you do with it all?'

I felt a bit abashed. I used to give a lot of it to Sofija, but since she left, it's just hanging in my dressing room. There are only so many great pieces a woman can wear, after all.

'You should do an event for Jess and Andy. Like a fashion show. People could come here and have drinks and nibbles and then browse through it all. I'll help.'

Lauren has the best ideas! I agreed to think about doing something in the autumn and we selected a beautifully cut pair of charcoal straight-leg trousers, a cornflower-blue top and a dark-grey boyfriend jacket. I went easy on the accessories, choosing my favourite hoop earrings and a chunky statement ring. I slicked on bright-red lipstick, sprayed myself with my favourite perfume and pulled on a pair of ankle boots.

Lauren is the same size as me, so waving aside her protests, I styled her up. Though I say it myself, I am very good at it, and by the time I'd finished, she looked amazing. We sashayed down the stairs to show ourselves off to Silvia and the girls.

'You look so pretty, Mummy!' Elsie hugged me fiercely and inhaled my perfume. 'I can't wait to be a grown-up so that I can be beautiful like you.'

Is Ipswich ready for Isabella M Smugge in party mode? Probably not. As we walked down the lane arm in arm, I took some deep breaths. I was feeling unaccountably nervous.

Squeezed in a minibus taxi with Lauren, Liane and seven other girls (thank heavens Hayley was in one of the other ones), I gave myself a stern talking-to. 'Stop being so wet, Isabella! You can do this. It's an honour to be asked.'

At the Grasshopper (sticky carpets and a funny smell in the ladies'), everyone drank vast amounts of white wine and tucked into large sharing platters of beige food. Everything appeared to be coated in lurid orange breadcrumbs. I asked if I could have a salad and Liane choked on her double vodka and orange.

'Get real, Smug! Have a spicy wedge. That counts as one of your five a day.'

Hayley was staring at me from the other end of the table. I had a choice. I could nibble a few mouthfuls, have a couple of wines and make my excuses, or dive in headfirst. I went for option two.

By the time we reached Fluid (neon lights, red velvet rope outside, so tacky), I was feeling delightfully over-refreshed. I had enjoyed (if you can call it that) two large glasses of house white before switching to double vodka and tonics. I had my breast pump in my oversized shoulder bag and would repair to the ladies' to siphon off my alcoholic milk if necessary.

Liane marched up to the doorman and did a complicated handshake. We handed over our money and we were in. It took me a while to accustom myself to the loud music, flashing lights and the proximity to so many sweaty bodies. However, in for a penny, in for a pound. I approached the bar person and ordered drinks for everyone. Money is no object, after all. I made the mistake of saying this in Liane's hearing.

'Not down to your last couple of million then, Smug?'

She gave me a dirty look, downed her double vodka and orange in three gulps and began gyrating on the dance floor. What had I done? I consulted Lauren.

'Why is Liane cross with me?'

'What?'

'I said, why is Liane cross with me?'

'Can't hear you, babes.'

'I SAID, WHY ON EARTH IS LIANE CROSS WITH ME?'

Lauren shrugged.

'DON'T WORRY ABOUT IT. SHE READ THAT THING IN THE PAPER WHEN YOU SAID YOU'D FORGIVEN THE WOMAN WITH THE PLAIT. SHE'LL GET OVER IT.'

Conversation in a nightclub is nigh-on impossible. I had forgotten this. I had three choices.

1.   Leave

2.   Prop up the bar like a saddo

3.   Drink heavily, drown my sorrows and dance myself dizzy

I selected option three.

Drinking and dancing and then drinking some more is so much fun! Why did I listen to stupid Johnnie in the first place? The pounding beat vibrated through my body and I forgot everything as I danced and danced and danced. A man came up to me and said something in my ear. I couldn't hear him. He kept saying it until eventually he gave up and went away.

The only trouble with drinking lots is that you have to go to the loo repeatedly. As I wobbled into the ladies', it seemed that a lot more than emergency lipstick reapplication and girly chat was going on. Liane Bloomfield, her face contorted with rage, had Hayley Robinson pinned up against the wall and was shouting at the top of her voice.

'Shut your face, you pathetic little worm!'

'You shut up!'

'No, you shut up!'

'Don't you tell me what to do, Liane Bloomfield!'

'If I throw a stick, will you take the hint and leave?'

Perhaps foolishly, I decided to intervene. My words were having a little trouble leaving my mouth in the correct order. I had meant to say something mature and helpful such as, 'Ladies, there's no need for this. Can I mediate?'

What actually came out was, 'Whoz goin' on? Why are you shouting a lot? S'not very nice, is it?'

Rather than pouring oil on troubled waters, I appeared to have hurled an inflammatory substance onto the flames.

'Don't poke your nose into what doesn't concern you!' Hayley was articulating clearly and appeared to be stone-cold sober. 'At least I haven't left my baby at home with goodness knows who so that I can go out and get drunk! My parents are looking after Lysander and Cressida. I can't fall back on my staff! What would your precious followers think of that?'

How rude! I attempted to reply, but again, was having some difficulty in expressing myself clearly. Liane jumped in, interrupting my slurred remarks.

'You had no right to do what you did! I'm telling everyone and I don't care. She might be a snob who lives in a huge house and writes a load of old rubbish, but she can't help being rich and posh. She was born that way. At least she's made an effort to fit in, not like you, Eyebrows!'

'I'll have you know I worked my socks off on the PTA for lazy, good-for-nothing parents like you who just stand around smoking and swearing! Why shouldn't I earn some extra money? I deserved that kitchen! She (here she jabbed her finger in my face, spitting out her words) took my job! The job I loved! She came swanning in where she wasn't wanted, throwing money around and pushing herself in. I hate her!'

Liane let out a cackle of laughter. 'Fêtes and tea towels? That's what this is all about? If you liked it that much, why didn't you just talk to her? I tried it and she's not as bad as you think. Bit wet, and talks a load of old waz sometimes, but she's all right underneath it all.'

'I don't have to stand here and listen to you! At least I own my own house and I can afford to have children instead of popping out one after another and sponging off the state!'

I winced. This was fighting talk, and with a woman who knew how to handle herself. There was a roar of rage from Liane's heavily lipsticked mouth and she hurled herself at Hayley. Sometimes at St Dymphna's there would be a punch-up, but never anything like this, with nails out, hair everywhere and the sound of Hayley's head meeting the hand-dryer at high speed. #catfight #wildnightout

Standing at the bar, I ordered another round of drinks. The vodka and tonic was going down a treat, and from the look on Liane's face, her drinks were going some way towards alleviating the discomfort of a rapidly swelling left eye and a split lip. Hayley had left and I wasn't quite sure where we stood. Nothing ventured, nothing gained. Isabella M Smugge didn't get where she is today by being pusillanimous.

'Thanks for standing up for me, Liane. Appreciate it.'

'What?'

'I SAID THANKS FOR STANDING UP FOR ME.'

'Don't mention it, Smug. Want to go outside? I need a fag.'

We stumbled into the chilly air and leaned against a wall which seemed to be moving slightly. Liane rolled a cigarette and stood puffing meditatively, gazing up at the sky.

'Did you mean that stuff you said about forgiving the woman with the plait? I hope you haven't gone soft on me again, Smug.'

I explained at some length that I did mean it.

'Cos I know you hang out with the vicar's wife, and she's a nice woman and everything, but you don't want to go believing all that nonsense. If we all forgave everyone who was horrible to us, where would we be?'

I wasn't too sure. Where *would* we be? Maybe in a world where we didn't stay up half the night crying and questioning ourselves or having fights in nightclub toilets.

My knees gave way and I slid down the wall, sitting down on the pavement with a thump. Liane joined me.

'I hated you when I met you, Smug. You know that, don't you? I thought you were so up yourself. You got my boy into trouble in Year 5 and you looked down your nose at me and I didn't want you around.' She flung her arm around my shoulder and let out a muffled burp. The aroma of partly digested garlic mushroom mixed with vodka drifted over. 'But I have to say you've got a lot better. You're still quite annoying but you make an effort not to be. And you're a single parent like me, even if you're not sponging off the state.'

'That was a horrible thing to say.' The fresh air had made my head spin but I was having less trouble articulating. 'Why is she so angry and bitter? You can have as many children as you like. None of her business.'

'You said it, Smug. None of her business. I only had the baby because my stupid partner promised me he'd go and get done

270

and I believed him.' She made a sudden movement with her hands. 'Two house-bricks and no anaesthetic. That's what was needed, looking back on it.'

A pair of feet clad in desperately on-trend sage thong mules appeared. I loved those shoes, but Lauren looked miles better in them than me.

'Are you two OK? Kicking-out time. Come on, let me help you up.'

'I'm starving! Time for the squirt wagon!' Liane pulled herself to her feet and smacked her lips.

I still didn't know what that was, but I too was extremely hungry and ready for refreshment. We piled into the minibus and drove through the streets of Ipswich, singing along to the radio at the top of our voices. Liane was sitting next to me and we seemed to be friends. Hooray! **#girlsnightout #issybouncesback #munchies**

Why did I think it was a good idea to drink all that vodka? Why? Struggling into consciousness, I clutched my head, into which someone appeared to have hammered some nine-inch nails. My legs were aching from all the dancing and my eyes were glued shut. I could feel milk (no doubt tainted with alcohol and unsuitable for consumption) leaking on to my pyjamas, and an alarming rumbling in my lower portions signalled the imminent exit of the repast I had so much enjoyed at the squirt wagon at 1.30 in the morning.

Sitting in my lovely en suite, I finally realised why they called it that. Thank heavens for the proprietary blend of ginger, rosemary and lemongrass filling my reed diffuser. I turned on the shower and stood underneath the boiling spray. I appeared to have a hangover of epic proportions. How would I get through the day?

Propped up on my pillows sipping a cup of tea brought up by my saintly mother-in-law ('I'd leave it for ten minutes if I were you, Silvia,' I warned her, waving a feeble hand at the en suite), I tried to make sense of what had gone on the night before. Liane had been cross with me, but she had also been cross with Hayley. Hayley was cross with me because I'd offered to become the secretary of the PTA. Liane was no longer cross with me. I finished my tea, closed my eyes and fell fast asleep. I really need a holiday.

Holidaying in the UK is not nearly as dull as I thought it would be. Isabella M Smugge is no stranger to the lambent reflection of winter sun on Swiss snow, nor the glittering azure expanse of the Aegean Sea. However, a week in a cottage in the Cotswolds was surprisingly enjoyable. We relaxed, swam, went out for dinner and enjoyed each other's company. I took lots of shots and posted them when I felt like it. My followers loved it. I feel a blog series coming on.

Who's relatable now, Lavinia Harcourt? **#staycation #familytime**

As I was unpacking from our holiday, my phone buzzed. It was a text from an unknown number. I knew who it was, of course. I sat down on my bed to read it. There was a lot to digest and a lot to think about. I'll reply, but I need to make sure I say exactly the right thing. **#scary**

I spent most of my twenties going to friends' weddings, my thirties going to their second ones and my forties not going to many at all. Being invited to a dear friend's nuptials is a huge thrill! Suze and I left the children with Silvia and Mummy and headed off for a weekend of glamping and gorgeousness!

Arriving at the site, I drank in the lake by the water meadow with the jetty where Minty and her fiancé would exchange their vows, the glamping village of bell tents, the huge swing hanging from the beech tree, the little island on the lake with the shepherd's hut where they would spend their wedding night and the huge, interlinked tipis on the grass. This was the way to do a wedding! Never mind your formal flower arrangements and little gold chairs. Friday night was spent enjoying dinner together and sitting around the fire bowl, reminiscing. Silas, Minty's husband-to-be, is absolutely lovely.

Just before we rolled into bed, Suze and I wandered around the site, holding our phones above our heads and trying to get a signal. That's the only downside to this kind of weekend. No internet. Lurking between the septic tank and a field full of cows, I finally managed to make contact with the mothership.

'Everything's fine here, my darling. You two just relax and have a wonderful time. The children are happy, your mother seems fine and we're off to the park tomorrow.'

I turned my phone off and slept the sleep of the just. And the slightly over-refreshed.

Saturday was an emotional day. We woke up early to the sound of cows mooing and the faint smell of manure. That might have been the septic tank. I don't know.

Over breakfast (bacon rolls and coffee provided by the venue – lovely people who think of everything), we reminisced about our childhood. Sitting on a rustic bench with my lovely sister, gazing out over the lake, I remembered all those games of hide-and-seek with Penny and Minty, the tree climbing, the bike rides, the endless chatting. All brought to a painful and abrupt halt by two people's decision. How helpless we were, looking back, at the mercy of our angry, bitter mother. I vowed never to be like that, whatever happened. I'd made my decision and I was going to stick to it, whatever people said.

At twelve, we gathered by the rose-decked arch on the jetty. Silas' parents own a nursery and they'd brought a trailer full of foliage and beautiful blooms to decorate the tipis and the arch the night before. I was very impressed. They'd used greenery and pretty flowering shrubs from their garden to create a magical atmosphere. Fairy lights were strung in the trees, a path of rose petals led from the tipis to the jetty and the giant swing creaked gently in the breeze.

Bertie Pryke-Darby, older and frailer than I had imagined, arrived at eleven. Our reunion was all I had hoped. I'm not ashamed to say I cried. As the father of my best friend and a close friend of my parents, he had been such a huge part of my childhood, and to see his face light up at the sight of me and Suze was more moving than I can tell you.

Watching him walk haltingly through the rose petals with Minty on his arm as music played was beautiful and heartbreaking all at once. I don't have much truck with self-written vows as a rule (so New Age), but Minty and Silas' words were so beautiful that I was in danger of crying off all my carefully applied eye make-up.

Once they were safely married, the wedding ran along more traditional lines. We drank champagne and ate the most delicious canapés, Spanish-style. Lots of Minty and Silas' friends are vegan and the caterer had invented the most heavenly toppings for some of their nibbles. Spicy aubergine pate, chickpea and spinach dip, a lovely dhal. It was all delicious and so delightfully informal. Johnnie and I used to talk about renewing our vows, and this would be exactly the kind of food I'd want if we did.

There were no formal speeches as such. Bertie stood up and spoke about his love for his girls, how much they all missed Arabella and what a joy and a delight it was to see his little Isabella and Suzanne again. One by one, people stood up and said what the newly married couple meant to them. It was quite unbelievably touching.

That night, we danced under the stars, sipped wine and watched as Minty's friend Jane gave an amazing performance of aerial silks, suspended from a majestic oak tree. It was breath-taking. We had a chat afterwards and I took her card. You never know when you might need a circus performer. **#janeleighsilks #amazingwedding**

On Sunday morning, lying in bed listening to the birdsong and the gentle mooing of the cows, Suze and I chatted quietly, drinking in the peace and quiet. Even the prospect of seeing Mummy later that day didn't seem too daunting. My new morning ritual of forgiving Lavinia could always be extended to forgiving her too, I supposed. I gave it a bash, and it felt pretty good.

I would never have believed that I could have enjoyed something so close to camping. Even though it hadn't been terribly glamorous (although we did have a proper bed, proper linen and an artisan goodie basket), I had found it a most pleasant experience.

There were tears and hugs all round as we said goodbye. The venue owners were on hand to make sure we'd had a good time and had everything we needed. Who would have thought that a water meadow next to a lake surrounded by cows would be such a magical place?

As I drove up the road with one last look back, both of our phones started going mad. Notification after notification. Which was only to be expected. Suze started checking hers and then let out a cry which nearly made me swerve into a ditch.

'Oh no! Bella, pull over. We've got to ring Silvia right away.'

When we got back to the Old Rectory, it was to find Silvia calm, but with traces of tears on her cheeks. Life is so precious, but you don't realise just how precious until something like this happens. I hugged my children tightly and told them I loved them, and cuddled my little Milo and gazed into his beautiful blue eyes.

Mummy had seemed her usual self, Silvia said, although she was a little confused at teatime and called her Arabella. Once the children were in bed, the two of them sat down in the family room with a cup of tea to watch television. Silvia went to the loo and as she came out, she heard a crash and found Mummy with her teacup and saucer shattered into a million pieces, her face drooping and flushed and her hands shaking. The ambulance came quickly, but not quickly enough. The stroke was a serious one and the crew did what they could, but she was in urgent need of medical care.

'I felt so terrible letting her go alone.' Silvia had given in to the tears and was sobbing. 'I promised her you'd be with her as soon as you could.'

We leapt back into the car and drove to the hospital, unsure of what we'd find there. #stroke #poormummy #shock

At our mother's bedside, we gazed in horror at what we saw. Mummy's face was pulled down on one side, she was dribbling and her eyes were vacant. The harried nurse told us that the consultant would be around at some point but couldn't say exactly when. In the meantime, she advised us to talk normally to Mummy and reassure her as much as we could.

'Hearing's the last thing to go. Your mother will recognise your voices. I'll ask someone to get you a cup of tea.'

And with that she was gone, off to deal with another devastated family.

'I'll stay on, Bella. I can't leave you to deal with this on your own.' Suze gave a watery smile. 'I'm sure Jeremy can work from home for a few days.'

'Are you sure?' I was hugely relieved. I felt quite unprepared to deal with a catastrophic situation of this magnitude. Having Suze with me made everything better.

After what seemed an eternity, the consultant arrived. Mummy's stroke was a severe one, she was expected to be in hospital for some time and when she came out, she would need intensive physiotherapy if she was to regain even part of her former health.

'Does your mother live locally? Where possible, we advise that stroke victims recuperate with a relative, if at all feasible. I'm afraid we have to prepare ourselves for some potential loss in her motor, cognition, language and sensory skills.'

I could feel Suze looking at me. I had the room. What possible excuse could I give for *not* having her living at my house?

'You've got four children, Isabella. And you work.' Suze is a gifted mind-reader and she was giving me a way out. But it was one I couldn't take.

'She can come and recuperate at my house. I'll manage somehow.' I swallowed hard. What on earth was I doing? What did I know about caring for stroke victims? #steppingintotheunknown #whathaveidone

It's late August. The fields are golden with wheat, studded with blood-red poppies. We've picked all the fruit and it's been made into jam, crumbles and jellies. Mummy is still in the hospital, a little better, but very ill. I've had one of my guest suites converted for her use when she's discharged. A ripple bed, walking frame and all the other things you don't know you need until your mother collapses and nearly dies. My friends have been amazing. I feel stunned, numb, not myself, and they've been there for me, every step of the way. I really am the luckiest girl in the world.

It doesn't look as if Mummy will be out until September at the very earliest, and until then, I'm living a strange half-life, dashing up to the hospital to see her and trying to look after the children and keep work going. Suze comes up every weekend and Silvia is always on hand if I need her.

It's so hard.

In the early days, when Johnnie first left, I'd have a recurring dream. I'd be sitting in the snug, gazing out of the window when I'd hear the crunch of wheels on the gravel. There he would be, jumping out of his car and running impatiently into the house to find me. He'd kneel in front of me, head on my knee, begging me for forgiveness and telling me it's always been me he loved, right from the start.

I would be overcome with a feeling of relief and happiness, but just as our lips met, I would wake up and lie in the darkness, crying and crying until I could cry no more.

That dream gave way to others, where I was running down a long, dark tunnel, or frantically swimming against a riptide or falling from a high place. Of late, I've been so focused on Mummy and the children that I've hardly thought of him at all.

Lavinia's horrible piece about friendship could only have been the result of Meredith stirring the pot with Kat. It hurt, but what could I do? I'd annoyed Meredith but I didn't care. I'd hurt Kat and I did care. Both of them had conspired against me with Lavinia, which I just had to take on the chin. I want to get in touch and apologise for his behaviour all those years ago, and to say sorry for standing up for him, but I don't know if I should.

Maybe I should pray about it.

The text I'd received as I unpacked from holiday, however, was from someone else altogether. Someone who had been as close as close can be to me. Her text had been most informative and we'd had a conversation that went on for some time. I know, I know, if you'd told me I'd be talking to her like this a few months ago, I'd have laughed in your face. But times change. And I've changed too.

The last weekend of the month is a Mummy weekend. It's nearly time to go back to school. Finn's uniform is all bought and labelled and he's beyond excited to be going to secondary school. The girls are ready for the daily routine again, but I don't feel that usual sense of relief. I'll miss them. Life is precious and time's raced by this year.

Sitting on the window seat in the drawing room gazing out across my beautifully kept lawn, I was jerked from my reverie by a text notification. It was from Johnnie.

'Iss, I know it's not my weekend, but I really need to see you. Can I come up? I'm half an hour away. Don't want to upset the kids, feel free to palm them off on friends if you think that's best xx'

I was alone, except for Milo. The girls were at Lauren's and Finn had gone to the park with Harry. What could Johnnie possibly want? I texted back.

'Only me and Milo here. Come over if you like.'

The sash window was open and a spicy, summer breeze drifted in and caressed my tired face. The lawn was still green and lush, thanks to Ted's efforts, and I could see down past the tennis courts to the farmer's fields beyond. I felt tired, heavy, alone. What did my future hold? How was I going to manage by myself? I closed my eyes.

'I haven't got the energy to do this. Please help me to do the right thing. Amen.'

I'm never going to win any prizes for my praying, but just saying the words seemed to help. My shoulders relaxed and I felt the slightest lift in my spirits. I went to check on Milo. He was fast asleep in his pram at the back door, his fluffy hair ruffling gently in the breeze and his smooth, perfect baby face relaxed and happy in sleep. I love him so much it hurts. That's true. I'm not just saying it because it's how I'm meant to feel.

I poured myself a glass of iced lemon water and returned to my perch on the window seat. Half an hour had elapsed and, sure enough, I heard the crunch of wheels on the gravel. The front door creaked open and I heard urgent footsteps in the hall.

'Iss! Where are you, Iss?'

And there he was, standing in the doorway, my handsome, charming husband, his hands outstretched. I smiled.

'Hello, Johnnie.'

Maybe dreams can come true. Sitting on the window seat looking down at my husband's bowed head, I listened to the words of love and passion pouring from him as if they would never stop.

'I was so wrong to do what I did, Iss. I've never loved anyone but you. She tricked me – she never loved me. She nearly broke up my family and destroyed my marriage. I've missed you every single day, my darling. Can you find it in your heart to forgive me and take me back?'

He gazed up at me, his strong hands holding mine and his sapphire-blue eyes gazing at me. My Johnnie. My first love. The father of my children.

I always knew he'd come back.

September

It's been two years since we upped sticks and left everything we knew to come up here. Two years of ups, downs, joys, sorrows, gain and loss. Sitting in church on Sunday morning, I closed my weary eyes and drank in the peace all around me. I find restoration and healing in the kindness and compassion that waits for me there. Claire has put Mummy and the whole horrible situation on something called the prayer chain, which means that lots of people are praying about it. I find that oddly comforting.

At the end of the service, Lauren brought me a cup of tea and a biscuit and I sat answering questions about Mummy's health. People seem to care, genuinely. I think that even if I hadn't given all that money to fix the roof they still would.

Back home, we had lunch and we all went to the beach. I held Milo above the waves and he giggled, peal after peal of helpless baby laughter as his toes touched the top of the waves. I could see people looking at us and smiling, watching as the perfect family enjoyed a perfect day at the seaside. I don't feel alone any more. I know I made the right decision.

I've been in touch with the care company in the village. They are marvellous. It seems that they will provide fully trained carers to come in and look after Mummy and offer any support I need. It all comes at a price, of course, but it's not as if I haven't got the money. Suze and Jeremy have offered to pay half.

Thank goodness the sale of Mummy's old house went through before she was taken ill. Her friends in the village are keeping an eye on the post, going into the new house once a week to dust and keeping us informed.

The children are back at school. Finn came out on the first day beaming, looking so smart and handsome in his uniform. He's already made some new friends. The girls are getting on just fine and my little Milo is cutting his first tooth and trying to roll over. Davina is constantly in touch, offering emotional support and being her usual wonderful self. The baby is due at the end of the month. If I can be spared, I'm going to go down and spend some time with them all.

On that hot, humid day in August, as I sat on the window seat in my delightfully proportioned drawing room, I looked down at my husband's penitent head and noticed, for the first time, a tiny sprinkling of grey hairs around his ears. The evocative scent of his aftershave drifted up to my nose. He's still using the same one he was wearing the night I met him. He calls it his signature fragrance, but isn't it a bit young for him now? I listened as he blamed Sofija for everything and begged for my forgiveness. The old me would have taken him back in a heartbeat. The new me wasn't too sure.

Johnnie sat back on his heels and gazed up at me, my hands still held firmly in his strong ones.

'So what do you say, Iss? Can you forgive me? I'll make it up to you every single day if you take me back, I promise.'

'Will you?' I gently disengaged my hands and looked down at him. 'How will you do that?'

'That's up to you, darling. I've got no right to ask you to take me back. I do know that. I've behaved appallingly to you. But if you can find it in your heart to start again, I'll change jobs, I'll work from home, I'll give you more support, spend more time with the children, anything you like. You're the love of my life,

Iss. All that stuff I said to you about you losing your edge when we had that fight last July wasn't true. Sofija tricked me, lured me in and I was so wrong to give in.'

My back was aching and my foot had gone to sleep. I don't know how Regency heroines do it. Perched on window seats in muslin gowns and ringlets accepting impassioned declarations of love from handsome, dashing men looks like lots of fun in those classic BBC drama serials, but in real life, the old back starts to give out. I stood up and declared my intention to move out into the garden.

We walked past our son, still fast asleep in his pram. Johnnie sighed deeply.

'I hardly know him. We really need to bond. Do you mind if I feed him when he wakes up?'

How could I say no? We walked down to the big bench under the weeping willow by the pond. I felt strangely calm.

'Listen, Johnnie, I still love you. I think I always will. But if I take you back now, it won't work. You cut me to the heart when you left and I still can't believe that Sofija could betray me like that. What do you mean when you say she tricked you?'

'Oh, you know, Iss. Flirting with me. Batting her eyelashes. Making it so obvious she was available.'

I frowned. 'But you didn't have to respond, did you?'

My husband gazed into my eyes and took my hand again. 'Let's not talk about her. What can I do to convince you to take me back?'

I took a deep breath. 'It's not that easy. When you left, I was heartbroken. I thought I'd fall apart without you, but I haven't. I'm stronger and I've got closer to the children. I can't take you back. Not yet, at least.'

Johnnie looked crestfallen. 'But what am I supposed to do in the meantime? I'm rattling around in the apartment by myself and it's so awkward with Hugo and Meredith. Go on, Iss. Please?'

I felt the courage of my convictions. All I needed was a fan to wave haughtily and a closing speech.

'No. It isn't that easy. Forgiveness is a process. I can't just forget everything you did. There would have to be some real changes. Suze, Sofija, Meredith trying it on with you – you've been busy, Johnnie. I've got Mummy coming to recuperate here, Finn in his first year at high school, the girls getting older, and a baby. I've got enough on my plate.'

My husband never did like being thwarted. Just for a minute, a shadow passed over his chiselled features and the beginnings of a frown gathered on his forehead.

'Iss, I'm throwing myself at your feet. Metaphorically speaking. You've got all the power. Please.'

What I would have given to have heard those words a few months ago. However, having read Sofija's text describing how she'd dumped Johnnie had made me look upon his sudden urge to return to the marital home with a cynical eye. That said, I didn't want to be unkind.

'You're the children's father, Johnnie, and they need you, and that would be the only reason I'd take you back at the moment. But I can't. Not yet. I need time. Please respect that.'

I don't think he did, but that's too bad. Issy Smugge Says: I Didn't Come Down With the Last Shower. **#itsaprocess #selfrespect**

Sofija and I are back in sporadic contact. She left Johnnie in August. In July, she'd texted me. Just five words. '*How old is the baby?*'

I gambled on the fact that telling her the truth would expose Johnnie for the liar that he is. And so it did. He'd assured her that I was very overdue with Milo, taking the chance that she was so blinded by love that she wouldn't do her sums. In my heart of hearts, I did it because I wanted her to leave him. Even now, the thought of the person I viewed as one of my closest friends betraying me so utterly hurts unbearably. But then, it takes two to tango.

I've had a chat with the children and explained that their father and I are talking regularly, are working through our issues and that none of it is their fault and that we love them unconditionally, whatever happens. I now know that children need constant reassurance. Just because I didn't get it doesn't mean that I can't give it.

Sofija tells me that it was obvious that Meredith was flirting with Johnnie. She had challenged him about it several times, but he always insisted it was just a bit of fun between old friends. One night at Meredith and Hugo's, Sofija came out of the loo to find her hostess trying it on with Johnnie in the darkened hall. Johnnie was rather drunk and turned her down flat, unaware of Sofija lurking in the shadows. I'm sure that's why she went tattling to Lavinia about Kat and Josh. I always knew Meredith had her eye on him! **#socalledfriend #muttondressedaslamb**

I'm thankful for so much in my life. Good friends, supportive family, a lovely house, church just next door (so convenient) and restored relationships with my dear Penny and Minty. Who knows what the next year holds? I don't know how I'm going to cope with Mummy in the house, but at least I've got support.

I have to go now. Sofija's ringing me at 8.30 and I want to pour myself a drink and enjoy the last of the evening light in the garden. **#soblessed #decisions #forgiveness**

Author's note

Jess and Andy are based on my dear friends Alan and Jane Hutt who really did leave a comfortable life in Suffolk to found a loving home for young mothers and their babies in Kenya. They rescue and restore girls who find themselves pregnant through no fault of their own, help to get them back into education and to find vocational work. If you want to find out more about them, you can visit their website: www.beehiveafrica.org